The Greene

Б

Once Upon a Midnight Dreary

M. KATHERINE CLARK

Other Works by M. Katherine Clark

The Greene and Shields Files:

> Blood is Thicker Than Water
>
> Once Upon a Midnight Dreary
>
> Old Sins Cast Long Shadows
>
> Tales from the Heart, Novelettes

Soundless Silence a Sherlock Holmes Novel

Love Among the Shamrocks Collection:

> Under the Irish Sky
>
> Across the Irish Sea
>
> On the River Shannon
>
> The Land Across the Sea

Love Among the Shamrocks Collection, the Next Generation:

> In Dublin Fair City – Coming Soon
>
> The Song of Heart's Desire – Coming Soon
>
> Chasing After Moonbeams – Coming Soon

The Wolf's Bane Saga:

> Wolf's Bane
>
> Lonely Moon
>
> Midnight Sky
>
> Star Crossed
>
> Moon Rise
>
> Moon Song

Silent Whispers, a Scottish Ghost Story

Heart of Fire

For my family, fans and all those who love Poe

ONWARD, ONWARD, ONWARD HE LED

"Once upon a Midnight Dreary"
Poe sang to me quiet and eerie.
Together we sat beside the fire,
Reading of kings and of their pyre.
Jumping at shadows, continuing I read,
Onward, onward, onward he led.

To death and dreams,
Through crying and screams.
Onward, onward, onward he led.
Time passed on, my mind was gone.
My fingers walked the page,
As men grew into a rage.

Bereft of breath,
I turned to what was left.

Onward, onward, onward he led.
The stories ended far and dead.
Together we sat beside the fire,
Reading of kings and of their pyre.

Not Shakespeare, Frost, nor Wordsworth, I read,
But Poe, Poe, Poe ran through my head.

She could barely work. The blood from her rope-blistered wrists had trickled down her fingers. Laying back when she heard it coming again, god, she didn't want to die, she nearly shouted. *So close. Too close,* she thought. Even though she couldn't see very well, she knew what it was.

As soon as it was safe, she went back to working the ropes that bound her ankles to the table. They wouldn't budge. Her fingers were going numb and her heart pounded with fear, adrenaline and pain. The next chink of metal resounded in the silence.

This was it.

She knew how low it was. This was it. She was going to die. Closing her eyes for a moment, she took a deep breath waiting for it.

The swoosh of air just above her made her gasp. Opening her eyes, she saw the pendulum wasn't nearly as close as she thought.

With renewed energy, she frantically looked around her. A broken piece of glass was right below the table, if she could just... reach.

CHAPTER ONE

Detective Courtney Shields looked up from the bloody mess at her feet when she heard her partner's car drive up. Lieutenant Jonathan Greene stepped out of his black Escalade and straightened his suit jacket around his gun. His black wavy hair, greying at the temples, lent to the dominance of his image. His deep, mesmerizing green eyes, rivaled the Irish countryside where he called home. Standing a few inches over six feet, Jon was built like the rugby player he was; broad shoulders tapering to a slender waist with a physique men half his age envied.

But that day, Courtney saw dark circles under his eyes, a tightness around his mouth and a stiffness in his movements. Hoping his insomnia had nothing to do with their previous case involving his own family and more to do with his girlfriend, Beth keeping him awake at night, Courtney watched as he walked toward the crime scene.

———◦◦———

Jon always kept everyone at arm's length, keeping his

emotions in check and letting only those he allowed in, recently Courtney had been able to sneak her way past his defenses. She was able to read him more and more each day. Schooling his reactions, he knew his most valiant efforts were thwarted by the heaviness in his eyes. It's not that he didn't want to tell anyone what he was feeling, it's just there were times he swore he saw *his* face... a dead man. Riley O'Grady, the man who was haunting him.

Pushing all thoughts aside, he knew nothing was as important as solving the case before him. Still walking over to his partner, he ducked under the police tape and nodded at her.

"What've we got, partner?" He asked.

Courtney smiled at him and accepted the coffee he handed her.

"Hey," she greeted. "Better ask the doc."

"Mornin', Grace," Jon smiled addressing the deputy coroner, Dr. Grace O'Malley. "What've we got?"

"Nothing like a gruesome murder to make you hate Mondays even more," she responded. "And where's my coffee?" she asked eyeing him.

"Another time," he answered, his eyes dancing as he gazed at her over the rim of the coffee cup and gave a wink.

"Uh huh," she answered, but he saw the slight pink color of her cheeks as she looked down. "All we really know for certain is that he is a Caucasian male, late 50s early 60s." O'Malley answered.

"Who found him?" Jon asked.

"Street artist came out early in the morning before the unis were on patrol," Courtney replied. She motioned to the young man standing beside the cop cars talking to a uniformed officer.

"All right, Grace, show me," Jon said.

"It's a little weird," Grace said turning back to the tarp. "Prepare yourself."

Jon gave a quick nod to the doctor and she lifted the sheet.

"Jesus," Jon breathed crouching down. "What could've

done that? A dog?"

"The worst kind of dog... a man," O'Malley answered.

"Not funny, Grace," he said looking over at her. "How could a man do that?"

"Not my territory, I'm afraid," she answered covering the victim back up. "The heart has been completely removed through the chest cavity."

"Have you located it, yet?" Jon asked.

"Not yet," she answered. "But it is possible the killer took it with him."

"Could it have been a woman?" Courtney asked.

"More than likely not," O'Malley said. "It would take a great deal of sheer force to break open a man's rib cage. It is not something I would say a woman would be able to do unaided."

"What about with the use of rib cutters or something a little more crude?" Courtney asked.

"No sign of any instrument," Grace answered. "But I won't know for certain until I get him back to the lab. It looks like the ribs were pulled and broken like one would break a wishbone from a turkey."

"Was he alive or dead at that time?" Jon asked.

"Dead," she confirmed. "It looks like he was struck on the back of the head roughly two to four hours ago."

"Making it between 5 and 7 this morning," Courtney stated.

"Can I take him now?" Grace asked.

"Let us know what you find out," Jon replied and turned to go. Before he took three steps, Courtney grabbed his arm.

"Wait," she said. Turning her head as if listening for something, she went on. "Do you hear that?"

"What?" He replied.

"Hey guys, quiet down for a second," she called out. No one was listening. Jon gave a shrill whistle that got everyone's attention.

"Everyone silent!" He shouted. Everyone in the area went quiet. After a moment, Courtney spoke.

"There," she whispered. "Hear it?"

A faint metallic heartbeat was coming from somewhere nearby. Grace looked around.

"It's near me," she whispered. Jon took a step closer to her and Courtney walked around to the other side of the pallets the body was laying on.

"Jon," Grace said. "It's directly under the body."

Jon beckoned her to come toward him. Taking his outstretched hand, she let him pull her forward and pushed her behind him. Taking a step closer, Courtney was opposite him. Jon held his hand up telling her to wait. Crouching, he gently pulled the tarp from covering the body.

The wooden pallets the body was on came into view and the sound seemed to be coming from directly below the victim and it was getting louder. Courtney nodded at her partner and reached beneath the wood, pulling out a small recorder. The sound of the heart beat played loudly on it by then.

"What kind of a sick joke?" Courtney asked Jon. He shook his head and looked back under the pallets.

"Grace," he called. "I think we found the heart."

O'Malley went up to him and bent low. Reaching for it with her gloved hands, she pulled the bloodied organ out from under the wooden slats.

"Looks like it," she answered. "And there's something attached to it. Looks like paper."

"It's too badly stained for us to read," Courtney answered, taking a look at it. "I'll send it to forensics, maybe they can retrieve something."

"This is very odd," Jon said. "I'm going to go talk to the witness." The uniform nodded as Jon and Courtney walked up.

"Thank you, Harper," Jon greeted the officer before turning his attention to the young man. "My name is Lieutenant Greene, this is my partner Detective Shields, Mister—?"

"That dude was just lying there. I mean he was just lying there and I saw all the blood and I don't remember—"

"It's all right, my partner and I are just trying to understand what happened here," Jon said. "Can you tell us what you saw?"

"The dude's dead!" His voice cracked as it went higher. "I mean his chest and the blood and did they say his heart was missing?"

"Yes," Jon said. "It was a very brutal attack and you are the only one who can tell us what happened before we arrived. What's your name?"

The young man looked at him suspiciously. "John," he answered.

"Is that your real name?" Jon asked. The street artist swallowed and his eyes drifted to his bag of graffiti tools. "We're not here for your street art," Jon said. "We don't care about that. Just tell us what happened."

He looked past Jon to the body being pulled onto the gurney in the coroner's body bag.

"I was walkin' through here," he said. "And I looked over and saw this guy lyin' on the ground and I see he ain't movin'. So I call out to him, and he doesn't answer. So I go a little closer, and I call out again, then I see he's definitely not movin' so I go a little closer and I see the blood and his chest and I – I think I scream or somethin'. I see one of the cop cars and I take off running toward them!"

"Did you see anyone else around the body?" Jon asked.

"Nah man! It was just him. He was lying there all cut up," he cried.

"Thank you, now I will need you to go with the officers to the precinct and get your statement in writing," Jon said indicating the police officers.

Courtney waited until the patrol car was driving away before she turned to Jon.

"You don't think he did it, do you?" she asked. Jon shook his head. "Yeah, me neither," she answered. "That heartbeat was some kind of sick joke."

"Let's get that letter down to forensics see if they can recover anything and have them try to lift a print off of the recorder," Jon said.

CHAPTER TWO

"What are you doing?" Bradley Henderson asked his brother, Quinn as he pulled one of the drapes closed.

"We gotta lay low," Quinn said tugging the other one and bathing them both in muted light. "Things gotta cool off. There's dozens of troopers looking for us."

"How long are we staying here?" Brad complained looking around the hotel room. "It's no better than prison."

"We're free that's what matters," Quinn said.

"Not for very long," Brad replied.

"I know what you're thinking and the answer is no," Quinn answered. "We have to lay low and wait for it all to pass."

They may have been only a few minutes apart with Quinn being the eldest but they thought the same.

"You know I'll look after you," Quinn went on. "Didn't I while we were upstate?"

"I'm tired of running," Brad replied. "I thought giving them what they wanted would give us free reign."

"Free reign?" Quinn replied. "Shit, what are you, an idiot? What did you think would happen? A full pardon? Clean slate? A medal? C'mon man," Quinn reasoned. "We're cop killers."

"That was over ten years ago," Brad said.

"Do you think that matters?" Quinn demanded.

"We didn't pull the damn trigger!" Brad defended.

"What do you—" Quinn was interrupted by a knock at the door. Putting a finger to his lips, Quinn motioned his brother to be quiet.

"Who is it?" Quinn called out.

"Come now, Quinn," a voice from their past surprised them. "Open the door like a good little criminal and let me in."

Quinn locked eyes with Brad. Suppressing his nervous swallow, Quinn took a deep breath and opened the door.

"Paul?" Quinn questioned, not recognizing the man before him.

"Tsk, tsk, tsk, you boys have been bad," Paul said. "And by the way... it's Rob from now on." Pushing past the much taller man, Paul stepped into the hotel room. "Nice place you've got here," he said looking around.

"Yeah they don't exactly allow escaped felons into the Ritz," Quinn countered, bolting and chaining the door.

"How have you been, Bradley?" Rob asked. Brad shrugged. "And you Quinn?" Rob turned to him. "You look thinner than last time."

"Prison food will do that to you," Quinn answered.

"How about a nice steak dinner? On me, of course," Rob offered.

"We can't be seen out and about, half the state is looking for us," Quinn answered.

"Ah no, see, Quinn and Bradley Henderson cannot be seen out and about," Rob unbolted the door and removed the chain. "But two nephews come to visit me? No one will bat an eyelash. But we need to clean you up." Opening the door, Rob let three women into the room carrying dry cleaning and one backpack each.

"Enjoy, boys," Rob said. "They're already paid for. Meet

me at this location when you're finished," he handed them a folded piece of paper. "Take your time, though. Ladies," Rob called to them. "Take *good* care of them. They've been locked up far too long and have probably missed a woman's touch. Enjoy!"

———————

There was a knock at Jon's and Courtney's office door and a moment later Officer Callen walked in.

"Excuse me, Sir, Ma'am," he said. "The forensics came back. John Doe is not in the system and the recorder had traces of latex. The paper had a couple words that forensics *were* able to make out but the entirety of the note was unreadable."

Callen handed Courtney the file and once he left, Courtney looked over at Jon.

"Listen to this," she started. "The three readable words were 'deed' 'planks' 'hideous'."

"Very interesting," Jon thought a moment. "And rather old language. Who really says *hideous* any more or *planks* for that matter?"

"Something about this whole thing seems strangely familiar," Courtney replied. "Almost like I've read about it," intrigued, she turned to the computer. "I need to check something." Typing into her search bar, Jon stood near her waiting for the search. Finally the results she was expecting popped up. "Ha! That's why it seemed familiar! It's from *Tell Tale Heart* by Poe," she explained.

"It's been a while for me, love," Jon said. "It's been since Primary School since I've read a Poe. Remind me about that one?"

Just as Courtney started to speak, Jon's cell phone rang. "Hey, Ryan," Jon answered.

"Hey, Uncle Jon," Ryan replied. "Sorry for the delay, the lab was backed up but I have those paternity test results you asked me for when Uncle Mat was in the hospital a couple weeks ago."

9

Jon's stomach twisted and he felt himself go pale. It had finally come. The moment he had been waiting for, for the past thirty-six years had finally come. The answer to the question; was Steven Anderson, Beth's eldest son, his son too?

"Do you want me to meet you, or do you want me to just tell you?" Ryan asked.

Jon debated for a second.

"Courtney, could you give me a second?" He asked. Nodding, she grabbed her water bottle and left the room. "Just tell me..." Jon finally said.

———◦◦◦———

Steven took a big risk joining Jon for lunch just before he went off on another assignment. But as he remembered their conversation, he knew it was worth it. Jon's words echoed in Steven's ears as he drove.

"As much as I wish this to be false... it looks like I am *not* your father," Jon said.

"You're saying that Paul Anderson is my father?" Steven demanded. When Jon nodded, Steven cursed angrily and stood.

He had always known. But now that it was fact, he wished he never agreed to that damn test in the first place. Was it better not knowing and... hoping? Three words escaped his lips before any others.

"Don't tell mom," he had said softly.

CHAPTER THREE

After Jon and Steven parted ways, Jon called Dave and Courtney and cashed in a favor. He couldn't go back to work, not now, not after everything. Maybe it was a mistake to go home but Jon needed a good glass of whiskey, some alone time and a long run to clear his head. Dropping his keys on the washroom ledge, he took off his shoes, tie and suit jacket and walked through the house to the living room.

Gazing at Scott's picture, he was relieved. He only had one son, and that's all he wanted. He enjoyed being a father *figure* to any man who asked, but he would only ever have one son.

Unbuttoning his collar, Jon went to the bar and poured a glass of whiskey. He breathed in the scent of the golden liquor and took a gulp reveling in the slow burn of the alcohol. Even though he was relieved, a part of him still hurt, especially for Steven. The man had just realized that he was the product of Paul Anderson's brutal rape of his mother. Jon knew, even before Steven had asked him not to, he could never tell Beth, it would tear her apart.

Knowing he needed to speak with someone about the thoughts whirling around his brain, he pulled out his phone and dialed a well-remembered number.

"Dr. Hinkle's office, how may I assist you?" the receptionist answered.

"Dr. Hinkle, please," Jon said.

"May I ask who is calling?" she asked pleasantly.

"Jonathan Greene," he answered.

"Thank you, Mr. Greene, one moment please."

"Jon?" The doctor answered a moment later.

"Hiya, Doc, got me on the *high priority* list, eh?" Jon asked.

"Off the *suicide watch*, that's as far as you're getting," the doctor chuckled. "You outta be happy you're only on my *immediate answer* list for now."

Jon had to laugh but there was no humor in it. The doctor had been on the receiving end of Jon's suicidal rants more than once.

"Are you busy?" Jon asked.

"I have a patient coming in ten minutes. What's up?" Hinkle asked.

"I finally found out about Steven," Jon said.

The doctor was silent for a moment.

"Give me a second," he finally said. Putting his side on mute, Hinkle told his secretary to cancel his day's appointments.

Quinn: He called his shrink.

Rob had to smile as he read Quinn's text report. Jon was cracking.

Rob: What was the theme?

Quinn: Mostly that he isn't some guy's father.

Rob smirked.

Rob: Who's?

Quinn: Some guy named Steven.

Rob laughed in triumph.

"Oh Beth, all those times you tried to use that against me…

I could've told ya he wasn't Jon's. Just look at him," Rob chuckled. Taking his phone, he texted Bradley.

Rob: Keep Steven in your sights. Report back to me what he's doing.

Brad: He passed the airport, heading to his hotel. I'm following. What does this guy do?

Rob: He's CIA.

Rob looking up at his computer screen at one of the pictures of Steven and Jon from their lunch earlier that day. "And he's mine."

———————

Steven found the hotel programed into his GPS off to a left of the divided highway. As he waited for oncoming traffic to break, his eyes consciously drifted up to his rearview mirror.

Car: Toyota, sedan, tan, lightly tinted windows, 2004 model.

Driver: late 30s, blonde, shaggy hair, sunglasses, Colt's hat, clean-shaven, alone.

Following: not so well, since the Indianapolis airport.

Amateur, Steven shook his head.

Pulling into the first parking spot he saw, Steven paused before getting out. He spied his handler's car. Knowing the code if something was wrong, Steven pulled out his phone and shouldered it, pretending to have a conversation as he walked around his car to the trunk. Pulling out his suitcase and hooking his computer bag over his neck, Steven walked into the hotel.

"Good afternoon," the desk clerk greeted Steven cheerily as he lowered his phone from his ear.

"Hey, how ya doing?" He asked quickly. "Checking in."

"Absolutely, what name is the reservation under, Sir?" She asked typing something into the computer.

"Craig Stevens," he answered.

"Do you have your driver's license on you, Mr. Stevens?" she asked.

"Yeah absolutely," he pulled out his wallet and handed her the fake, government issued ID. Looking down at his phone as it buzzed in his hand,

Flash: I'm shipping up to Boston.

Steven was glad to see his handler's code letting him know everyone was in position. Stealthily glancing around the room, he saw the man who had followed him for the past hour looking nonchalantly at magazines at the entryway table.

"Welcome Mr. Stevens," the hotel receptionist went on. "We have your room ready for you. Will this be on the same card you reserved with us?"

"Yes," he answered. The desk clerk handed him the paperwork and he looked it over.

"Damn," he said teasingly. "Didn't know I'd be signing my life away."

She giggled causing him to glance up at her through his rectangular framed glasses and smirk. He knew he looked good. Ralph Lauren would have been proud. It was his job to always look sexy.

"All set," he replied after signing his name.

"Here's your key, Mr. Stevens. You'll be in room 208. I hope you have a pleasant stay." She said.

"It's been pretty great so far," he answered winking at her.

She grinned at him. "If there's anything else I can do, please don't hesitate to let me know," she said suggestively.

"You'll be the first," he replied.

Turning, he looked around for the signs to the stairwell. Waiting on the second landing for a couple minutes, he listened. No one followed him. Exiting the stairs, he saw Zoe, one of his colleagues, dressed as a hotel maid and another agent, Cliff dressed in pool attire with a towel draped over his shoulders. He nodded at

Steven as they passed each other and Cliff went into the elevator.

Once Steven reached room 208, he slid in the keycard into the lock and the smell of cinnamon filled the air.

"You're late," he heard from the other side of the wall. Gordon stepped into his view.

"Dammit, Flash, give me a second to put my bags down," Steven said, using Gordon's code name as he walked over to the TV and set his computer bag on the desk beside it.

"What was the business downstairs?" Gordon asked chewing his signature cinnamon chewing gum. "Should I tell them to stand down?"

Steven pulled off his leather jacket and draped it over the back of the desk chair.

"I don't know," he answered. "Tell them to keep an eye out." Steven described the tail as he walked over to Gordon and pointed out the sedan in the parking lot. Gordon gave the announcement over the walkie. He read off the driver's license for Mac, their techie, to run.

"So, any change to the plan?" Steven asked sitting in the oversized chair in the corner.

———※———

Bradley got a room on the ground floor directly below Steven's room. He sat on the bed and pulled out his phone.

Brad: He just checked into his hotel. I couldn't get anywhere near his room. Too many guys with earwigs.

As he waited, he pulled off his jacket and shirt. His phone buzzed on the bed.

Rob: I warned you already. Don't get too close.

"Yeah I know," he muttered harshly. Going to the bathroom, he ran the shower. It was nice to have his own room, his own bathroom, his own space. After ten years in prison, he reveled in taking a shower without anyone watching him.

CHAPTER FOUR

Courtney looked down at her engagement ring remembering how Ryan had proposed in Ireland the month before. As she waited for him to answer his cell, she thought about how cute he looked all bundled up in an Irish wool sweater, cap, scarf, and jeans the day they visited the Cliffs of Moher. Then his voice came over the phone and she melted.

"What are you doing up, baby?" he asked. Her eyes drifted to the clock over the mantle, noticing the time.

"Hi," she bit her lower lip to prevent the stupid grin that spread across her face. He chuckled and she heard him sigh as if he just sat down. "How's your shift?"

"Just a bit out of breath. Jogged three times to the other side of the hospital for STAT calls," he replied.

"Everything all right?"

"Yeah, crazy day though. Massive wreck on thirty-one and some idiot chopping onions along with my other patients."

"You sound tired, baby," she said concerned.

"I am," he sighed. "You remember my mentor, Fred?"

"Yeah," she answered.

"Well, he's taking more of a backseat in my training. I think the hospital board is wanting to see how I do on my own."

"You'll do great," she said sincerely. "You've already impressed them or they wouldn't have offered you Assistant Head of Surgery once your residency is up."

"Yeah, it's nice having a set plan for the future, for our future." Tingles still coursed through Courtney when he said those words.

"Yeah," she sighed. "Our future. A future where I will greet you when you get home in nothing more than high heels..." He groaned. "Or maybe, in your favorite lingerie..."

"High heels are good, less work for me," he replied. She laughed. "You do know what you're doing to me right?"

"Helping you get through the day?" she answered innocently.

"Right," he teased. "So in order to save me from the thoughts that are distracting me... You didn't answer my question. Why are you up so late?" he asked.

"I'm working on a John Doe case Jon and I got this morning," she answered.

"Are you at home or at the precinct?" he asked.

"Home," she replied.

"Anything interesting?" He asked.

"Kinda," she replied. "I had to pull out my college lit books and refresh my memory on Poe."

"Wasn't he your focus?" Ryan asked.

"When I was a lit major, yeah, he and Brontë," she explained. "But this case... it's eerily similar to one of his works so I'm pulling out my old notes and my print-outs of my professor's lectures and dissertations."

"Wow, you still have that stuff?" Ryan teased.

"Of course," she grinned.

"Who knew Poe would be so useful in everyday crime fighting."

"He was the original master of detective procedure, Dr. Marcellino."

"I stand corrected. It's kinda sexy."

"Kinda?"

"Okay, okay very."

"Better," she answered. "You're off in what, ten hours?"

"Yeah."

"How about you come over and I'll cook you your favorite; Belgium waffles and turkey bacon?"

"I can be there at nine," he answered.

"I'll be up at eight," she grinned. "Oh are you, Jon and Scott going grocery shopping?" she smiled.

"Yeah but not tomorrow," he said. "Going to get stuff for Scott's *get better sooner* party,"

"How's he doing?"

"He says he's feeling a lot better. He's gaining more mobility but the bullet did a number on his tissues more than muscle and sometimes that's worse because of the scar tissue build up and scraping that away could be very painful," Ryan explained.

"I don't want to know what you mean by that," she shuddered.

"No, you really don't," he answered.

"I know Jon worries about him."

"Yeah."

"Is he okay?" She asked.

"Who?"

"Jon."

"Why do you ask?"

"He left work earlier today, just after he got that phone call from you. Is he okay?"

"You know I couldn't say anything, even if there was something to say," Ryan said.

"So he's not sick?"

"Not to my knowledge."

"Okay, I was just worried about him. He never takes personal days."

"Everyone needs some sometime," he answered.

"I know," she agreed.

"Dr. Marcellino to the ER, STAT, Dr. Marcellino to the ER, STAT," they both heard the intercom above him. He felt his pager buzzing at his hip.

"I gotta go, babe," he said. "I love you and I can't wait to see you."

"Love you too," she replied just before he hung up.

———◦◦◦———

"You seem a little distracted tonight, baby," Beth said looking at Jon over her wine glass. "Is something wrong?"

"Sorry, babe," he replied. "Just a little preoccupied tonight."

"Anything I can help with?"

Don't tell mom. Steven's voice rang in Jon's ears and he forced a smile.

"Oh no, I won't ruin your night with my troubles," he replied. "Just some police business."

"You are a terrible liar," she said. He chuckled, stood and took her plate.

"More wine?"

Sighing she leaned back in her chair, "are you trying to get me drunk, Lieutenant Greene?"

"Never needed to before?" He winked. She nodded and watched him walk away from her. "I can feel your eyes on my arse," he called over his shoulder.

"And a very nice ass it is too," she called back. He chuckled but looked at her through the opening above the kitchen bar.

"Hot tub?" he asked.

"Love it," she replied. "But I don't have my suit."

"Who said anything about a swimsuit?" he asked.

She slowly licked her lips. "Bring the bottle, leave the dishes," she said. Jon grabbed the wine bottle and chased after her as she squealed running to the door and down the steps to the garden enclosed hot tub.

CHAPTER FIVE

Steven turned off the water in the shower and wrapped a towel around his hips. Gordon had kept him up late, briefing him on the case. Wanting nothing more than a good night's rest and maybe raiding a Bourbon shot from the mini bar, Steven stepped into the main room of the hotel suite, glancing at the door as he passed. The chain and dead bolt were still in place as was the emergency call button Gordon had installed on the wall by the light switch. He walked over to his suitcase and pulled out a pair of sweat pants. Pulling them on, he towel dried his hair but paused when he heard the doorknob rattle.

Grabbing his gun from his carryon, he slowly walked to the door and listened. A scraping sound met his ears, pushing the alarm on the wall, he alerted the agent on duty that something was happening. Not a moment later, his hand reached for the bolt and chain and silently slid them both back. Cocking his gun, he turned the doorknob. Gordon pushed in and shut the door in one swift movement.

"Jesus, Gordon, what the hell?" Steven demanded.

"Some drunk who couldn't read the room number. Nothing to worry about," Gordon said.

"You sure?"

Gordon nodded once. "Got your alert. All clear. Go to bed. We'll talk in the morning."

Gordon opened the door and walked down the hall, disappearing into his room. Steven's job was to sniff out lies and Gordon just lied to him. Not knowing the full picture could lead to an agent's death. Yawning, he put the safety back on the gun and placed it under his pillow. Turning off all the lights, the room was bathed in darkness, just the way Steven liked it. Closing his eyes, he let the events of the day lull him to sleep, but they didn't.

Tossing and turning most of the night, he finally gave up when the clock read four in the morning. Sitting up, he grabbed his laptop and opened it up. Unbeknownst to the Company, Steven had started writing his memoirs in fiction form. Letting the story take over, he typed up a good five chapters before he heard the knock on his door for wakeup call.

———◦———

"And just who might you be?" Gordon asked the man tied to a chair.

The shaggy haired man looked older without his Colt's cap. The man looked up at him and sneered. Gordon's fist collided with his jaw.

"Boss," one of Gordon's men called to him. "His ID."

Taking the driver's license, he squinted at the name.

"It says here that you're from Boston, Mister… uh… Hendricks? Clearly a fake. Run it." Gordon handed the license back to his agent. "So," Gordon pulled another chair and sat in it backwards as his agent called in the ID to Mac. "Within five minutes we will have every piece of your life on our computers. High school, college, work history, mother's maiden name, father's criminal record, your first girlfriend's credit report, and everywhere you have been since 2001. You have exactly that amount of time to tell me what I want to know. Why have you been following the man in room 208 since early this afternoon?"

Bradley looked at him but said nothing. Spitting out some blood from his busted lip, it landed on Gordon's shirt.

"I liked this shirt," Gordon said flicking the spit off and backhanding him again, causing him to fall to the floor, chair and all. Looking over at the two men standing by the door, "See what you can get out of him." One of them tied a gag around Henderson's mouth, the other grabbed his arms and tied them behind his back. They forced him out of the room and into Zoe's laundry cart.

———◦◦◦———

Rob looked at his phone for the tenth time in as many minutes. Finally grabbing it, he sent a text.

Rob: Have you heard from Brad?

Quinn: No, why?

Rob: He hasn't checked in.

Rob set his phone on his desk as the cleaning crew passed his office.

"Burning the midnight oil, sir?" One of them asked.

"Some work knows no time limit," Rob answered back trying to stay in the character of the alias the man knew.

"I wanted to thank you for what you told me to tell my boy the other day, sir. It really helped his case with Immigration," the man said. "It looks like they will not deport him."

"Glad to help. They had no case. He had all the correct papers. They like to scare," Rob smiled.

"Thank you. Good night, sir," he replied.

"Good night," Rob answered as the man left the doorframe.

Once he was alone, Rob let out a breath. *Far too many aliases to keep straight.*

CHAPTER SIX

Courtney awoke that next morning on her couch. Straightening, she flinched when her back and neck cracked. Rubbing her neck she looked around and saw all of her papers still set out. Slowly, she got up and went to her bathroom. Running the water for a hot shower, she left the room to grab a towel from the dryer just outside the door. The steam from the hot water was rising and drifting into the hallway. Just as she was about to slip back into her bathroom, she heard her front door open and close.

"Ryan?" she called. "I'll be out in a minute. I have some juice in the kitchen."

When he didn't answer her, she looked at the time. It wasn't even seven o'clock yet. Ryan wouldn't be there for another two hours. Silently she went to the bookshelf in her bedroom and grabbed her spare gun from her hollowed out book.

"How was your shift today, baby?" she called out hoping to distract whoever it was coming up her stairs.

Peeking out from behind her bedroom door, she saw a man in a black leather jacket enter her bathroom. His back was to her and she watched as he pulled out a thin fish wire. Wrapping it around his hands, he created a garrote. A shiver ran down her spine, but hearing the bath curtain being yanked back, her training kicked in. When he rushed out of the bathroom, eyes wild jumping from side to side, Courtney emerged from her hiding place and pointed her gun at him.

"Don't move," she said. He darted down the hallway and ran to the stairs. "IMPD! Freeze!" She yelled.

He didn't stop. Before he reached the front door, she fired hitting him in the right leg. He fell forward down the last five steps and landed in her entryway. She raced down to him and held him at gun point.

"I told you to freeze, asshole," she stated standing over him and dialing dispatch from her cell.

"I need a hospital!" he cried.

"You're not getting anything, yet," she said to the perp. Finally dispatch answered and Courtney continued into the phone. "Detective Courtney Shields, I have an intruder in my home. We'll need an ambulance too," she hung up and looked back as the man attempted to crawl to the door. "Hey," Courtney called stepping on the man's injured leg. "Unless you want like another bullet, I suggest you stay still. Now, who sent you?" He didn't say anything.

She aimed the gun closer to his forehead. "Tell me now, and I'll put in a good word for you with my partner," she said.

"Your partner? Why?"

"He'd be your executioner," she replied. "If you don't tell me what I want to know now, I will tell him you came to kill me. You would not last more than five seconds after he finds that out."

"I'm a dead man either way."

"I'm heartbroken," she answered sarcastically.

"I want immunity," he said.

She snorted. "You're not getting anything until you tell me who sent you."

Panicking her finger danced on trigger, he knew she would shoot him again. He mumbled something.

"Speak up!" she ordered.

"Rob," he said. "Rob sent me."

The name quickly registered as the one behind Riley a month ago. Her eyes flashed with anger. "Why?" She demanded.

"He said you didn't die when Riley shot at you. He said another cop got it, some rookie pushed you out of the way. Rob wanted to make sure it was done right this time. He wants you dead," he said.

Officer Justin Harding, flirt, renegade, hero... dead cop. He had pushed her out of the way when he saw the glint of Riley's rifle and had been awarded the Police Medal of Honor posthumously. She suppressed the shiver that raced up her spine.

"Why? What's it to him?" She questioned.

"He wants your partner," he gasped out as the pain in his leg grew and he saw his blood seep onto the marble tile floor.

"Why?" She yelled, her anger getting the better of her.

"Rob said your partner took something from him and he wants him to suffer for it," the man said, watching as her finger curled around the trigger again.

"Suffer for what?" She demanded leaning down and grasping the front of his shirt.

"I don't know," he cried. "I don't know, I swear! I'm just a hired gun."

"What else did he tell you? Speak!" She shouted.

"He told me to write something..."

"Write what?" she demanded. "Where?"

"On the bathroom mirror," he explained. "After I was done."

"What?" she demanded.

"'Ah, dream too bright to last,' that's all I know, I swear! I don't even know why. Or what it means."

It was from a Poe poem... more importantly it was from the poem *To One In Paradise*. A poem Poe experts believe was written about his love who had died.

Sirens blared in the parking lot as the EMTs arrived at Courtney's apartment building. She opened her door and saw the St. Vincent EMTs rushing toward her apartment.

"Shit," she mumbled. It wouldn't be long before Ryan would hear about this. "Hey, Todd," she said to the senior technician.

"Jesus, Courtney, I thought this address was familiar," he went to her and placed comforting hands on her arms. His expert gaze passed over her. "Are you all right?"

"Fine," she shrugged, comforted by his beefy, teddy bear arms. "Pissed, but fine." Todd quickly took in the scene around him. "Just... don't tell Ryan would ya?" She asked.

"He probably already knows," he answered. "I was eating breakfast in the lounge and he came in for a coffee him. We were talking when I got the call."

"Damn," she muttered. That was exactly what she didn't need. Her overprotective partner *and* her fiancé hovering making sure she was all right.

"You want us to get this guy to Wishard... or should we just leave the door open on I-465?" Todd grinned.

She gave a small laugh but the guy on the floor overheard and started making a fuss.

"Shut up, you," she said to him. Turning back to Todd, she continued. "Wishard is fine. I'll make sure there's a guard."

She saw the police officers get out of their cars and head toward the apartment. Todd followed her gaze.

"You want me to stay with you?" Todd, the former offensive lineman for Notre Dame, asked. She smiled at Ryan's fraternity brother.

"Nah, I think I can handle it," she replied. "Thanks, but you might text Ryan to let him know I'm okay. I'll tell him but he won't believe me."

He nodded and gave her arms a brotherly squeeze. When he turned to see how his team was doing, she took her phone from the shelf beside her. It had buzzed several times already. Ryan was trying to get a hold of her.

Courtney: I'm fine. I will call you in a little bit.

She didn't have time for all the sweet talk but having a familiar face nearby gave her the courage to face the man she knew would break every law trying to get to her. Clicking out of her texts, she dialed Jon's number.

"Dear god, are you all right?" Jon's voice demanded.

"Yeah I'm fine but I've got an entourage of police, EMTs and a bleeding perp in my entryway."

"I know, Jesus I'm on my way. Dispatch called me. Are you all right?" She heard tires squealing and a horn honking.

"Slow down, I'm fine," she tried to say. "I hoped you hadn't heard yet. Don't break any laws getting here. I'll see you soon," she kept her voice level, while watching the EMTs work. It was time to call Ryan. Looking back at Todd who glanced her way again, he gave her a sympathetic look but turned back to his team. Stepping up, she sat on her stairs, out of the way of the forensics team and dialed Ryan's number.

After what seemed like hours, the EMTs got the perp onto the gurney and out of her apartment. Todd went back to her and handed her the electronic clipboard, which she signed. Courtney was trying to calm Ryan down, preventing him from leaving work early and potentially getting in trouble. Todd gave her one last sympathetic look and winked. She tried to smile back at him but as she finished up talking with Ryan, she heard squealing tires in the parking lot and looked up to see Jon pulling into a spot, getting out and running to her. He pushed the other officers out of his way. She met him just outside.

"Are you okay? What happened?" He demanded. It all came crashing down. She gripped her phone tighter preventing him from seeing them shake. He caught the move and crushed her into a hug. She wrapped her arms around his back and held on. Her whole body shook. Swallowing, as her attempt to speak failed, Jon soothed her but then pulled back. "Talk to me," he ordered, his eyes burning and yet comforting.

"That asshole just tried to kill me," she replied bluntly gesturing to the gurney being loaded onto the ambulance.

Jon's face gave nothing away. His hand clenched into a fist and he turned on his heels with the sole purpose of heading to the ambulance. Courtney pulled him back.

"He'll keep. Calm down. I'm fine," she said.

His whole body was rigid with anger. The ambulance pulled out and headed to the hospital.

"Tell me what happened," he said turning back to her. They went into her apartment, skirting the crime scene markers and the officers snapping pictures.

They reached the top of the stairs and went to the kitchen. Jon poured a cup of coffee for her as she watched from the archway. He set the cup down on her bar counter and forced her to sit on one of the stools. He came around and straddled the other one.

"Tell me what happened, Courtney," Jon said not looking at her.

She took a sip of the coffee and her face contorted when she tasted just how much sugar he had put in it. "Uh, god, a little coffee with my sugar please?" she replied.

"It's good for you especially right now," he said indicating the stairs. "Now talk."

"I was going to take a shower when I heard the front door open."

"Jesus, Courtney," he breathed running a hand over his face. "Security system?"

"Right like I'm that stupid to leave it off?" She demanded. He held up his hands in surrender. "Sorry," she said. "I set it last night, he must have overridden it. He said Rob sent him and told him to write something. A quote from a Poe poem."

"Courtney," he warned.

"Someone told me once to never ignore coincidences," she said.

"I knew those words would wind up biting me in the arse," Jon sighed.

She giggled. Very rarely did his childhood Irish accent show itself but when he was angry, animated, or for words American's never use, did she hear it.

"At least that made you laugh," Jon said. "Now, are you prepared to tell your story again?"

She turned to see a detective from their precinct but different division walk up the stairs.

"Officer Parks," she said slipping off the stool.

"Detective," he answered formally. "What the hell happened here?"

"Long story," she answered.

CHAPTER SEVEN

Steven sat in his hotel room early that next morning looking down at the profile of his next mark. No sleep was starting to catch up with him, but he gratefully accepted Cliff's offer of a coffee run. Hotel coffee wasn't his favorite but when the agent offered to buy a round of Starbucks just down the strip mall behind the hotel, Steven thanked him profusely. His triple Americano teased his nose as he brought it to his lips. Gordon stood over him, arms crossed over his chest, chewing his signature cinnamon bubble gum.

"The kid?" Steven asked.

"Joshua," Gordon explained, showing a picture in the file. "He's seven. You'll meet him on your run around the park tomorrow. You need to earn his trust and get him to invite you to his game tomorrow where you'll get his mother, Jade – possible Al Qaeda operative – to invite you home... you think you can handle yourself from that point on?"

"Yeah," he said. "I think I can manage."

Gordon barked a laugh. "You know you're my hero, right?" Gordon teased. Steven glanced over at Cliff who had fumbled with the container of sweetener at the minibar. Cliff's eyes flashed to

Gordon but immediately looked down.

"Didn't realized you like women too," Steven replied. "I do what I have to for the country I love."

Gordon lowered his arms but didn't answer Steven's obvious taunt. Gordon had never told Steven he was gay but the signs were hard to miss, especially for a trained agent. "We've had her house under surveillance for three weeks now," Gordon went on. "Managed to piece some of it together. As far as we know, she's Monsauri's cousin. He leads an Al Qaeda cell here in the good ole land of the free."

"What's the draw to Terre Haute? Small Town, USA?" Steven asked.

"That's what you need to figure out," Gordon said. "Think Casanova can get it out of her during pillow talk or maybe during something a little more *active?*"

Steven's eyes were blank as he looked up at his handler.

"Yeah, I think I can," he answered.

"Cameras have already been set up in her house. She loves dogs, the color orange and has a soft spot for little Chinese porcelain dolls," Gordon said.

"That's… creepy," Steven replied.

"Any questions?" he asked.

Steven leaned back in his chair and took a drink of the caffeinated life nectar. "Everything cleared with the local FBI?"

"Of course," Steven couldn't tell if he was lying. "They'll be on hand if an arrest is needed," Gordon replied.

"So, this kid," Steven said. "Is he hers?"

"As far as we can tell," Gordon replied. "Birth records have been sealed."

"Sealed?" Steven asked.

"Couldn't get much," he answered.

"So he could be Monsauri's?" Steven asked.

"Possibly, and his cousin is just looking after him or they

may use the cousin thing as a cover and be lovers. Who knows?" he answered. "Might even be lovers *and* cousins. But I don't have to tell you to watch out. You know firsthand how Al Qaeda uses kids."

Steven paused. Shooting pain raced across his chest and before he could stop himself, his hand went up to the wound that was causing him so much phantom pain. The scar was years old, but the pain was fresh. He closed his eyes and took a deep breath.

"Enjoy the day, Casanova," Gordon said. "We'll be on hand if you need us."

Knowing the moment Gordon and Cliff left the room, Steven let his mind wander back to the sandy blood-soaked city. He felt the heaviness of his combat uniform, the M-4 in his hand, the chafing of the helmet strap under his chin, the surety of his laced up combat boots, the friction of the sand in every crevice of his body and the searing pain as the bullet pierced his chest.

His thoughts began to consume him and he raced to the bathroom. Dry heaving into the toilet, coughing up what little coffee he had gotten down, his whole body shook. *Damn you, Gordon!* He wanted to shout as the smell of rancid coffee mixed with the smell of sand, blood and organs. Groaning a shout, Steven went to the sink and ran cold water. The putrid smell would not leave his nose. Gripping the edge of the sink with shaking hands, he looked up at his reflection in the mirror. For a moment he saw himself in his fatigues, his squad stood behind him just as they looked before the bomb went off. They all looked at him and he felt their blood on his hands.

Then one person stepped forward and he locked eyes with her. She stared at him for a moment then opened her mouth and let out a terrifying scream. Steven roared and punched the mirror. In that moment, everything went back to normal. His bathroom was empty, the sink was running and the smell of coffee burned his nose. Looking down at his shaking hand, he saw a large piece of glass sticking out between his knuckles, pulling it out, he latched on to the pain. He grabbed a hotel towel and wrapped it around his hand. Leaving the bathroom, he found his jacket and keys.

"The hell with it," he said heading to the door and out to the elevator. His hand needed stitches anyway, but he wasn't staying there and having one of the agents do it.

———————◦◦———————

Jon strode through Wishard Hospital with one goal. He reached the door to the man's hospital room and saw the uniform cop standing guard.

"You look like you could use a cup of coffee, Sergeant," Jon said.

"I'm all right, sir, thank you," the officer replied.

"You look like you could use a cup of coffee," Jon stressed. "On me," he said handing him a twenty dollar bill.

The officer looked at him and slowly nodded as understanding dawned.

"Oh, yes, sir, I think I could. Thank you, sir," he answered and took the money. The officer left and after looking down both corridors, Jon slipped into the room.

The perp was asleep and handcuffed to the hospital bed. His leg was bandaged and had Jon not been so dead set on getting answers, he may have smiled. Stepping forward, he gripped the wound tightly. The man awoke with a start.

"Shit, man," he cried. "Who the hell are you?"

"I am the partner of the detective you tried to kill," Jon answered. The man paled. "Ah, I see you've heard of me."

"Look it wasn't nothing personal," he said.

"Really?" Jon asked looking around the room. "It seemed pretty personal. They say you had some fish wire on you. What exactly were you going to do with it?"

"I was… uh…" he said.

"You made it personal. Is this your morphine control?" Jon

asked softly taking it from the side of the bed.

"Hey, hey, hey leave that alone!" He cried.

"You know, funny thing about these things, it's so easy to set it to the right levels but also so easy to stop the flow," Jon pressed a button. Seeing the man flinching as he started to feel his wound, Jon squeezed his leg again.

"Shit!" He cried out. Jon's grip increased. "What the hell do you want?"

"Information," Jon said. "Who sent you?"

"Rob! Rob paid me to kill her," he replied.

"How much did he pay you?" He didn't answer. Jon squeezed harder.

"A hundred grand," he cried out.

"And how much is your life worth to you?" Jon asked. The man looked up confused as Jon shrugged. "You failed him. I wouldn't want to be you when he finds that out. You tell me everything you know and I'll make sure you are in protective custody."

"I don't know anything," he said.

Jon's fingers gripped his leg, digging into it with his nails. The man bucked up and cried out.

"All I know is that he has other men too. Two brothers," he said.

"Names?" Jon barked.

"I don't know," he cried out. Blood began to soak the white gauze on the man's leg.

"Seriously, he never said. I never met them," the man replied, his eyes trailing down and widening when he saw the blood.

"Why?" Jon demanded.

"They weren't there when I was given the job," he said. "He said to take her out. He said she was *of value to you*. This is some sort of payback."

"What is Rob's real name?" Jon asked.

"Oh, come on man, I don't know," he replied. Before Jon could increase his grip, the man bucked up to stop him. "I seriously don't! I swear!"

Jon watched him and finally released his grip.

"I believe you," Jon said. "Now, I need you to give Rob a message for me before he kills you."

"You said I would have protective custody!" he cried.

"I lied," Jon replied. "Tell him to stay away from my partner, my woman, my son, and my nephew. If he touches my family, he will wish for death before I'm done with him."

"You're a cop what are you going to do?" He scoffed.

"I wasn't always a cop. Tell him I know who he is and I will get him."

"You don't know anything," he replied.

"I know it is Paul Anderson," Jon whispered. The man's countenance changed as he looked up at Jon. "You tell him to stay away from Beth."

"He doesn't want her," the man said. "He wants you."

"Tell him he can't have me," he said.

"He'll never give up," the man replied.

Jon pulled back and pocketed his knife. "Then I'm counting on your acting ability to convince him," Jon said heading to the door.

The officer handed Jon a cup of coffee when he walked out of the room.

"Did he tell you anything?" the officer asked.

"Not enough," Jon replied then looked down at the cup. "Thanks for the coffee."

"Anytime," he smiled and watched Jon walked down the corridor to the exit.

CHAPTER EIGHT

"Okay, so what do you think about green and yellow?" Kim asked Courtney while they changed in the store's dressing rooms. Courtney pulled off the top she was trying on in her room across from Kim's.

"Packers," she answered.

Kim paused pulling on another blouse. "Shit," she replied. "You're right…"

Courtney just smiled. Shopping for their honeymoon clothes had to be the best Post Traumatic Stress Therapy imaginable.

"What about green and purple?" Kim replied looking in the mirror.

"High school prom," Courtney replied.

"Courtney," Kim said exasperated. "You're not helping."

"You know, shouldn't you be talking to your fiancé about the colors for your wedding?" She laughed pulling on the next outfit. "Or at least have a date picked before you talk colors?"

"He doesn't feel up to talking. I've tried, but with the pain meds, he says he doesn't always remember what I just said. Yeah, right… But he is willing to help with the venue, I guess. When I bring up colors he says 'whatever you want, love, as long as it has the traditional Irish green color, I'll love it.'" Kim deepened her voice to mimic Scott's. Courtney laughed. "As for the dates, we don't want to wait until the new year. We want to get married this year but everything is booked. We're seriously thinking about having a destination wedding and flying everyone to Ireland. The estate is perfect."

"Why not?" Courtney asked. "I would love to get married in a castle."

"Well... don't tell anyone but we're seriously considering moving there after the wedding. Scott's already talked about selling the law firm. Last time we were over there, he realized how important it was to run the estate hand in hand with Iollan when the time comes. We've talked a lot about it so I wasn't sure if we wanted to get married there and besides it's a lot of work for Kathleen. She's not as young as she likes to make us all think she is," Kim said speaking of Scott's grandmother.

"Well, I know Jon is considering retiring soon, maybe all of you will move together." Even as Courtney said the words there was a pang in her chest. She couldn't imagine not seeing Jon every day, or having the freedom of texting Kim at seven o'clock at night just to see if she wanted to meet up for a glass of wine. "And don't let Kathleen fool you, she's got plenty of fight left in her and I'm sure she'd love to help plan it."

"I know," Kim sighed. "But honestly... ugh, I've even mentioned going down to the courthouse and getting married there or at one of those same day wedding places downtown. Scott refuses. He says he did that the first time around, he won't do it again." Scott's marriage to Meredith Ventmore, his sophomore year in college gave him his daughter Sarah but ended in a messy divorce when she cheated on him with his friend, Alex.

"I think we can understand that," Courtney said.

"Yeah, but honestly I just don't care. As long as I get to

marry my best friend and have one hell of a wedding night that's all I care about."

The women giggled as they gathered their things and met outside their dressing rooms.

"How's Scott doing?" Courtney asked as they stood in the checkout line.

"He's getting there. I mean it's only been a couple of weeks. But he says he's feeling better. He's been working half-days every other day and says he wants to go back to full time on Monday. Jon and I are working on keeping him only half-days this week and going full time next week but he doesn't like that. His therapist says to just take one day at a time and not do anything too soon but you know Scott, he's like his father and he doesn't listen to anyone when it comes to his health."

"Oh god, don't I know it! Jon *never* listens to me!" Courtney said.

"How about you and Ryan?" Kim asked. "There's a ring involved now…" she reminded her of the promise she had told Kim last month. Courtney never slept with anyone and refused until there was a ring involved. Courtney blushed but shook her head.

"There's been some… almosts but never…" she replied. "I guess I'm still a little nervous. My grandmother's voice is ringing in my head with her old school logic that a woman is only so good as her morality and to wait until marriage."

"There's nothing wrong with old school morality," Kim replied. "But there's also nothing wrong with a grown woman making her own decisions. Personally, I don't think you need to worry about measuring yourself to that."

"I guess as much as I want to, I'm scared. What if I do it… badly?"

Kim laughed. "That could happen even in the longest relationships. Don't worry. Ryan doesn't strike me as the kind of guy who doesn't know what he's doing."

Courtney blushed again and looked away. "We're in the same boat..." she admitted.

"What?" Kim asked shocked. "Ryan's never?"

Courtney shook her head. "First it was his Catholic background, then his parents died, then school and then residency. He hasn't had time for a serious relationship."

"I definitely didn't see that coming," Kim replied.

"Don't tell him I told you," Courtney begged.

"Hey, of course not," she answered. "Girl talk, remember? No guys allowed." They stopped talking long enough to pay for their clothes and headed out the store.

"Kim," Courtney started as they walked together down the sidewalk of the outdoor outlet mall. "Do you know anything about Poe?"

"Yeah," she answered. "He's one of mom's favorite authors."

"Really?" Courtney asked. Kim nodded. "Well, I was just curious, if I told you that there was a guy whose murder looked similar to *Tell Tale Heart* and someone said something later that was a quote from the poem *To One in Paradise*, do you think that's enough to make a connection to Poe?"

"What does Jon say?"

"He's telling me to keep an open mind, but I can't ignore the evidence that's staring me in the face."

"As a lawyer, we're taught to never ignore a coincidence and to find a connection, no matter how vague, but to follow the evidence wherever it leads. But," she went on seeing a spark in her friend's eyes. "Maybe he's right and you should keep an open mind."

"He's keeping an open mind, I'm gonna follow the connection. I can't ignore it,"

"No one is asking you to," Kim replied. "Look, I'm dying for a glass of wine. Let's take a load off and get some late lunch."

"Sounds amazing!" Courtney replied shifting her bags to

the other hand and finding her keys in her purse to open her jeep as they passed by leaving the bags inside the trunk.

———◦◦———

Jon's private line was ringing in his office downstairs. The reserved line was for calls overseas to Ireland. Opening the double smoky glass doors just in time, he answered the phone in his usual manner.

"Jonathan Greene," he said.

"Howya, Jon," he heard the voice of his Steward say on the other end.

"Keelan," Jon smiled. "Doing well, and yourself?"

"I'm… all right," he answered. They had hardly spoken more than twice since Riley's death. Jon treaded gently with his old friend.

"How's Aislín?" Jon asked after his Steward's wife.

"She has good days and bad," he answered. "She's still in Dublin to be with her sister for a couple weeks." Losing a child was unbearable. Losing the same child twice was unthinkable. But knowing that child had murdered his own brother in cold blood was incomprehensible.

"I'm sorry, Kee," he said. "I know that's never what you wanted."

"We've been on rocky soil for a while," he admitted. "Ever since Riley's… *Brendan's* death."

"I know you never admitted it before, but I knew," Jon said. "I'm sorry it's been rough."

"I didn't want to burden you," Keelan replied.

"It's no burden, Kee."

"I didn't want the lads to know."

"I understand that."

There was a pause for a long time before Keelan spoke again. "She's left me, Jon… I don't think she's coming back."

41

"I'm so sorry," Jon breathed.

"She won't answer my calls. She won't talk to me… I have to call her sister just to make sure she's all right," he revealed. "And Maggie has to take the call when Aislín isn't there or Aislín…"

"She just needs time," Jon replied.

Keelan breathed deeply. "I know. But I'm hurting just as much as she is. He was my son too!"

"Is there anything I can do?"

"No," he replied. "I'm sorry, I do not blame you. I just… I need to handle this. I was a father of five lads and now… I love my sons, I do deeply but…"

"You love them all the same," Jon answered. "But the ones who passed will always have a special place and you do not want the others to feel like they mean less to you."

"How do you always know my thoughts?" Keelan chuckled humorlessly.

"Because I have the same and I know you," Jon replied. "And trust me when I say, I know Iollan. He does not feel that way. He feels very honored to be the next steward, at least, that's what Scott tells me."

"I know he does," Keelan said proudly. "I called to let you know, too, Iollan passed his last final exam and is set to graduate."

"That's fantastic!" Jon answered. "I had no doubt he would. He's a smart lad. Has he proposed to Meeghan yet?"

"Not yet, but he has asked for me mother's ring, so it is only a matter of time," Keelan explained.

"Let me know when he does," Jon smiled.

"I will," Keelan answered. Again there was a pause and Jon knew his friend had something else on his mind but dared not pressure him. "I also wanted to tell you," Keelan started again. "I was going through the things you were able to get out of evidence… for Riley, and I came across something." When Jon remained silent, Keelan continued. "I found his diary." Again Jon said nothing letting him continue at his leisure. "Other than murderous threats against you and Scott, and rants about me," Keelan's voice shook. "There is something in here that talks about someone else. It doesn't give a full name just a nickname... Rob."

Jon's brows furrowed. Rob, the name Riley had mentioned before he died. The man who wanted Jon dead. The man Jon suspected was Paul Anderson, Beth's rapist ex-husband and father of her three children.

"Rob?" Jon repeated.

"That's all he says," Keelan said.

"Could you make copies and email them over to me?" Jon asked.

"I'll send it as soon as I can," Keelan offered.

"Cheers, thanks," Jon answered. "Can I ask you, does he say anything about Poe? Edgar Allan Poe?"

"No," Keelan sounded a little confused. "Why?"

"A theory," Jon replied. "Not important."

"Jon," Keelan said, his voice telling Jon what he was about say was what he truly called about. "My son tried to kill you. Do you still trust me as you did before?"

"Yes," Jon answered without hesitation.

"How can you?"

"Because you are not your son, Keelan," Jon replied. "You are my friend. We're practically brothers. I know you as well as you know me and you know me far too well."

Keelan breathed a relieved laugh. "Not as well as my sister knows you," he teased, a breath of fresh air filling the space between them.

"Eh," Jon groaned. "Yeah, let's not go there," Keelan chuckled. "Riley, I personally believe, had a psychological break and fixated on me. He blamed me."

"I wish I could've talked to him, one more time. Maybe I could have understood him or even talked him out of this... Is it true he followed you to Ireland last month?" Keelan asked.

"Yes, he did," Jon said. "He was the one who shot at Scott and Kim on her birthday."

Keelan took a deep shaky breath.

"Did he want to take more from us?" Keelan nearly yelled.

"I honestly think he wanted to get at me. He knew if anything happened to Kim, Scott and I would go after him. If anything would happen to Scott, I'd never rest until I found him and then, at my weakest moment, he would strike. His whole plan was to get back at me," Jon explained.

"But why?" Keelan asked.

"I don't know," he answered. "The police found a well-worn picture of the Green Man above a door of a dilapidated cottage on the land. Any idea why he would have it or what it meant to him?"

"The pagan symbol?" Keelan asked.

"Yeah," Jon answered.

"Jon, the Green Man represents rebirth," Keelan said. "You know this, it is the symbol of our island to mean creator and destroyer. He was the hunter. If Riley had a picture of him in his pocket, he was more lost than I thought. If Riley felt a kinship with the Green Man..." Keelan shook his head.

"It makes sense," Jon offered.

"In a twisted sort of way, I'm afraid you're right," Keelan replied. "And his diary makes sense now too. He started to refer to himself as *The Hunter*." He cleared his throat when his voice cracked on the last word.

"Keelan," Jon said softly. "There is nothing you could have done differently."

"I keep telling myself that," he got out. "But it doesn't help."

"No, of course not," Jon replied.

"He killed his brother," Keelan said. "He shot Scott. He

nearly killed you. Somewhere along the line I must have failed him. Oh Christ…"

"You did not fail," Jon said.

"I feel like I did," Keelan replied. "I don't know what to do, Jon. My life is falling apart around me and all I can do is watch it crumble."

"Then you rely on your friends and family to help you through," Jon said.

"When did you get so good at this?" Keelan asked.

"Since my own life crashed down around me," Jon offered.

They were quiet for a little while before Keelan spoke again.

"I still have my three sons; I should not be like this. I should be thankful to have them… I'll copy the pages and send them to you."

"Thanks," Jon said.

Keelan took a deep breath. "Thanks for letting me talk."

"Anytime," Jon replied. "Call me if you need me."

"I will, cheers."

CHAPTER NINE

After getting three stitches in the gash in his hand, Steven grabbed a beer at a dive bar and caught a bit of dinner at a place with peanut shells on the floor, a mechanical bull and watered down bourbon. Steven staggered back to his hotel, hardly drunk enough to forget the shattered mirror in his bathroom or the reason behind it standing in the room beside the window.

"That's coming out of your salary, you know," Gordon said indicating the mirror in the bathroom.

"The hell it is," Steven replied. "You know what you did."

"I didn't do anything," Gordon answered flatly.

"Go to hell," Steven said.

"I'm already there having to deal with you," Gordon replied.

"You know what? Fine, get me another handler," Steven ordered.

"No one else will put up with you, you know that," Gordon said.

"I'm sick of your shit, Gordon," Steven replied.

"Bradley Henderson," Gordon said. "Know him?"

"Never heard of him," Steven replied. "Now get the hell out

of my room or are you gonna share my bed tonight? Don't think Cliff would like that." Steven's eyes trailed to the agent standing to Gordon's right.

Cliff took a menacing step forward, Gordon pulled him back.

"I'm getting pretty tired of your shit too, Steven," Gordon said.

In his current state, Steven didn't see Gordon's right hook until it was too late to dodge. He was sent reeling back and collided with the wall behind him. They didn't talk but Steven barreled into him knocking him onto the bed. Immediately, Cliff and Brian, the other agent on duty, pulled Steven off. Not going down without a fight, Steven swung catching Gordon square in the jaw and elbowing Brian just above the eye.

"You have no right to mess with my life like this!" Steven shouted twisting out of Cliff's grasp.

"We're the US government, Steven," Gordon wiped the blood off his lower lip. "We don't need *rights*. Hold him." Brian, a former linebacker with a grudge, grabbed Steven and Clifford, just an inch shy of Steven's six-foot two-inch frame, gripped his wrists.

"Sorry, boys," Steven grunted. "I don't go that way."

Gordon let off three hard hits to Steven's ribs before pulling him away and tossing him into the chair. His ribs ached, but Gordon was strategic enough not to break any bones.

"Now, are you feeling a bit better? Got your jabs in?" Gordon sneered wiping more blood off his lips.

"Try that again and I will not hesitate to kill you," Steven said.

"So dramatic, Casanova," Gordon taunted leaning closer to him. "Keep up the good work and you'll stay alive. But one more stunt like this and Uncle Sam will thank you for your most valuable service and feed you to the dogs. Do I make myself clear?"

Steven head butted him and smirked when he heard the

very satisfying crack of Gordon's nose breaking.

———◦◦———

Jon spied Courtney at the kitchen table and headed over. Even though Scott's *get well soon* party was in full swing, he still saw the tightness around her eyes as they darted about taking in everyone around her. Making his way over to her, he pulled her into a tight hug. "How ya doing?" He asked.

"I'm fine," she mumbled into his chest.

"Okay," he knew better than to push. "There's your favorite Cosmo on the bar."

She gifted him with a brilliant smile and a peck on the cheek.

"You know the way to my heart," she replied.

"That's good luck, you know, to kiss an Irishman," he said.

"I know, I've had it every day since I first kissed Ryan," she teased.

"My nephew is only half Irish," he replied winking. She laughed but eyed his apron.

"*Kiss me I'm the Irish cook...* real subtle, Jon," she replied.

He laughed and looked back to the kitchen when he heard his name. "Baby," Beth called. "The burger patties are ready."

"Comin', love," he answered. "I'm putting some burgers on the grill, how do you like yours cooked?"

"I'm really not that hungry," she replied walking with him to the kitchen.

"Oh come on," he said.

Turning back to Courtney, he kissed her forehead and squeezed her shoulders. "You're safe, have some fun today."

She nodded and watched him walk away. "Medium," she called after him. He turned back to her confused. "My burger, medium."

"Ah, well like all my stuff it'll be good and charred," he

teased. "Tell that boy o' mine to put on some music, eh?"

She watched as he lifted the lid to the already smoking grill and added the burgers beside the bratwursts and salmon. Looking past him to the early spring clouds that came rolling in, Courtney couldn't help reflecting on the battle the sunlight was having. One moment it was bright, the next it was hidden behind a dark cloud.

Someone walked up behind her and wrapped his arms around her. She knew immediately who it was and snuggled back into him.

"Guess who," he teased.

"My doctor," she whispered reaching behind her to cup his face in her hand. He rested his chin on her shoulder.

"How's my favorite cop?" He asked kissing the shell of her ear.

"Better now I'm in the hands of a very good doctor," she grinned.

He chuckled. "You seem a million miles away, love. What are you thinking about?"

"How lonely I'd be if you weren't here," she replied.

"No, seriously," he said softly.

"Seriously? I was thinking about how wonderful it is to have such a great friend and partner all rolled into one," she answered looking back at Jon smiling at something Dave Weston had said.

"You know I'm not jealous," Ryan replied.

She wiggled her way around and looked up at him confused.

"What do you mean?" She asked, her arms wrapping around his neck.

"About how you feel about Uncle Jon," he answered. "I know what he means to you and I would never get in the way of that. He's a good guy to have around."

"Ryan…" she started. "What are you saying?"

"It's okay," he answered. "I'm not saying anything. It just helps me to know Uncle Jon would do anything to keep you safe."

"I love *you*, you know that, right?" she asked leaning up to kiss him. Ryan's eyes tightened.

"Yes, I do," he answered. "But I also know you love him."

"That's not true," she shook her head. "And I really don't need this right now."

"I know, I know, I'm sorry. You know, I never questioned your ability to be a cop, but… I swear I got a few grey hairs when I heard what happened to you. And when you told me not to come to help you because Uncle Jon was there, it just… made me question."

"Question what?" she asked.

"Why him?" She heaved a sigh and looked away. He pulled her chin back to him. "Just tell me you love me again and put my mind at ease," he said.

"If you really knew me, you would know why I said what I did," she replied. "I told you not to come because you were at work. You are not on board entirely yet and I didn't want you to get into trouble for it. I told you Jon was there because it's his job to be there. Really, Ryan." She tried to pull away but he held her to him.

"I'm sorry," he said. "I just… I'm an asshole."

"On that we agree," she answered. He nodded, leaned down and kissed her gently. She pressed her lips together and did not kiss him back.

"I'm glad you're safe," he said.

"I'm still pissed off at you," she said.

"With reason," he answered. "But can I ask you something?" his eyes lit up playfully. She was a sucker for those bright blue eyes and he knew it, damn him.

"What?" she asked trying not to let him get to her.

"Whenever we have an argument, talk to me first, don't just shoot me," he said.

"Hmm... I'll have to think about it," she replied. He laughed and kissed her once more. That time, she kissed him back but just slightly.

"But the handcuffs? Keep those," he whispered. She laughed then, shook her head, punched his shoulder gently and kissed him deeply.

"Get a room you two," Scott passed them and headed for Kim waiting for him at the screened-in porch.

Ryan and Courtney pulled back.

"I love you but sometimes you are an insensitive ass," she said.

"I know," he sighed. "I have zero bedside manner."

"Doctor," she rolled her eyes.

He winked but then his face turned serious. "I love you," he said. "And when I found out, I nearly died. I couldn't get to you and I..."

"I know, hey, it's over. I'm fine," she replied. He nodded but a seam on her shirt seemed to have captured his attention even though she knew he wasn't looking at it.

"If anything happened to you," he started.

"Stop, please," she said. "It's okay, nothing will happen to me."

"This Poe thing... it worries me," he answered.

"What's the worst that can happen? The Pit and the Pendulum? Seriously, baby, I'll be fine."

CHAPTER TEN

Something was buzzing. Jon's eyes shot open and Beth stirred beside him, wrapping her leg tighter around his. She flung her arm across his chest and burrowed her head into his neck, still asleep. Realizing his cell phone was charging on the nightstand and someone was calling him, Jon grabbed it before it woke Beth and put it to his ear.

"Jonathan Greene," he said clearing his throat.

"Hey Jon, it's Jason," he heard on the other end.

"Hey Jay," Jon said recognizing his godson's voice and pulling the phone away from his ear to check the number. "I didn't recognize the number."

"I'm calling from the new house phone. I wanted you to have the number." Jason said.

"Oh great, thanks," Jon smiled. He looked at the time. It was two in the morning. "You okay? You sound a little strained?"

There was a pause on the other end. "Did I wake you?"

"Uh... it's two in the morning, Jay. What'd ya think?" Jon teased rubbing his eyes.

"I'm sorry," he answered.

"Don't be. What's up? You okay?"

"Yeah, not really. I needed to talk to someone and I was hoping I could talk to my godfather."

"Of course," Jon said sliding his arm out from under Beth's head and sitting up.

"I know it's late, but would it be okay if I came over?" Jason asked.

"Absolutely," Jon replied. "Come on by. Is it a coffee or a whiskey kind of night?"

There was a pause on Jason's end. "Maybe both."

"Sounds good to me."

———◦———

"Whoa wait," Quinn Henderson saw a car pull into Jon's driveway. "Who are you?" He checked his file. That car did not belong to anyone he recognized. Pulling out his phone, he took a quick photo of the car and sent it to Rob.

———◦———

Jon saw headlights flash through the front door windows as a car pulled into the driveway. Walking over, he turned off the alarm and opened the front door.

"Clairvoyant?" Jason called as he walked up the walkway.

"Saw the headlights," Jon smiled. They pulled each other into a tight hug and thumped one another on the back. "Damn, it's good to see you."

"You too," Jason replied. "It's been too long."

"It has. Coffee just finished and I've pulled out a bottle of Green Spot."

"My favorite," Jason smiled following Jon into the house. "You can't get whiskey like that in the states."

"Don't I know it," Jon replied. "How's your supply?"

"Running a little low if I'm being honest," Jason answered.

"You should take a couple bottles while you're here. You

know I ship it by the crate."

"Thanks," then looking around, Jason went on. "Is Scott here?"

"No, he's staying over at Ryan's tonight." Jon explained. "He's been keeping an extra eye on Scott's recovery and it was one of their *guy nights*."

"Ah I see, how's he doing?" Jason asked.

"Better, I believe," Jon answered. "Go ahead and sit. I'll get some coffee." Jon said heading into the kitchen. "Would you rather have the whiskey first?" He called over his shoulder.

"Would ya kill me if I asked for some whiskey *in* the coffee?" Jason asked.

"Not at all. I'll make up some Irish Coffee. Your dad used to like that." Jon smiled fondly at the memory of his childhood best friend.

"I wish I had gotten to meet him," Jason said sadly straddling one of the barstools.

"You're just like him," Jon replied getting the mugs from the cupboard. "You even look like his twin."

"You and Dad were close, right?" Jason asked.

"I was privileged to call him my best friend." Jon said.

"You never talk about... *it*. Were you with him?" Jason asked. "Were you there when he...?"

Jon paused pulling the heavy cream out of the refrigerator. Jason had never asked before. For a moment, Jon could smell the intensely pungent odor of the Vietnam jungle mixed with the overwhelmingly putrid smell of decaying, unwashed flesh. He heard the pop of gun fire, men screaming in agony as their life's blood seeped out of open jagged wounds. Flashes of faces he once knew raced through his mind, stopping on one face in particular, the face now mirrored in the man waiting patiently before him.

"Yes," Jon finally answered shutting the door of the fridge. "I was with him."

"Did he die... well?" Jason asked.

"No one dies well... but..." *lie to him.* Jon thought. "He didn't suffer... much."

Jason looked away. "Did he love my mom?"

Jon's face morphed into a frown but quickly relaxed when he saw genuine concern lining Jason's eyes.

"Oh yes," Jon answered gently. "He loved her more than anything. And you, he couldn't wait to get home to see you," Jon watched as Jason took a deep breath.

"I don't know how I can mourn someone I've never met, but there's always been this hole in my heart. I've always lacked a father." He looked up suddenly at Jon. "Not that I don't absolutely appreciate what you have done for me. Without you I'm sure I wouldn't know what it's like to be one. But there are so many times I want to talk to my dad. Especially now I am a father." Walking over to him, Jon put a comforting hand on his godson's arm.

"I know," Jon replied. "Believe me. I lost my da' before Scott was born and there were so many times I felt like a ship adrift but that's when I turned to Carol's dad who treated me as his own son. You can always talk to me. I know it's not the same as your own flesh and blood but I'm here for you, Jay."

"And I am so grateful," Jason answered. "You know, you may have *fathered* only Scott... but you have been a *dad* to so many others and I am honored to be one of them."

"I am privileged to have been a dad to you. I am so proud of the man you have become. Your father would be too," Jon smiled slightly. They were quiet for a little while as Jon finished the coffees and offered to go into the living room. Once settled in his chair, Jon took a sip of his coffee and looked at Jason. "So, why have you really come over? What happened?"

Jason huffed. "Mom's engaged again."

"Ah," Jon replied taking another sip. "Do you like this one at least?"

"I have never met him. She met him down in Florida."

"And you don't want your mom hurt again or..."

"Well there's that, but honestly it's a little more selfish than that."

"Tell me," Jon said.

"Every time she brings someone over I... I know it's irrational considering Dad's been dead for over thirty-five years but I hope..." Jon waited. "It's silly I know but still I wonder if this one could be him and when it's not I... it bothers me."

Jon nodded. "I can understand that. You've always missed that connection with the man who's blood flows in your veins. You have missed the connection of a father."

"I have and considering mom is on husband number five, I think she is too," he said.

"Your mother is a wonderful and strong woman. She loved your father and when he died she was devastated."

"Why..." Jason took another swallow before he continued. "Why didn't you and mom every... try it out?"

"Your mother and I could never do that for one very simple reason, your father," Jon explained. "We did try. You were just a baby. We went out on a date but halfway through we realized we were better as friends. Neither of us could put your dad to the side when we saw each other. Instead I offered to be there for you both and we agreed to go from there."

Jason nodded slowly. "You never went any further?"

"No," Jon shook his head. "We couldn't dishonor his memory."

"I don't think I've ever seen mom truly happy."

"She deserves to be, if this man is the one to make her happy will you stand in her way?" Jon asked gently.

"No, I couldn't," he shook his head. "She deserves a chance and if he's going to be the one then I will stand by her."

"Good," Jon drank again and waited.

"What about you?" Jason asked leaning back on the couch. "Any news on your end?"

"Nothing much," Jon replied.

"Sorry again that I couldn't make Scott's party," Jason apologized. "Sally was out of town and I was taking care of Anna."

"No worries," Jon shook his head. "How's that going? I know it was tough for you after the divorce."

"It's fine," he replied. "I… signed up for online dating."

"Did you? Good," Jon nodded. "Any bites yet?"

Jason chuckled. "Not so much, but there's one or two that's promising."

"Need me to run a background check on them?" Jon offered.

Jason laughed but shrugged. "I'll keep that in mind."

"Jon?" Beth appeared through the doorway of the living room, wrapped in a short, silk housecoat. "Oh, I'm so sorry, I didn't know you had company," she tightened the housecoat around her. "You weren't in bed and I saw the light on."

"You remember Jason, right, babe?" Jon asked. She looked over at the man who stood when she walked in.

"Of course," Beth replied smiling. "It's good to see you again Jason."

"And you, Ms. Nixon," Jason said. "I just finished your latest book. I really enjoyed it."

"Oh, thank you!" she acknowledged. "That's so sweet of you. And it's Beth."

"Jay called me earlier wanting to talk. I didn't want to wake you," Jon explained. "I know you were… tired."

Beth looked straight at him knowing he was trying to make her blush.

"I was, considering I had to do all the work," she replied and laughed when he looked down and cleared his throat, a nice pink tinge to his stubble covered cheeks. Jason chuckled.

"Well don't let me disturb you," she said. "I'll just get some water and head back up."

"I'll be up a little later, baby," Jon replied.

"Take your time." She turned to go. "But be sure to wake me when you come to bed." Jon winked agreed. "It was nice to see you again, Jason."

"And you, Beth," Jason replied still chuckling at the exchange he witnessed. Once she was gone, Jason turned back to Jon. "You old dog," Jason smirked.

"Old?" Jon questioned.

"How long has *that* been going on?" He asked.

"Not long," Jon answered. "Since... St. Patrick's Day actually..."

"That's great!" Jason smiled. "You should've told me, I would never have come over and interrupted."

"You didn't interrupt anything. Besides, it's always good to see you."

"Well," Jason drained his coffee. "I'll not keep you down here when you have a beautiful woman warming your bed."

"I appreciate that," Jon laughed. "Let me get you a couple bottles of Green Spot."

"Oh yes, I'll at least have *that* to keep *me* warm tonight," Jason winked.

CHAPTER ELEVEN

"Dad?" Scott called as he and Ryan opened the front door.

"Kitchen," Jon called back.

"Hey," Scott smiled as he rounded the bend and saw Jon and Beth. "I didn't know you were over, Beth."

Beth greeted them with a kiss on the cheek. "Jon and I were just thinking about what to make for breakfast," she explained. "After he made me a wonderful cup of espresso."

"I bet," Ryan stated. "I wanted to take you all out to breakfast. Courtney and Kim are already on their way. We're to meet up at Le Peep."

"Oh grand," Jon replied.

"That's so sweet of you!" Beth said. "I need to change. Give me one second."

"Saves me doing the dishes," Jon winked and followed her up the stairs to his room.

───◦───

Rob sat in his car watching everyone pile into Jon's

Escalade and drive off. The man he had hired to kill Courtney had told him about the conversation he had with Jon in the hospital. At least, he did before Rob pulled the trigger and watched the bullet pierce him between the eyes. He knew Jon had guessed who he was, but he kept his distance. It was fun now they were on a semi-equal playing field.

Putting away his headphones, he waited until Jon drove down the hill and turned out to the main road. Rob pulled on his fake IMPD jacket and baseball cap from the trunk of the car.

The service door to the garage gave way and he went in quickly. Knowing he had tripped the silent alarm, he opened the door to the main house and went in. Setting the manila envelope he had under his jacket on the kitchen island, he hurried upstairs.

Going into Jon's bedroom, he noticed the bed was made in Jon's standard militaristic style, no clothes hung on the chair beside the small bookcase, but there were two empty wine glasses and an empty bottle on the nightstand. The closet door was open and he saw some of Beth's clothes hanging next to Jon's. Taking one of her shirts in his hand, he pressed it to his nose. She still smelled the same and it made his body jump to life. The shirt was soft in his hands and he remembered the first time she was wearing that same color. He smirked as he thought of how their first meeting had created Steven.

But knowing he only had a few seconds left to finish the task at hand, he dropped the shirt and hurried down the stairs, out of the house, through the garage, closing the door tightly after him. He walked calmly to his car as he heard police sirens blaring in the distance.

Jon stood in the living room of his home with the police officer who responded to the silent alarm.

"You know we'll find whoever did this, Lieutenant," the

officer smiled. Jon nodded. He knew who had done it, but he could not say anything yet.

"I appreciate your promptness," Jon thanked him.

The officer nodded, saluted and headed to the door. Scott and Ryan walked up to stand beside him.

"What the hell happened, dad?" Scott asked.

"I don't know," Jon replied.

"We know you're lying, Uncle Jon," Ryan went on. "We understand but we wanna help. Is it to do with this case?"

Jon did not look at his boys. He kept his eyes on Courtney as she walked into the room.

"They just finished their sweep," she said locking eyes with her partner. "I found this…" she held up Beth's shirt. "It was on the floor just outside the closet door. Knowing you, it wouldn't have just been left there." Beth froze.

Jon shook his head and turned slightly toward Beth.

"No, that was hanging in the closet," Jon replied. "I'm sure of it."

"I hung it up last night," Beth confirmed.

"We won't get anything off of it," Courtney said. "Have you opened the envelope?" Jon shook his head. "It's addressed to you," she went on.

"I know," he answered glancing back at Beth.

"Kim," Beth began, standing. "Let's get home, love. You boys come too, if you'd like. We haven't had breakfast yet. I'll cook. Come on." She went up to Jon, pulled him close to her and kissed him. "I love you. Please be careful."

"I will," he answered. "Love you, too." He watched as the four of them left and turned to Courtney.

"Do you want me to open it?" She asked.

"No," he answered. "I'll do it."

He took the envelope, pulled up the prongs and opened the lip. Photos and a stack of papers, fell out.

"When were these taken?" Courtney asked looking at the surveillance pictures. Jon looked over.

"After Riley was killed," he explained.

"And this one?" She pointed to another one.

Jon looked down. "That was when I had lunch with Steven."

Courtney flipped to the last few and Jon immediately took them from her. She blinked a few times, then looked up at him.

"Tell me that's not what I think it was…" she said.

"'Fraid so," he answered hiding them.

"Try and remember to draw the curtains next time, Romeo," she stated. "It's a side of you I didn't think I'd ever see."

Jon cleared his throat. "This means he's been watching the house."

"Clearly," she replied. "At *all* hours of the night."

Ignoring her ribbing, Jon looked through the last of the photos. "These were taken on different nights this month."

"What's in there?" She indicated the clipped papers he set on the counter.

"It's a criminal file," Jon replied.

"There's a note on it," Courtney indicated the folded piece of paper taped to the front.

Jon pulled it off and read it.

"'Thought you'd like a little clue, isn't this fun? He's of no use to me now. Prefect'," Jon read.

"Prefect?" Courtney asked. Jon opened the file and froze. "What is it?" She asked.

"It's the file on a man named Bradley Henderson," Jon replied haltingly.

"Who's that?" Courtney asked.

"A man involved in the murder of… my wife," he answered.

<hr />

"You son-of-a-bitch!" Quinn burst into Rob's room.

"Hello, Quinn," Rob said looking at him in the mirror while he shaved.

"I swear if you got my brother killed, I'll kill you, you bastard!" Quinn shouted.

"I told him to keep his distance, he didn't listen." Rob explained sarcastically then shrugged. "Is it my fault the CIA caught him? No. Cut our losses and move on."

"I swore I'd have his back," Quinn seethed.

"Touching," Rob said. "I think I'm gonna tear up."

"You can't just use him," Quinn went on.

"Really?" Rob asked. "Or you'll what? Leave? A little late for that option. Last I checked, you owe me. Don't forget I can call in as a concerned citizen. An escaped felon on the loose? Please hurry! I think they have a hostage!" Rob changed his voice just to prove his point.

"Don't think just because you have a little bit of power over me, I'll hesitate in killing you." Quinn said.

"Oh, I have no doubt of it," Rob replied. "But before you do, you might want to watch where you step."

Quinn looked down and saw a handgun under the sink aimed at him with a trip wire strung across the doorway.

"Now, go finish surveillance like a good boy," Rob said. "I'll call you when I'm ready to relieve you."

CHAPTER TWELVE

Steven nursed his bruised ribs with a long soak in the tub, pain meds with a bourbon chaser, and rest. His bed was comfortable as usual, but he couldn't fall asleep for longer than an hour. When he tossed again and eleven o'clock shone on the alarm clock, he gave up. Taking his phone, he sent a text to Gordon.

Casanova: Is the hotel phone okay to use? Or should I use my cell for personal calls?

Hating having to ask permission, he sucked it up and his ribs thanked him. After a few minutes, Gordon replied.

Flash: Hotel phone is better if you must. We swept the room this afternoon. Make it quick.

Taking the phone, he dialed a number.

"Jonathan Greene," Jon answered on the second ring.

"Hey, it's me," Steven said.

"You okay?" Jon asked.

"Yeah. Just couldn't sleep. Did I wake you?"

"No, I couldn't sleep either. How are things going?"

"I think something is going on," Steven answered.

"I'm listening."

"I was followed here by a man, I do not know his name,

and it could be nothing, but my handler is acting strangely," Steven explained.

There was a pause on the other end. "There's something you need to know," Jon finally said. "My house was broken into earlier today. And in the kitchen, there was a manila envelope with pictures and a few of them were of us at lunch. Bradley Henderson's file was left along with a note saying he's of no use anymore. Henderson was an armed robber and Meth dealer. He was implicated in Carol's death. He was one of the ones behind the drug ring that killed her. I'm fairly certain the guy who sent it is Rob, the same one Riley talked about before he died."

"My handler mentioned that name to me this afternoon," Steven said. "Do you think he was the one who followed me?"

"Possibly," Jon answered. "I'm going to look at his file but I'm having difficulty. Watch your back, Bradley had a twin brother, Quinn. If one of them is out, he might be too. And I wouldn't put it past Rob to have hired them both."

"Have you gotten any closer to figuring out who Rob is?" Steven asked.

"I promised I would never lie to you. You can't ask me that, not right now. You need to keep your head in the game," Jon replied.

"C'mon, you gotta level with me here, Jon."

"I don't have any evidence," Jon began.

"But you have a suspicion," Steven interrupted.

"Yes."

"Tell me."

"Not yet," Jon answered. "I do not want anything to distract you from the task at hand. I swear to you the moment you call telling me it's over, I will tell you everything."

"Fine," Steven acquiesced.

"Get some sleep," Jon ordered. "Everything will be all right. I promise. Be safe."

"You too," Steven said before he hung up.

Steven settled into the bed and took a deep breath. Jon wasn't telling him everything and that made Steven question who he thought Rob was. There was only one man Jon would think would distract him from his job. Paul Anderson. His real father. Steven gripped the remote tightly in his hand. If his father was back to hurt Beth, Steven would stop at nothing, save a bullet in the chest, to protect her.

Sleep obviously illusive, Steven got up, pulled on sweats and tennis shoes. He texted Gordon that he was going for a run. He wasn't surprised when Brian and Zoe fell into step with him, both dressed for a workout.

"Worst time gets to buy a round," Zoe said.

"Done," both men replied as they headed out into the night air and began their jog.

———◦◦◦———

Courtney sat at her desk that next morning, pouring over the paperwork she had to fill out for her home invasion shooting. The words were running together and all she wanted to put down was *guy got into my home and tried to kill me, so I shot him.* Knowing the police shrink wouldn't look too well on that explanation, she tried to focus.

Eventually, her eyes drifted to the file on Jon's desk. The John Doe case that resembled *Tell Tale Heart* by Poe. She pulled out the notes she had taken from her college days and began writing down what the three cases; John Doe, her home invasion, and Jon's break-in had in common. Poe was a running theme in each of them. The name *Prefect* from the note left in Jon's kitchen had bothered her.

"Hey," Jon called.

She jumped slightly and looked up from her notes.

"Hey," she said. "How long have you been standing there?"

"Not long, but long enough to know your paperwork is not as interesting to you as my files or what you're writing," he pushed off the doorway and walked over to her carrying two coffees. "Will this help?" He asked, handing her one of the cups.

"Mm, thanks," she sighed, smelling the coffee. She casually sat back in her chair. Jon leaned against her desk and watched her.

"Anything wrong?" he asked sipping his coffee, the smell of hazelnut filled the air. Courtney knew she had two options. Lie to him or tell him why she was going through his files.

"I was just thinking about how much these cases resemble Poe... I know, I know, so sue me. I'm your partner and I see the connection. You be the level headed one," she stated.

"Clearly," he answered pushing off her desk and walking to his. Opening the file she had been looking at, he continued. "What did I miss? Any more news on the forensics from John Doe?"

"Dr. O'Malley says death was from blunt force trauma as she had mentioned at the scene. The chest cavity was ripped apart apparently with bare hands, but remarkably the heart shows little tampering."

"So we're looking for a surgeon or someone used to handling human organs," Jon offered.

"Possibly," she agreed. "But Grace also thinks death was definitely between five and six o'clock that morning."

"So our street artist is out of the picture," Jon said. "He was having breakfast with about five other people."

"Agreed. Grace said John Doe's prints were not in the system and he had recently had a good dinner, including Chateau Bordeaux within several hours of his death."

"Got the vintage?" Jon teased.

"She's good, but not that good," Courtney replied.

"So, what — wined and dined before death?"

"Steak and lobster," Courtney revealed. "Reminds me of *The Cask of Amontillado*."

"Shields," Jon warned. "Check out all the places within a five-mile radius that has those three items on the menu," Jon said.

"Jon, he was found at New York and Penn, that's about every decent restaurant downtown," Courtney replied.

"Might get lucky," Jon answered. "Start at the intersection and work out."

"Oy," she breathed and turned to her computer.

After hanging up with the sixth restaurant, Courtney desperately needed a refill on her coffee. Just as she was about to suffer through the precinct's coffee, her cell rang.

"Shields," she answered. Listening a moment, she looked over at Jon and met his gaze. "We're on our way." She hung up as she finished writing something down. Jon stood and gathered their jackets. "Homicide," she explained accepting her coat from him. "This one's a little odd."

"What else is new?" Jon asked as they rode the elevator down to the garage.

"It's in a church," she said. "6900 North Meridian."

Jon froze when the elevator doors opened and Courtney stepped out.

"What?" She asked looking back at him.

"What's the name of the church?" Jon asked.

"Meridian Street Lutheran," she said looking at the name, then back up at him "Why?"

Jon's eyes hardened. "Who's the victim?" He asked coolly.

"John Doe for right now," she replied.

He nodded and eventually walked with her.

Driving silently for a little while, Jon's jaw flexed a few times beneath his black and grey stubble. Courtney watched as a myriad of emotions crossed his face as he drove. Unconsciously or not, Courtney noticed how he always looked down at Carol's picture on the dashboard.

"Meridian Street Lutheran was Carol's and my home church when we moved here. Though I was Catholic and Carol was Non-denominational, we agreed to raise Scott in a church," Jon finally said. "Father Isaac presided over Carol's funeral. I haven't been back since she died," Courtney said nothing. "I left the church on somewhat bad terms after Carol died. I swore I would never go back."

"I can get us reassigned," Courtney offered.

"No," he answered. "It's a case, we're cops. I can deal with this." Jon was quiet for another few minutes. Finally, he cleared his throat once and spoke. "Fill me in. Why is this one weird?" He asked.

"It looks like the priest who found him and called 911, only said one word before there was silence on the other end," Courtney explained

"What did he say?"

"Witchcraft..." Courtney replied. Jon's hands gripped the steering wheel tighter. "When the uniforms arrived, they found the priest passed out, prostrate in front of the altar."

"Who's the priest?" Jon asked.

Courtney looked down at her notes. Looking back up at him, she took a breath before answering.

"Father Isaac..." she finally said.

Jon licked his suddenly dry lips and nodded slightly. "Where is he?"

"Looks like he regained consciousness but refused to go to the hospital. He stayed at the church. The EMTs have cleared him, but he's still agitated."

"With reason," Jon replied.

"Agreed," Courtney answered. "You got this?"

"Fate can be cruel sometimes. I remember when I left that church, I told Mat it would take a miracle to get me back," he chuckled humorlessly. "I guess it's true what they say about mysterious ways."

CHAPTER THIRTEEN

The morning was hazy, almost eerie. Steven passed Gordon's van but didn't stop, only rapped his knuckles against the side three times.

"We read you, Casanova, loud and clear," he heard Gordon over his earbud. "*Potty Training* is go."

"Whoever names these missions should not give up their day job," Steven replied.

Still jogging, Steven started to feel a cramp in his side. Maybe that jog the night before wasn't such a good idea after all. Pulling up short at the entrance to the soccer field at the park, Steven wiped his forehead with his shirt and stretched.

"Make your move, Casanova," Gordon said.

Looking over, he saw a boy he recognized from the file, practicing his goal shot. Steven walked to the gate, put his arms over it and took out his headphones. For a moment, he just watched the kid as he tried to make another goal and missed.

"Looks like you could use some help," Steven called out to him.

The kid turned toward him and took a couple steps back.

"I've got a game tomorrow and our best player got sick," he

replied.

"You know, my dad taught me how to shoot a goal," he lied. "There's a pretty cool trick to kicking the ball that will get it in nearly every time."

"Really?" Josh asked.

"Yeah. My name's Craig," Steven said. "What's yours?"

"Josh," he replied. "But my friends call me JC."

"Well, Josh," Steven said. "How about I show you?" Josh looked around and stepped back again. "Would your parents be all right with it?" Steven amended.

"My mom had to answer her phone, but she'll be right back," Josh said.

Smart kid, Steven thought. *Doesn't know me, doesn't trust me.*

Eventually Josh looked at him and nodded warily. Steven unlatched the fence and headed toward him.

Jon walked through the church toward the sanctuary. Far too many memories flooded his mind as Courtney followed silently behind him. Reaching the main doors of the sanctuary, they saw two officers guarding the entrance.

Gritting his teeth against the memory of Carol's casket at the end of the aisle, his legs were heavy and his mouth went dry. Jon turned away and rushed into the men's restroom. Courtney followed him without thinking. Hearing him heaving in one of the stalls, she wet a couple paper towels and took it over to him. With shaking fingers, he pressed it against his pale face. He couldn't bring himself to look at his partner, but Courtney gently touched his arm.

"So much for the tough guy approach," Jon whispered. He finally looked down at her. "You told me once, you would never pity me," he went on. "Don't start now."

"I don't pity you, Jon, you know me better than that. I just am so sorry…" she said.

"For what? Following me into the men's restroom?" he tried to tease.

"Shut up," she punched his arm gently. "I know you hate to appear, what you think, is weak. But Jon you are the strongest man I know. I just wish I could have been there for you."

"You would have been thirteen years old. You would have wanted to help but wouldn't have known how."

"I would have taken your hands, like this," she intertwined her fingers with his. "I would have looked in your eyes," she held his gaze. "And I would have said… the sun'll come out tomorrow." Jon burst out laughing. "What?" Courtney asked with a twinkle in her eye.

"My god," he said. "You can't stop singing, can you?"

She laughed. "Nope, never. So are we going to tap dance with Daddy Warbucks or go and be cops?"

He smiled crookedly, wadding up the paper towel and throwing it into the waste basket.

"Cops," he confirmed. "I don't tap dance."

Walking out of the men's restroom, they made their way down the aisle toward the priest sitting in one of the pews. Before addressing the older man, Jon took a deep breath.

"Father Isaac," he finally said, though the name tasted bitter on his tongue.

The priest looked over and slowly stood. "Jonathan Greene…" the priest breathed. There was a pause. "Thank god you're here, but we do seem to meet under the most unpleasant circumstances." Father Isaac extended his hand to Jon who, though guarded, took it in a firm handshake. "It's been too long," Isaac continued. "Far too long. How are you? How's Scott?"

"We're both doing well, thank you," Jon replied curtly. Father Isaac dropped his gaze.

"Always the cop…" he muttered. "I know this is not social

call."

"No, it's not," Jon answered, irritated at the old man's jab. "I need to ask you what you saw."

"The devil is in the belfry, Jon," Isaac said. "It's witchcraft."

"What did you see?" Jon questioned.

"The devil," he answered. Swaying back and forth, the priest slipped back down in the pew. "Death."

Jon sighed and looked over at Courtney. She took it as an opportunity to intervene.

"Father Isaac," she smiled. "Let's try starting at the beginning, shall we?"

"He's still a little shaken, ma'am," the female cop replied. "He hasn't said much."

"Well then," Jon answered, eager to get away from the man who brought back memories he wasn't ready to deal with yet. "Perhaps we should go up to the belfry and have a look for ourselves."

<hr />

"How many steps do you think that was?" Courtney asked when they finally reached the top of the stairs.

"One hundred and forty," Jon replied. "Ten stories. No elevators when this was built," he chuckled. "All right?"

"Yeah," Courtney breathed. "Wow, gotta do more cardio, I think."

They entered the room at the top of the stairs and paused. Jon, the Irish Catholic altar boy in him, signed the cross on himself when he saw what was before them. A body hanged from the rafters of the room. The corpse wore a Halloween costume complete with red suit, tail, and red mask with horns. A chair had fallen to its side on the floor.

"He was right about one thing, Jon," Courtney said. Jon looked over at her. "The devil is in the belfry."

Dr. Grace O'Malley walked over to them. "Well," she said. "Why is it you guys always get the weird ones?"

"Do we have a cause of death?" Courtney asked.

"You mean, besides the obvious; strangulation?" O'Malley asked. "Haven't really had a chance to look at him."

"ID?" Jon asked.

"Not much. We didn't find a wallet anywhere. I can tell you he was dead between ten or eleven hours ago though," she replied.

"Putting the time of death at around midnight last night," Jon said.

"Could it have been a suicide?" Courtney asked noting the fallen chair.

"Possibly but I won't know more until I can examine him," the doctor said. "Can we take him down now?"

Jon nodded. Once the body was on the floor, they could see that the mask was only covering his face three-fourths of the way and it was clearly a man, as he had a closely trimmed goatee. The coroner crouched down beside the body.

"It looks like he was pulled up onto that chair," she said.

"How can you tell?" Courtney asked.

"You see how the bruising pattern isn't uniform? If someone stood on the chair and kicked it out from under him, the bruising would be pretty even all the way around the neck. Here you can see that there is more bruising at the hyoid bone, pinching the jugular vein, but here the bruising fades out toward the back of the ear and the neck." Dr. O'Malley explained.

"What does that indicate?" Courtney asked.

"Well, I haven't examined him but I have seen something similar in a case back in '99. A man was dragged on his back by a rope. The bruising pattern is similar."

"Indicating there was another person in the room with him and they pulled him up by the rope," Jon explained. "Would he have been conscious at the time?"

"Hard to tell," the coroner replied. "I won't know until I get him back to the lab."

"Make sure you test that rope for physical evidence. If he was pulled onto that chair, we might get lucky and the killer left some skin cells behind." Jon said.

"Can we take the mask off now?" Courtney asked. The coroner nodded and removed it.

"Pastor Hollywell," Jon breathed rubbing a hand across his jaw.

"You know him?" Grace asked.

"Greg Hollywell. He was my son's youth pastor many years ago. God, what kind of a sick monster would hang a pastor in the belfry dressed as the devil?" Jon asked.

"Let's find out," Courtney said indicating the security camera mounted in the corner.

CHAPTER FOURTEEN

Steven noticed a woman running toward them just as he praised Josh for shooting the ball into the goal for the third time. Her dark brown hair flew behind her, her piercing light eyes were a mixture of angry and concern. From his peripheral, he made a checklist in his mind.

Tall

Early to mid-30s

Strikingly beautiful

Lioness

That last one was proven the second she reached them and grabbed Josh, pushing him behind her.

"Who the hell are you?" she challenged Steven.

The fire in her eyes struck him directly in the chest. It was a feeling he hadn't felt for a long time. It nearly knocked him over. Her long hair falling below her shoulders, her body looked perfect under jeans and a sweater. But her eyes. They pierced through him making him forget her question. He hadn't felt the rush of blood through his veins for a very long time. Swallowing against the physical reaction he was having, he smiled a forced version of his *Casanova* smile.

"My name's Craig. I was just on a run and saw Josh struggling. My dad taught me how to kick a soccer ball, so I thought I could—"

"Did you?" She demanded. "I know exactly what you thought you could do. Who sent you? Mahmoud? Abdulla? Who?"

"Now hang on, I don't know anyone named Mahmoud or Abdulla," Steven replied raising his hands in the psychological gesture of innocence. She was getting to him and he had to take the conversation back. "Craig Stevens," he introduced again with a hand extended. "I'm on a business trip for my insurance firm. I—"

"I don't give a damn who you are or what you're doing here!" She yelled. *Clearly that didn't work.* He thought. "Joshua, I told you to never talk to strangers while I am on the phone," she turned to her son but kept Steven in her sights.

"But, Mom!" Josh protested. "He was just trying to help."

"No buts, Joshua," she said thrusting her car keys in his face. "Now get to the car." Josh took her keys and stormed off. Again, she turned her fire-filled eyes on Steven. "Next time you feel like stopping by," she bit. "Don't. I have very powerful friends. I can and will destroy your life."

Change of play. Steven crossed his arms over his chest and stood to his full height, half a foot taller than her. Intimidation normally didn't win women over, but she was not like most women and he had to change his game.

"Just because you have a guilty conscience about leaving him alone, you don't have to take it out on me. I was just trying to help your kid, where clearly his father lacked the time or effort to do so."

"Excuse me?" her tone was dangerously soft.

"Do you think," Steven went on, taking a step toward her. "If I was some kind of kidnapper or pedophile, I would have stuck around until his mother came back?" he let that thought sink in. "Not everyone is as bad as you might think they are. Some people are actually decent," he stated. Steven turned around, put his ear buds back into his ear and walked away.

"Casanova," Gordon came over his earpiece. "What the hell are you doing? Get back there!"

Steven didn't answer. He knew exactly what he was doing. And he was right.

"Hey! Craig, was it?" Steven turned slowly covering the smirk of triumph that covered his lips. Jade walked over to him. "I apologize. I was worried for my son. I should not have accused you."

"I get it, you know," he replied. "If I came back and saw my kid with some strange guy I'd never seen before, I would probably freak out too. But not everyone is bad."

"You're right," she said. "I'm not used to having people be nice to us considering..."

"Considering what?" He prompted.

"We're not from around here," she answered cryptically. "Listen, let me make it up to you, come to Josh's game tomorrow morning."

Steven paused a moment. "What time?"

"Nine," she said.

"You sure you're not going to call the cops if I show up?"

"No promises," she laughed.

"I'd like to come," he smiled. "My meetings aren't until Wednesday. Thought I'd come down early—"

"For some fun?" she asked eyeing him. Never before had he had such a blatant look from a woman. Sure, the women he was with for the Company thought he was attractive, most women did. He was tall, over six feet, well-built with muscles only seen on TV. His eyes were light blue and his hair was light brown. Most women he knew, called him handsome. And he prided himself on knowing exactly what those women wanted when they gave him bedroom eyes. But Jade? *Damn.* He thought. He might just get eaten alive.

"Something like that," he replied.

"Good," she answered. "Then I'll see you tomorrow."

The moment she turned and left him was the moment he realized she took his breath with her.

———◦◦———

Footage from the belfry's security cameras jumped and pixelated on the screen. Jon and Courtney watched as the church's public relations coordinator rewound the tapes until the previous evening.

Feeling Jon's tension, Courtney tried to distract both men in the room by asking, "Why do you have security cameras set up in the belfry?"

"We've had some issues with local kids breaking in. We had cameras set up in all corners of the church to dissuade any... *teenage* activity."

They fell silent once more as the video rewound some more.

"There," Jon finally said seeing the time tick over on the lower right-hand side of the screen. "Let it run."

They watched as a man, the coordinator confirmed was Pastor Hollywell, walked up the steps and appeared in the doorway.

"He's looking around. Maybe he heard something?" Courtney said. Jon nodded slowly but did not take his eyes off the screen.

Suddenly, the pastor was struck over the head and fell to the ground. The person was just out of view of the camera. The pastor was dragged away and did not reappear until he was dressed in the devil costume and there was a noose around his neck, being pulled up to stand on a chair.

"Looks like he was unconscious until there," Jon said as he watched the pastor slowly lift his head.

"His hands were tied," Courtney replied. "That's why there were no scratch marks on his throat."

The pastor looked around and they saw his mouth moving as if he was talking to someone. Then the camera shook and they saw the pastor start to scream and twist uncontrollably trying to get free.

"What's going on?" Jon asked calmly.

"Don't know," Courtney breathed.

Almost in answer to his question, the bells started to chime the hour. Jon and Courtney stared at each other for a moment.

"Oh, you don't think..." Courtney's voice trailed off. Jon nodded slowly.

"Pull the feed of that same room now," Jon directed. The coordinator switched over.

"The same shaking of the camera," Courtney replied. "It's the vibration of the bells."

"Go back to Hollywell," Jon ordered. "Count them with me."

...Thirteen.

"Thirteen?" the PR coordinator asked confused. "That's not right."

"Pastor Hollywell stopped moving after the bells stopped..." Courtney said. "There," she pointed to the screen. "They pushed the chair out from under him. Always out of eyesight, it's like they knew where the cameras were."

"They're not hidden," the man said.

"The bells must've been deafening up in the belfry. It's less than a story above it," Jon surmised.

"He didn't die from being hanged," Courtney replied.

"No, he died from the noise." Jon stated.

"Causing a brain aneurysm," Courtney continued.

"But why thirteen?" Jon asked. "It doesn't make any sense."

"Wait, it kind of does..." she said. "Thirteen chimes, the devil in the belfry... Bear with me, Jon, I have an idea."

—————

"Courtney," Jon shook his head as they sat outside the Starbucks on Butler University's campus two miles south of the church and Courtney's *Alma Mater*. "I thought we agreed to keep an open mind."

"And I thought you agreed to bear with me," Courtney replied. "It makes sense," she stressed.

"Well, yeah, but so does that Sherlock Holmes movie where the clock strikes thirteen before a death," Jon said. "So do a lot of tales and folklore from my home country. I don't think we should rule anything out or say it's strictly Poe just yet."

"God, Jon you are pigheaded sometimes!" Courtney sighed exasperated. "The evidence is right there before your eyes and you still can't accept it. Why? What more do you need? A pendulum sweeping above you? Being bricked up inside some walls? Finding a black cat? What? *The Devil in the Belfry* is the title of a Poe story. Prefect, the name that was in the letter left by Rob, that is the name of someone who helps C. Auguste Dupin, Poe's detective, in *The Murders in the Rue Morgue* and *The Purloined Letter*. *The Tell-Tale Heart?* John Doe and the whole heart ripped out and put under the planks? The poem that guy was gonna write on my mirror after he killed me? That's from *To One in Paradise...* They're all Poe."

Jon was silent as he took a drink of his coffee. Courtney watched him as he worked through the idea. For a moment she thought she had convinced him but then she saw the look change on his face and her stomach fell.

"I appreciate that you see the connection, Courtney," he said. "But I just want to keep an open mind. This could all be a –"

"You say coincidence and I'll be walking away," she replied. "I don't understand your reticence."

"And I don't understand your brashness. Courtney, if there is one thing I've learned in my fifty-six years, thirty of which were on the force, it is that looks can be deceiving and if you pigeonhole your evidence to fit your first and most of the time, wrong instinct, then you ignore valuable and essential evidence that is not linked to your original thought. I'm not saying it's not a good idea, and god knows you are the expert on Poe, but I'm saying I need, no, *have to* keep an open mind."

Courtney took in a deep breath and looked at her partner. "You've asked me to trust you on less evidence than this and I have, wholeheartedly because you are my partner and friend. I'm asking you to give me the same courtesy. I am not a child, Jon. I am your partner and I have never known you to ignore a coincidence."

"I'm not saying I don't trust you, Courtney," Jon said.

"No, you're just saying I am blinded by my belief this is Poe. That's fine," she stood and took her coffee. "I'll meet you back at the precinct."

"Courtney, wait," Jon stood as well.

"No," she held up a hand. "Don't. I want to be alone right now."

"How are you going to get there?" Jon asked.

"I'll call a taxi," she answered then walked down the sidewalk.

Jon sighed as he watched her but couldn't bring himself to go after her. The truth was, this scared him. Beth had told him, Paul Anderson was an expert on Poe.

CHAPTER FIFTEEN

Jon walked with Eddie Freeman, a friend of his in Organized Crime. When Courtney left Starbucks earlier that day, Jon had texted her to make sure she was all right. She did not answer but he saw the read receipt she had set on her texts. After she did not answer his phone call, he dialed Eddie's number. His friend worked the deep family mafia type crimes. And those boys always had a flare for the dramatic.

"Hanged in a devil costume in a belfry with the bells as the murder weapon? And some guy getting his heart ripped out?" Eddie got to his office and sat at his desk. "Sorry, Jon, can't say that rings any bells... forgive the pun."

"Do you think you could circulate the MO to your CIs to see if anything pops?" Jon asked.

"Sure," Eddie replied. "No promises though, it sounds like something out of an Edgar Allen Poe story."

"Yeah," Jon replied on a sigh. "Let me know if you find anything."

"Will do," Eddie answered.

"I owe you one," Jon said.

"Yes, and you can pay by getting me another bottle of that

whiskey you donated to the Christmas raffle last year," Eddie said.

Jon chuckled. "I'll see what I can do."

"Watch your back, Jon."

"You too."

<hr>

When Jon got back to his office and Courtney wasn't there, he began to worry. Pulling out his phone he again dialed her number. The call rang out and went to voicemail.

"Courtney, it's me, look I'm getting a little worried about you. You have every right to be angry with me, I was an arse and I'm sorry. Just let me know that you're okay. I've got your back, partner. I'm sorry I haven't shown it recently. The truth is, I'm worried about this. Call me back and I'll tell you why. But at least send me a text saying you're okay, would ya? I'll be here if you need me."

He hung up and sighed. She was angry at him. He knew he had not trusted her but what she didn't understand was he saw the connection too and it scared him. Paul or Rob or whatever his name was, was trying to get his attention. He already was too close. Greg Hollywell was a good man. Jon knew the moment he saw him lying there, he had been killed because his murder was something Paul knew Jon would want to solve. What was next? He did not want Courtney too close to this. But not telling her was worse. She would go on her own and he could not stop her, short of telling her the truth.

<hr>

Steven arrived at the park ten minutes before Josh's game started. He saw his mark standing near the bleachers and headed that way.

"Hey, Craig!" Josh shouted when he saw him.

"Hey, Buddy," Steven smiled as Josh rushed to him and

threw his arms around his waist. Steven tried to prevent the surge of fatherly need that rushed through him. If his life had gone the way he had planned, he would have had maybe three or four kids by then and they would all greet him like that when he came to their games. Clearing his mind, he needed to stay focused as Craig. "You ready for this?"

"Totally," he replied pulling back.

"All right, now what did I teach you?" Steven asked.

"Right foot, left slide," he repeated.

"That's right, Big Man, up high," Steven said giving him a high-five. "You're gonna be great."

"Honey, why don't you go ahead onto the field, it looks like Coach Williams is calling all of the guys together," Jade said as she walked up to them.

"Okay," Josh replied smiling up at Steven and giving another high five before he ran back to the coach.

"I'm glad you could make it," Jade said to Steven. He looked at her with one eyebrow raised. "Yeah, yeah, I said it," she laughed. "But Josh was very upset last night. He wanted you here. I'm sorry I immediately jumped to the wrong conclusion about you."

"It's okay," Steven said.

"You seem like a decent guy."

"I am."

"And oh so humble," she teased.

"Completely," he goaded. "So, how old is he?"

"Seven."

"Good age."

"Yeah," she sighed. "He's my little man."

"And his dad?" Steven asked gently. She went quiet. "I'm sorry, it's not my place to ask. And I should never have said what I did, but I was angry you immediately assumed I was some bad guy."

"No, it's okay. Let's move past the fiasco that was yesterday.

His dad was an old college fling," she explained. "Got himself killed on the way home to his wife after our… indiscretion. Hit by a truck who ran a red light."

"I'm sorry. That's gotta be tough," he said.

"It was," she replied. "But I wouldn't trade my Josh for anything."

"No, he's a great kid," Steven said.

"Do you have children?" She asked.

"None that I'm aware of," he teased. She laughed as they sat together.

"Playboy huh? A little Casanova?"

He let out a strangled chuckle. "Something like that." She had set his nerves on end the moment the word came out of her mouth.

"What about family?" She asked.

"Well, my parents died a long time ago, it's just been my sister and me since," Steven explained Craig's story.

"How old is your sister?" She asked.

"Older than me," he grinned.

"Ha! Nice dodge. And how old are you?"

"I'm 36," he answered. Normally, he would be leery of anyone asking so many questions, but unlike Steven, Craig wasn't the secretive or suspicious type and he was known to rattle off a lot of personal details.

"Now you get to tell me how old you are and none of this *you never ask a woman that* shit. Question for question."

"Tit for tat, huh?" She smiled. "Josh is seven and I had him when I was twenty-seven. Do the math," she replied smiling.

"Not bad," he replied eyeing her up and down. She rolled her eyes but smiled. "Any man in your life now?"

She looked over at Josh on the field. "Nope, just me and my little man," she answered. "My father died a few years ago and my mother takes care of my autistic brother."

"Sorry about your dad," Steven said.

"It happens," she shrugged. "But I've had another guy recently in my life who is like a father to me."

"Oh?" Steven asked.

"But I don't get to see him as much as I would like," she said.

"Why?"

"He's in Iraq."

"Oh, I'm sorry. Deployed?"

She shook her head. "He lives there," she answered simply. "It's his home."

Steven decided not to ask any more questions about Monsauri. She was opening up to him and he didn't want her to be suspicious. Luckily, the game was about to start. She turned to him changing the subject.

"Again, I wanted to say I'm sorry about yesterday," she said.

"Hey," he replied smiling his Casanova smile. "Don't worry about it. It's okay. I'm sorry too."

"Would you want to come over for dinner tonight? I'm making Italian and I'd like to make it up to you," she offered.

"Dinner would be great," he said. "As long as you really want me, I'd love to come."

"I think Josh would like that," she said. "He's kinda taken a shine to you."

That thought twisted his heart like a dull knife. "And... you?"

"Yeah, I kinda like you too," she replied.

CHAPTER SIXTEEN

Rob watched as person after person walked through the bar. He was waiting for someone very specific, someone he would know when he saw them. A backup plan. A Queen bee. A black Queen on the chessboard he had created. No one knew. No one could know. It was a plan he had had in his head for a while. Rob needed to take another approach if he was to keep Steven and Jon apart.

Finally, the door opened and she walked in. He had forgotten how stunning she was. Her blonde flowing hair billowed down her back in gentle curls, her figure was one any model would kill for and her face had to be chiseled by a god. Their eyes met and he raised his glass to her. Recognition crossed her face when she saw him. He smirked as he drank, never dropping her eyes. He was glad she remembered him. But she only remembered one part of him, the identity he still kept secret from everyone else. Waving her over, her eyes narrowed but she was intrigued, he could tell by the way she looked around her.

Falling into the seat in front of him, she crossed her arms, inadvertently pulling her shirt down tantalizingly enough for him to see the round curves of her breasts. He knew what he would require as payment and it was not money.

"What do you want?" she demanded.

"The Greene family ruined and Jonathan dead," he answered simply. She froze but then her practiced Mata-Hari face smoothed her surprise.

"Oh?" she asked slowly sitting up. "But aren't you buddy-buddy with one of them?"

"Weren't you married to one of them?" he retorted.

"Yeah, you know how that turned out," she scoffed.

"I have a plan to take them down," Rob continued. "Are you in?"

"What's in it for me?"

"Well..." he clinked his wedding ring against the glass. "In addition to seeing them ruined, you get thirty thousand and new IDs."

She thought a moment. "Make it fifty and I'll consider it," she replied.

"Forty," he answered. "Trust me, I'll make up for the rest."

"And just how do you plan on doing that?" she asked.

"Don't you trust me?"

"With our history?" She asked rhetorically. "No."

"Oh, I'm hurt. I would have thought you trusted me a little."

"Well, I don't," she replied. He chuckled.

"So... how about forty, those new IDs I told you about and you get to boss around a couple men I have working for me," he offered. "You can command them to do whatever your little heart desires." His lips quirked up in a lustful smirk. "But you know... age is always better."

She eyed him. "Think you could keep up, old man?"

"You'll have to wait and see," he answered, tossing back his drink. "Do we have a deal?"

"And am I *your* payment?" she asked.

"Yes," he shrugged.

She laughed. "You like the straight approach."

"Always have," he answered.

"As long as the ultimate goal, getting the Greene's to pay, is completed, you can take me to bed however many times you want," she said.

"How about a little down payment then?" he asked standing and offering his hand.

<hr />

Pulling into Jade's driveway, Steven watched Gordon's van park on the opposite side of the street.

The neighborhood was typical American Midwest middle-class, the kind where the subdivision got together for BBQs, pool parties and holidays. The kind of place where you would let your kid run around with the neighbors' kids and not worry if they weren't home by dusk. This was the kind of place, Steven noted, that would be perfect for an Al Qaeda agent and her kid to settle for a time. *Probably a lot of hard working American Dreams in this place,* Steven thought. The audacity of the terrorists turned his stomach sometimes.

Licking his lips, he tasted the beeswax lip balm he wore and grimaced, never liking the taste. Taking a deep breath, he checked the front of his orange polo shirt picked especially by Gordon because of Jade's favorite color. He didn't know why he was nervous, it wasn't as if he had never done this before. Seeing something move in the corner of his eye, Steven was immediately on alert. Luckily it was nothing important. A young couple walked their dog and newborn along the sidewalk. Smiling at him as they passed like traditional Midwesterners, Steven waved back then rubbed the back of his pointer finger over his upper lip giving the tell to Gordon, all may not be as it seemed when he spied what looked like a .45 tucked in the back of the man's jeans.

Turning back to the front door, he rang the bell and waited.

"Hey, buddy," Steven smiled when Josh pulled the door open.

"Craig!" Josh threw his arms around him again. "Mom! Craig's here!"

Jade came out of the kitchen to greet him and Steven froze. He felt the heat rise to his cheeks. He hadn't blushed since he was a teenager, his training as a spy had kicked any unconscious tells out of him. But Jade looked stunning. Dangerously so. Her hair was pulled up into a twist and she wore tight skinny jeans that left absolutely nothing to his imagination. Her tight, form fitting, red, scoop neck shirt revealed a figure that her bulky sweatshirt that morning and sweater the other day had hidden well. The shirt dipped dangerously passed *night at home* to *sexy as hell* and Steven found himself swallowing and taking a deep breath.

"Craig," she smiled then looked at his shirt. "I love orange, good choice."

"I've been told I can pull it off."

"The color, or the shirt?" she asked.

"Both," he answered.

"Good," she turned and headed back into the kitchen but giving her hips a little swing. Steven's eyes immediately went lower and didn't leave until he felt Josh's hand slip into his.

"Wanna see my Xbox?" he asked.

"Sure, bud," he answered.

"Josh, give Craig a chance to come in," Jade called from the kitchen. "Did you ask him if he wanted anything?"

"Mom," he whined. But he looked up at Steven and sheepishly asked. "Do you want anything to drink?"

"I'm good for right now, buddy," he answered. "Thanks."

"Good," Josh gripped his hand tighter and tugged him up the stairs to his game room.

One thing was certain... tonight he had to keep his wits

about him and that would definitely not be easy.

———————◦◦◦———————

Rob stood in the bathroom of his hotel room, concentrating on his face in the mirror. The shaving cream was lathered up and partially shaved away when her voice came from the doorway.

"I think I may have misjudged older men," she said. Their eyes caught in the mirror and he smirked seeing her in nothing but his t-shirt.

"No, just me," he stated.

"Clearly," she answered pushing off the doorframe and walking over to him. She pushed him back to sit on the toilet. Grabbing his razor, she straddled his lap. He raised his jaw allowing her to shave his neck.

They were quiet for a long time as she shaved his face.

"Are you this endearing to all the men you sleep with?" Rob asked.

"Only if they've given me what I want, as you have," she replied focusing on his upper lip.

"It's easily done," he stated. "We both know what we like."

"Still," she replied. "It's been a while since I've felt that sort of satisfaction."

"Not since Scott?" he asked.

She paused and looked into his eyes. "He was cute kid when I met him."

"And since?"

"Since? I've waited for this moment where someone tells me they're planning to kill him," she said.

"How boring."

"It has its moments," she shrugged.

When she finished, she ran the hot tap and dampened a towel. Coming back to him, she again straddled his lap and wiped the towel across his face cleaning it from the remainder of the shaving cream. Rob caught her wrist and kissed her palm. Once she was done, she sat back and observed her handiwork.

"The best shave I have ever had," he said. "From the hand of a goddess." He leaned forward and kissed her neck.

"Now what do you need me to do?" she asked.

"Need?" he asked then shook his head. "What I would like you to do, for the good of the plan is to distract my son, Steven Anderson the only way you can."

CHAPTER SEVENTEEN

The cases were a jumble, Jon decided as he walked through his house holding a glass of wine. Did they have a serial killer that used Poe? Were these just odd occurrences that could be easily explained? Could it be Paul? Where the hell was Courtney? She had texted him after his voicemail. The text was short and just said; *I'm fine*. But she didn't answer when he called her.

Stopping at the music room door, he stared at his piano. He walked around to sit at the bench, setting his wine down on the table beside him. The instrument had been in his family for generations and as he loving touched the ivories, he felt his father's presence there with him.

"Hoh, da'," Jon sighed. "I miss you. Wish I could talk to you tonight. Why does this all not make sense?"

His fingers gently touched the keys. He closed his eyes as a smirk came over his lips when he remembered the feel of his father's hand on his child-sized one, spreading his fingers on the keys and showing him the feather light touch technique that his father had taught him.

"Listen to the sound she makes, Jonny boy," his father had said. *"Don't just play it, feel it. It's like no other. You can't just play the piano.*

You have to love *the piano. Together you work as one. Make love to it. It's all about the simple things, lad. It's the littlest things, most of the time, the things which you don't think matter, that matter the most."*

Jon opened his eyes suddenly and grinned. "Cheers, da'. Ya're a genius!" He raced to his bookshelf in his study.

"Poe... Poe... Poe," he muttered to himself as he read each name of the authors. "Hell, where are ya Poe?"

He went to the library and searched there too. Nothing. Into the living room. Nothing. Media room in the basement. Still nothing. He knew he had a copy somewhere.

"Okay, da', you helped me think of the littlest thing. It's the things that I don't think matter that are important... so... where's my book of Poe?" Grabbing his phone, he texted Beth.

Jon: Hey babe, do you know where my book of Poe is?

It was a second before she answered.

Beth: Sorry, do you need it? I borrowed it. My character was trying to quote him and I couldn't remember the exact quote. After looking it up online, I realized this was taking a turn toward Poe and needed a refresh. I have it here at my office. I can bring it by later.

Jon: No worries, you hold on to it, I'll look it up online. Love you.

Beth: Love you too! Sorry!

She sent a frowny emoji followed by two heart eyes.

Just as he sat down at his desk, he heard the doorbell ring and his eyebrows drew together confused. Heading up the stairs, he looked through the window on the side of the door to see Courtney standing outside. Turning off the alarm, he immediately opened the door.

"Christ Almighty, Courtney, you'll catch yer death," he cried ushering her in as the rain pelted the porch. "What in God's name are ya doin' out there?"

Courtney looked at him confused. "Why are you speaking

with an Irish accent?" She asked.

"I'm no'," he replied.

"I think ya are," she mimicked.

"Ach, lay off," he said. "Get in 'ere afore ya soak." Stepping into the entryway, she suppressed the grin that was making its way to her lips. She loved it when he broke into his Irish brogue, it only happened when he spoke to Keelan for a long time or when he was thinking of his father. Courtney didn't know which scenario had happened but she was still angry with him and put a mask of indifference on her face.

"Listen, I know you don't think it is Poe, but I have to show you something," she said.

"I want to hear everythin', but ya need to warm yerself."

He took her to the living room and started the gas fireplace.

"I'm okay, really," she said. "I'll warm up soon."

"No, you're soaked. You've got to get out of those wet clothes," he ordered. Rushing up to Ryan's old room he grabbed a pair of sweatpants and one of his numerous Notre Dame t-shirts. Courtney had peeled out of her shoes and wet socks. Placing her soaking wet shrug with her socks and tennis shoes in a plastic bag she had found, she gladly took the dry clothes he offered.

"Thanks," she said.

"I'll make ya a whiskey toddy, that'll warm ya up. Change into those," he ordered.

He hadn't dropped his accent yet and she found herself grinning as she went to the restroom to change into the warm dry clothes. Staring at her face in the mirror, she schooled her expression. She was supposed to be mad at him not grinning like a buffoon simply because he was speaking in a different accent. Setting the plastic bag with her wet things on one of the kitchen table chairs, she went over to him.

"I wanted to tell you something," she said.

"Let's get you warm and go into the living room," Jon

stopped her, pouring the hot whiskey concoction into a glass and handing it to her before they walked into the living room and sat together.

"I owe you an apology," Jon started. "I want to hear everything you need to tell me, but I first wanted to say I'm sorry. You are right, you are my partner and I should never have said what I did. I have asked you to trust me and you have every time. I am sorry I did not. Can you forgive me?"

She looked at him and nodded slightly. "Yes, Jon," she said. "Thank you."

"Good," he smiled. "Now, what was it you want to tell me?"

"Well, I have a theory, only a theory, but I wanted to run it past you," she said.

"Go on," he prompted.

"Going back to the original case, the one back in March with Riley and Rob and all of that business with Hannah and the Captain… if we go with that and see Rob hasn't been caught, he is still out to get you like he was last month. Flash forward several weeks later, we have somewhat moved past that case. Budget cuts and everything, we don't have any reason to continue with a cold case. So, what if Rob doesn't like that he's not getting attention from you? What if he wants to stir up something that is so intriguing all our attention is focused on that? That way he gets us, *you*, to himself again.

"So, what does he do? He knows – somehow – I am a student of Poe. He creates a series of murders I recognize using little things like Prefect, *Tell Tale Heart*, *To One in Paradise*, thirteen chimes of the bell and the devil costume to make me see the similarity, that way insuring we get the case and all your attention is on him. He needs that. He feeds on it. He has to have you right where he wants you. You and I getting into an argument, I bet he loved that. He wants you alone."

Jon nodded. "He wants me involved, that is clear by the

photos he sent me," he replied back to his traditional American accent.

"Do you still have those photos?" She asked.

"Yes."

"Can we look at them again?"

"All of them?" he raised an eyebrow.

"No," she replied. "I've seen all of you from those pictures already and as handsome as you are…"

"Right, I'll take those out," he replied standing and heading upstairs.

Chapter Eighteen

Josh had fallen asleep on the couch after dinner with his head in his mother's lap. Jade locked eyes with Steven. "I should take him upstairs."

"Need help?" he asked.

"I got it, thanks, he's not that big yet," she answered, slipping out from under her son's head.

Steven watched as she picked Josh up, cradled him against her and headed up the stairs. As soon as her footsteps retreated, Steven jumped into action. He rushed to the computer in the kitchen and put in the flash drive Gordon had given him.

"Come on, come on." Steven muttered as the hard drive was taking its time downloading. Steven constantly looked over his shoulder to see when she would come down. His ears were tuned to the stairs. Any noise and he would have to stop the transfer midway. Luckily, the files finished downloading and he pulled the flash drive out of the computer and shut the lid. Walking back to his seat, he had just sat down when he heard her coming down the stairs.

With each mission it got easier. He wasn't out of breath as he was on his first few. The adrenaline was pumping but he was able to calm himself down quicker and keep his mind focused. At least until Jade walked into the room. She had let her hair down from its twist and let it fall soft and silky across her chest. Steven stood and cleared his throat.

"So," he said, pretending to be getting ready to leave. "I guess we should call it a night?"

She looked at him, with a look any man could read. "Care for a night cap before you go?" Her voice was low and sultry.

"Uhh… Sure," he answered. "What've you got?"

"You a scotch drinker?" She asked. "I only pour doubles."

"I could go for that," he answered. She disappeared to the bar. Steven tried to calm his breathing and slow the blood rushing and pounding in his veins. This mark was not going to be difficult to desire.

Walking back to the room, she handed him his drink, sitting on the couch and indicating the spot next to her. His arm lined the back of the couch and her body rested in the crease of his shoulder. "What do we drink to?" He asked.

She looked over at him, a look of pure lust in her eyes.

"New friends?" She offered.

"New friends it is," he answered. She turned on some music as they drank in silence for a little bit. He started mindlessly rubbing her arm with his fingertips.

"Craig," she said.

He looked over at her as she leaned forward and set her scotch on the table.

"Yeah?" he asked taking a sip.

"I don't normally do this."

"Do what?"

She looked at him and leaned in. He didn't pull away. Taking his glass from him, she ran her fingers through his hair. He wrapped his arm around her waist and pulled her toward him. Her lips were hungry as they latched onto his.

Jon walked into the living room carrying the manila envelope with the photos Rob had left earlier that week. Courtney stood from the couch and took it from him.

"Don't worry, I took the embarrassing ones out," he replied.

"Good," she answered. He had to laugh at the look on her face. She sat on the floor and spread them all out as Jon sat in the chair near her.

"If you let me know what you are looking for, I might be able to help," he offered.

"I don't know yet, but if there's something hidden here, we have to be able to find it. Maybe he gave us a clue," she said.

Her eyes flashed from one picture to the other. She didn't know what she was looking for, but she was certain she would know it when she saw it.

"What I want to know is, who is this Rob person?" Courtney asked. Jon felt his stomach twist. He hadn't told her about his visit to the hospital or his suspicion it was Beth's ex-husband Paul who was behind this and he was starting to regret it. Knowing it was time to tell her, he leaned forward, but she went on. "I mean, he has to be someone we know. That guy who broke into my house and tried to kill me, told me you stole something from him and he wants it back. What could he mean?" She didn't look up at him.

"Courtney, there's something I need to tell you," Jon started.

"I mean, if he was someone from your past, wouldn't you know him?" She went on, not listening to him. "Why does he want you to suffer? What could he possibly think you have done to deserve this?"

"Courtney, I really need to tell you something," Jon started again.

"Could there have been something in your life you have overlooked? Could you have arrested him? Is that what you stole from him? Some years of his life while he was behind bars? Maybe we should look at your previous cases. See if there was anyone named Rob you put away for a while."

"Courtney," he started.

"I mean clearly this has been dormant and planned for many years, so could he have just gotten parole?" She asked.

"Courtney," Jon tried again.

"Do you have access to the database? I want to check all those who have been released recently—"

"Saints, Courtney, for the love of god, will ya shut up for a second," he said, his Irish accent and temper flaring.

She froze and looked at him. "Sorry," she replied.

"Listen to me, there's something I need to tell you. I don't know if you got my voicemail but it's time I tell you what I was thinking. I know who he is. I've had a theory for a little while now, but I didn't want to mention it because I didn't have evidence. Now, I have talked to the guy who broke into your house and I have the confirmation I need."

"Who is it?" She asked sliding across the floor to sit near him.

"Like I said it's a theory, but he did not correct me when I mentioned the name," Jon replied.

"I get it, tell me," she said.

———

"That was amazing," Jade sighed.

"Yeah," Steven breathed. "I haven't had that for a while."

"Oh no," she teased. "Did I break some celibacy law you were under?"

"No," he chuckled. "Just haven't had a good one in a while."

They were quiet for a little while as she traced the outline of a scar in the shape of a bullet on his chest.

"Where did you get this?" She asked softly.

"Afghanistan," he answered.

"You were in the military?" She leaned up and looked down at him.

He nodded pushing her hair back from her face. "Two tours," he answered.

"What did you think about it over there?"

He sighed running his hands through her hair and down her bare back.

"Well, it was dry and hot, and god knows that sand gets everywhere," he said. Chuckling, she laid her head back on his chest and kissed the scar.

"No, I mean, did you believe in what you were fighting for?" She asked.

"I think every side should be considered," he answered. He had been through enough situations like this one to know not to answer with how he really felt.

"Do you really?" She asked.

"Yeah, I mean, the things I saw over there," he went on. "I don't believe they're the bad guy."

"You're sympathetic to Al Qaeda?" She asked.

"Well," he shrugged. "Maybe, I'm not sure."

"Did you convert to Islam while you were over there?" She asked.

"I had some friends who did," he answered. "I went with them to the Mosque a few times. I thought it was an interesting idea."

"You're more sympathetic to them than you are a part of them?" She asked.

"Well, I mean I don't know," he replied. "I guess I'm not educated enough on it. I'd give it a shot if the right woman helped me." He smiled and kissed her hair.

"Yeah?" She asked leaning up and looking down at him

again. "You'd convert to Islam? Maybe even fight for them?"

"Yeah," he replied. "I think I would."

"That's good to know," she answered. Leaning down and kissing him again, she moved over him and for a moment he thought they were going to have a repeat of what they just did. But suddenly, she pulled back and Steven felt the barrel of a .45 kiss his forehead. He froze. Knowing he could take her, he instinctually almost grabbed her in a wrestler's hold to flip her over on her back and pin her down, until he heard the words out of her mouth.

"FBI, you're under arrest. Let me see your hands," she said.

Oh, Gordon, you idiot! Gordon had failed to contact local FBI. He remembered the young couple out for a walk earlier and the gun he had seen tucked in the man's back. The all too eager way she shared information about her *father figure* in Iraq. How she was pressing him about converting to Islam. *Ah, hell...* he couldn't help but admire her. *Damn, she's good.*

"I said let me see your hands!" She ordered.

"I think you know where they are," he answered.

"Show me your hands," she demanded. He slowly raised them. "Easy!" She cautioned with her gun still to his forehead.

"You wanted to see my hands, here they are," he said. "Now, will you let me tell you who I am?"

"I don't care. You are under arrest," she replied.

"For what?" He asked.

"Suspicion of terrorism," she replied.

"Me?" he asked rhetorically.

"Craig Stevens, or whatever your real name is, you are under arrest. You do not deserve your Miranda Rights, but I'm sure you know them—"

"Easy, Jade," Steven interrupted. "We're on the same side here."

"I don't think so," she answered.

"I'm CIA," he replied.

"If you were CIA, you would never tell me that," she said. "No agent would ever reveal that."

"We do when there is a gun pointed at our head by a friendly," he replied. "Now, listen I'm wearing my ear bud let me take it out and you can talk to my handler."

"I don't think so," she said. He slowly moved his hand to his ear. "Watch it!"

"What? You think I've got a gun hidden somewhere? I don't know if you realize this, but you would know if I was carrying a gun," he said.

She looked down at him realizing that was true and nodded. Then the thought entered his mind. "Where the hell did you have yours?"

"None of your business," she replied. Without answering, he pulled his ear bud and handed it to her. She hesitated for a second then took hers out and handed it to him.

"This is Special Agent Ian Kendrick with the FBI, to whom am I speaking?" Steven heard over her ear bud.

"This is Special Agent Steven Anderson, CIA, badge number 87-32," he stated. "My handler is talking to your agent."

There was a pause on the other end. "Special Agent Anderson your badge checks out, sorry for the inconvenience. You are free to go," Agent Kendrick said over the earpiece. "Is your handler in a white van three doors down from our agent's house?"

"Yes," he answered.

"Would you tell him I would like to speak to him?" Kendrick asked.

"Sure," Steven replied sarcastically.

Steven and Jade exchanged ear buds. Jade moved off him and wrapped the bed sheet around her chest and body.

"Oops," Gordon said in Steven's ear.

"Really? Ya think?" Steven demanded. "Take a step out of your van, Gordon. Her boss is waiting for you outside. Please explain your error to him."

"Yeah, yeah," Gordon replied. Steven stood and grabbed his clothes.

Jade looked over at him as she pulled on the last of her clothes.

"So," she said coldly. "Casanova, huh?" He froze pulling on his shirt and turned to her. "You may think you are God's gift to women, but trust me, you have a long way to go," she said.

"I was just doing a job," he answered harshly grabbing his phone.

"Yeah, me too," she replied. "And Casanova?" He turned from the door. "I've had better."

"No, you haven't. You can lie to me all you want, but your body can't. And I'll tell you something, I wasn't lying when I said I haven't had that in a while. You were dangerous and I was attracted to you. But now I see that was a just a façade. Pity, never thought I'd actually like the terrorist more than the FBI agent. You want to succeed in this business, don't be so high and mighty, it'll only tear you down. Good night." He didn't look at her as he left the room.

CHAPTER NINETEEN

"Why didn't you tell me this before?" Courtney demanded. "If you knew this was Paul Anderson then why didn't you tell me? I had a right to know as your partner!"

"I know, you have every right to be upset with me. I withheld important information from you, but the thing is, I don't know for *certain*, I only think it *could* be," Jon replied. "I have no evidence just a gut feeling."

"You always told me gut feelings are usually right," she said. "Hell, that's why I focused on my Poe theory."

"And why I needed to be the different voice, I need that from you. I didn't want to put the idea your head. When you get started on something you don't stop. You're like a juggernaut, you will stop at nothing to get the truth."

"*I'm* the juggernaut? Have you looked in the mirror?" she demanded. "You get a small inkling of something and off you go, ready to stop at nothing but your death.

"I needed you to have a fresh approach and an unbiased viewpoint," Jon went on. "If you saw something that didn't make sense with my theory then…"

"I get that," she answered. "But still. Have you told Beth?"

"Oh, god no," Jon said. "It would destroy her."

"She's stronger than she looks," she replied.

"I appreciate your whole *girl power*, but you don't know their history," Jon said. "Beth is strong, but when it comes to him, she's not."

"Why?" Courtney asked. "What's the history?"

"I – I don't feel comfortable talking about this without her permission to do so. I only learned about it on our St. Patrick's Day trip."

"Jon, if you think it would make me look at her differently, then you don't know me," Courtney said. "I am a cop first and foremost. I am your partner. If you know something we both need to know for the case, then you sure as hell better tell me."

"Dammit," Jon breathed. "Fine, you're right. You remember me telling you a while ago about the really bad break up I went through with my girl back in New York after I came home from Vietnam?" she nodded. "Well, Beth was the girl. We were together for about three years. I asked her to marry me the night before I shipped out. When I got back, she was married to someone else and had a baby, Steven. You've met him. He killed Riley."

"Her son," Courtney confirmed. "Tall, dark hair, fit, underwear model?"

Jon breathed a laugh. "I'll have to tell him you said that, he'll get a kick out of it."

"Mark was the one who came to Ireland, right?" she asked.

"Yes, he's the pediatrician," Jon said. "And the middle child."

"What does Steven do?" Courtney asked.

"If I could tell you, I would," Jon replied. "But I can't."

"Why not?" she asked suspiciously.

"Jesus, Courtney just take my word for it?" he ordered.

"Okay," Courtney answered. "So, government position, got it. Psychoanalysis, paramilitary or spy?"

"The middle one."

"Woah."

"Paul Anderson, as you know was Beth's husband and father of Steven, Mark and Kim. But what she revealed to me last month was that he was physically abusive and would rape her consistently." Courtney felt a wave of anger wash over her. "At a party her parents threw, he forced himself on her. It was two weeks after I left. She never told me."

"Jon," Courtney looked at him. "Steven's not yours, is he?"

He looked down and drank his whiskey toddy. "No," he answered. "I had Ryan run the test. That's the phone call I got from him the other day. Do not tell Beth. She knows but she doesn't *know* for certain."

"She wants to believe he is from love not rape," Courtney surmised.

"Exactly. I met Carol later that year. We didn't marry until she was twenty, five years later and had Scott two years after that. When Mat," her brother and their former captain, "moved up here, we followed. Scott was ten and he had made friends with Kim and Alex at school. Carol and I hosted a Super bowl party that following February. We invited Scott's school mates and their families. I hadn't seen or spoken to her since we broke up. I called *Mrs. Anderson* not knowing anything other than she was the mother of my son's friend. She realized immediately who I was. It was... interesting to say the least."

"I bet," Courtney interjected. "How did Carol take it?"

"Carol knew about our history and they actually became friends. I found out she had separated from her husband, leaving him in New York when her first book hit bestsellers lists, over five years ago at the time. She and Carol would have weekly breakfast and coffee meet ups. I even think they went to the gym together." He broke off as a memory entered his mind and he chuckled fondly, then grew serious.

"But it was a little over a year after we had become friends again and one night, we got a call from Beth. I'll never forget it. She sounded so scared. Paul had found her. He was forcing his way into her house. The boys were on a school trip and Kim was staying over at a friend's house. She had locked herself in her bathroom. I got over there too late. Paul had forced himself on her again and vanished. Beth was shattered. After that, Carol and I were instrumental in getting her to go to a friend of ours on the force. She got a restraining order and a warrant out on him. She also filed for divorce," Jon shook his head. "Last we had heard, he was never served the papers for divorce because they could not find him. The court put a stipulation in the divorce proceedings that if Paul Anderson was not found in ten years' time, the court would grant her full divorce. Ten years ago, she was free of him. Now, he's back."

Courtney sat in silence. The new information Jon shared about Beth's past had made her an even stronger woman in Courtney's eyes. Kim had mentioned her father a couple of times, and it was never fondly, but it did not prepare Courtney for the sheer emotion she felt at Jon's explanation. Tears gathered behind her eyes for the pain and suffering Beth had gone through, but she swallowed them away.

"Any man who rapes a woman should have his balls sawed off with a dull, rusty hand saw and fed to him," she said through clenched teeth.

"We can agree on that," Jon replied.

"So, he's after you because he found out you're together and he doesn't want any other man to have her. Maybe he's trying to tear you down and eventually kill you to get her alone again."

"My thoughts too," Jon replied.

"Makes sense," she said. "Does Beth have any family? Kim hasn't mentioned any."

"Her mother and father live in the Hamptons, but they'll

never help her when it comes to Paul. Her parents were instrumental in getting them together," Jon explained.

"What kind of parents would—?"

"Do not get me started on her parents."

"Bad blood?"

"More than you will ever know."

"Damn," she replied.

Before either of them spoke again, Jon's phone buzzed on the table beside him. He put it on speaker.

"Jonathan Greene," he said.

"Jon, hey it's Eddie," he heard the voice of his contact in Organized Crime. Courtney looked at him confused. He held up a finger to tell her he would explain in a minute.

"Hey Eddie, I've got you on speaker, my partner is with me," Jon said.

"Hey Shields," Eddie said.

"Eddie," she greeted.

"It's nearly midnight, what's up?" Jon asked.

"Sorry if I woke you two," Eddie started.

"You didn't," Jon replied.

"One of my CIs got in contact with me. He says he doesn't know the MO, but he knows something about the pastor who was killed."

Jon leaned forward. "And what is that?"

"It looks like your pastor was involved with some shady people," Eddie said. "But he won't tell me. He will only talk to you."

"We're on our way."

Courtney and Jon met Eddie in his office half an hour later. Leading them to the door of the lounge just down the hall, Eddie paused before going in.

"He asked to speak to you alone, Jon," Eddie said. "Are you comfortable with that?"

"My partner and I are one," he started. "I'm not going in there without her."

"I'll be out here if you need me," Eddie said.

Jon thanked him and opened the door. Jon and Courtney saw the informant lounging on the couch. He looked up when they walked in.

"Curtis, my name is—" Jon started.

"Jonathan Greene," Curtis finished his sentence for him then turned to Courtney. "And you must be the pearly white partner, Courtney Shields. Word on the street is that you two are more than just cop partners," Curtis winked at Jon. "I can see that, Jonny, she's smokin'."

"Show some respect," Jon ordered.

"I don't got to show her or you nothin'," he said. "I'm here 'cause I wanna be."

Courtney sat down across from him. "Why are you here, Curtis?" She asked.

He eyed her like a piece of meat and Courtney looked away. After Jon's story about Beth, she was in no mood for a man to look at her like that. But he had information they needed. "I'm here 'cause I know somethin'," he said.

"Something like what?" Courtney asked.

"Uh uh, not until I get my money," Curtis replied.

"You're not getting anything until you tell us what you know, then, and only then, will I consider how much you *might* get," Jon said.

Curtis looked at Courtney. "Is this what he's like in the sack, baby girl? You need somebody to show you somethin' better."

Reaching across to touch her, Curtis never saw Courtney move to grab his fingers until it was too late. She gripped and twisted. He yelped and fell off the couch to his knees.

"One, I'm not your baby girl," Courtney said calmly. "Two, I've had enough of your play. You dragged us here after midnight to tell us something. I would like to know what. I'm tired and I would like to go back home. So speak."

He nodded, his face twisting in pain. She released his fingers and he sat back up on the couch.

"Damn, girl," Curtis said. "You could've broken my fingers."

"Speak," Courtney ordered.

"Okay, okay, your priest," he started. "He was known to roll with the kid of Viktor Redorvsky; Viktor Viktorovich, or Viktor Junior."

"The son of the Russian mob head?" Jon clarified looking over at Courtney.

"What would Pastor Hollywell be doing with a well-known mobster's family member?" Courtney asked her partner. "Let alone his son."

"He *was* a youth pastor, maybe he was trying to reach out to him," Jon offered.

"From what I hear," Curtis said. "He was reaching out a little too far. He was spending too much time with Junior. Daddy wasn't too happy, said that if Preacher Man ever came near Junior again, he'd give him a quick pass to Heaven." Curtis laughed. "Get it? 'Cause he's a priest?"

Jon and Courtney looked at him. Curtis went quiet.

"I think we need to talk to Viktor," Jon replied.

"Whoa, no," Curtis replied. "You can't just go and talk to Viktor Redorvsky. He'd have you killed on the spot. Not to mention, he would know where the information came from. There'd be a price on my head, man," Curtis said.

"And tell me why that would be a bad thing?" Jon questioned.

"Because then I wouldn't be able to tell you something I know about Rob," Curtis said leaning back in his seat, resting his arm on the back of the sofa. "Why do you think I asked my contact to wait outside?"

"What do you know?" Jon questioned.

"Word is this Rob guy was putting the call out to anyone with a beef against you," Curtis explained.

"Who answered?" Jon asked.

"The Henderson brothers for one, and a few others you put away during your time in narcotics," Curtis replied.

"Do you know who Rob is?" Courtney asked.

"Nah," he answered. "He kept it all quiet, word of mouth sort of thing. They were screened before they met with him. Wanted to make sure there were no cops trying to get in."

"Screened by whom?" Jon asked.

"No idea," he answered. "I had no reason to go."

"Next time there's a call out, you go," Jon ordered. He pulled out his wallet and handed Curtis three one hundred dollar bills. "This stays between us."

Curtis took the cash. "Whatever you say, boss."

Jon and Courtney waited while Curtis gathered his things. Eddie opened the door seeing his informant getting ready to leave. When Jon and Courtney were finally alone, they turned to each other.

"Well?" She asked.

"Remind me to warn Ryan not to double cross you," Jon teased.

"I meant about Viktor Redorvsky," she replied.

"I know what you meant," Jon answered. "I don't know yet."

"Do you want to go talk to him?"

"Cops don't just talk to Viktor Redorvsky. Curtis is right. He'd kill us. But if we know someone who could get the info without being a cop... well then we just might have an in."

"And do we know someone who could get us the info without being a cop?" Courtney asked.

"I think I might know a guy," Jon replied.

"Of course you do," Courtney said.

Chapter Twenty

Steven slowly woke with a splitting headache. His phone buzzed on the nightstand beside him with a text from Gordon saying he had tried to get into the room earlier that morning, but couldn't. Steven was to meet him at the breakfast room when he got up. Fortunately, they were alone, apart from Cliff and Brian. Gordon sat, reading a newspaper, having a cup of coffee. Falling into the seat across from him, Steven stared at him.

"Well?" Steven asked when Gordon hadn't said anything.

"Well," Gordon replied not putting the paper down. "That didn't go as planned."

"Ya think?"

"Sometimes these things happen."

"That's all you have to say?" Steven asked. "'Sometimes these things happen'? I could have taken an innocent woman's life. Let alone, I could have been the one killed. Where did you get your intel on her? Who did you talk to in the FBI? I want answers."

Gordon looked over at him, put his paper down and took his coffee.

"That's classified," he replied nonchalantly.

"Don't give me that shit," Steven answered.

"I'm sorry, Steven," Gordon said apathetically. "You know the risks of the job and you know what is expected of you. You are not to question this."

Steven stood, but Gordon motioned Cliff and Brian over, they settled heavy hands on his shoulders. Steven shrugged them off.

"You won't always have your boy toys here to protect you," Steven said. "You screwed up, Gordon. You didn't contact the local FBI. It's your funeral. I will bury you."

Cliff landed a blow on Steven's solar plexus. In one swift move, Steven had twisted Cliff's arm painfully behind his back and slammed him against one of the walls. His eyes turned to Brian who was rushing to his partner's aid.

"Try it," Steven sneered. Brian stopped, raised his hands and backed away to where Gordon now stood. "Listen to me," Steven whispered into Cliff's ear. "I'm getting pretty damn tired of your bullshit, Cliff. I was serving this country when you were still wet behind the ears. If you think for one damn second you can get the drop on me, you will not like the consequences." He shoved him against the wall making Cliff grunt in pain. "I was training for this when you were doing nothing but checking out your fellow high school football players' asses in the locker room. You may think that by sleeping with him, Gordon will give you the best assignments, but you know what that snake does? He uses people. Best to cut it off before any more damage is done. Think about it, boy. You're a good agent, you're a shitty person but you are a good asset to the team. But if you hit me one more time, I swear I will break this arm in more places than you thought you had. Do I make myself clear?"

Cliff nodded quickly when his face contorted in pain. Steven shoved him again, making him cry out before pulling away and facing Gordon. His handler's face spoke volumes in its blank stare.

"You're done," Steven stated walking past him, pulling out his phone and dialing Headquarters.

———————

"Viktor Redorvsky?" Dave asked looking from Jon to Courtney then back to Jon. "Really? You want to go head to head with this guy?"

"We just want to see if he's involved in some way," Jon replied.

"I seriously doubt it," Dave said sitting down behind his desk. "But I'll see what I can do. Just be careful, this guy is not to be trifled with."

"Understood," Jon replied following Courtney out of the office. "Uh oh," Jon said watching her. "I know that look."

"What look?" She asked.

"That look... what are you thinking?" he asked.

"Lunch?" She replied.

Jon's brows furrowed. "Sure," he answered grabbing his coat. "Where?"

"I don't care," she asked.

"Okay," he replied.

———————

After they had ordered lunch, Jon leaned forward over the high-top table.

"So?" he asked. "What were you thinking about?"

"I was just wondering if this whole business with Viktor Redorvsky is a wild goose chase," she said.

"Why would you think that?"

"I know we have to follow up on every lead for Pastor Hollywell's murder but how do we know what Curtis gave us is legit? I mean, we basically know this is Rob, right? So, what does Redorvsky have to do with it?"

"We should follow up on every lead as you said, but I do

think we should at least speak to the son. I'm hoping if this was Rob or Paul or whatever, he may be able to tell us if Hollywell had a visitor."

"And get us the evidence we need," Courtney supplied.

"Exactly," Jon answered. "We have none. Up to this point he has covered his tracks so well we have nothing to go on except a gut feeling."

Courtney nodded slowly and leaned back as the waitress put her lunch order before her. Once she had left, Courtney spoke.

"Do we know why Paul is using Poe?" she asked. "Has Beth said anything about him having a fascination or something with it?"

"We don't really talk about her ex-husband," Jon replied.

"From what I saw in those pictures, you don't do much *talking* anyway," she teased dipping her fry in ketchup.

"Cute," Jon said sarcastically. "Unfortunately, I do know the answer to this. Paul is a Poe aficionado."

Courtney nearly choked. "What?" She gasped. "Again, why didn't you tell me this?"

"I wanted to, but we got sidetracked talking with Curtis. Last case there were clues I could understand with chess, now–?"

"It's clues I would understand," she replied. "Do you think he wants me to figure this out?"

"I think he wants us monopolized with this right now for some reason," he said. "Let's find out if Rob or Paul made an appearance at the church."

"Then let's talk to Viktor," she said taking a bite out of her steak and avocado wrap.

CHAPTER TWENTY-ONE

Steven hung up with HQ and was told to report to Gordon's boss's office in two weeks' time. They wanted a full report on what Gordon was doing but granted Steven his two weeks off as usual after a case. When Steven passed Gordon's room, a maid was cleaning it out.

Going down to the breakfast room for something to eat, his eyes scanned the main area. Luckily, he was late by normal standards for breakfast and there were not that many people around. Still his training kicked in and he viewed each and every one of them as a threat until he was proven otherwise. Gathering his breakfast on the plain white plate, he chose a seat at the window where he could view the whole room.

As he sat eating overdone eggs and undercooked bacon, Steven sighed. He missed his mother's cooking. When he got home, he knew he wouldn't have to ask her to make his favorite; blueberry pancakes, crisp – almost burnt – bacon, eggs scrambled with diced peppers, onions, cheese, and ham and if he was really lucky or his mother had missed him terribly, he would get her fresh squeezed homemade orange juice. The mere thought of his mother's cooking made his mouth water and his stomach growl.

Knowing a hotel breakfast, though complimentary, would never measure up to his mother's expertise, he finished his meal, wiped his mouth and headed back up to his room to change into his swim trunks.

After one hundred laps in the pool, he went to the workout room for another hour. It felt good to let the stress melt away. Running five miles in just over thirty-five minutes, the sweat poured down his face and it felt liberating.

Two weeks to himself. He could go home and let his mother take care of him. Maybe hang out with his brother and scare the shit out of his future brother-in-law. He smirked at that. Scott was a good guy, but he wasn't always. And Steven wanted to make sure his baby sister was taken care of.

Just after lunchtime he drove around the city and stopped at a steakhouse. The thought of a good rare steak was just what the doctor ordered. Sitting at one of the high-top tables at the bar, his eyes ran every face, making sure he didn't have any trouble headed his way. As he did, his eyes fell on two women in their early thirties who were eyeing him. Taking a drink of his all-American beer, he called the bar waiter over and ordered them another round of drinks. It had been a while since he flirted without having an earbud in his ear.

The dark haired woman giggled at something her blonde friend said when the drinks he ordered arrived. The blonde slipped off her stool and walked over to him.

"Hello," she smiled, standing in front of him.

"Hey," he answered.

"I'm Meredith," she said.

"Craig." Even though he was not on assignment, he never answered with his real name until he knew the woman was cleared to know it.

"Thanks for the drink," she said taking a slow drink through the straw stir, never breaking eye contact with him.

"No problem. Gin and tonic?"

"Vodka tonic," she replied. He smirked and offered her the seat opposite him.

"You live here?" He asked.

"Just visiting, you?"

"Business trip."

"Really?" She hiked up her miniskirt and crossed her legs. "What do you do?"

"Oh, a bit of this, a bit of that," he answered his eyes going down her legs.

"Man of mystery," she said leaning forward, putting her elbows on the table and her other best assets on display. His eyes ventured up her legs and stopped on her flaunted bits.

"Actually, I'm a spy," he answered finally raising his eyes to hers.

"Ooh," she teased, her eyes passing over him. "Like James Bond?"

"Similar, yeah," he answered.

"And you're here on a top secret mission?"

"Pretty much."

"Well, Mr. Bond," she said. "Don't you always get the girl?"

"Most of the time."

"Well, I've always wanted to be a Bond girl," she said clutching his hand. He chuckled. She looked more like the Bond bad girl, the one James fell for, who actually was the killer. But the idea of a good one-night stand with someone other than who he was assigned to sleep with, was tempting. She was beautiful and willing. "You want to get out of here?" she went on. "My hotel is just around the corner."

He leaned back when his lunch came and smiled. He debated for a moment. Then something in her eyes made him question it. She was too eager to hear his answer. Call it a sixth sense but something didn't feel right.

"I'm flattered, really, but – uh – actually have plans," he replied. She looked disappointed.

"Well, I might see you later," she said as she slipped off the chair. Steven watched the swing of her hips as she walked back to her friend.

CHAPTER TWENTY-TWO

Viktor Viktorovich Redorvsky, Viktor Junior was on his way in to talk with Jon and Courtney. Having spoken to the teenager earlier that day, Jon stressed the importance of meeting with him. Viktor agreed but asked to meet later in the afternoon, so he could slip in and out without his father knowing. As they were waiting for him to arrive, Jon pulled their chairs together and again went through the pictures he had received from Rob.

"If only I knew what I was looking for," Courtney said.

"You're the Poe expert not me," he replied. "Sorry I'm not more help."

"It's just tough seeing all these pictures, knowing someone was watching us and there's something I'm not able to put my finger on."

"Well, if you do find something, let me—" Jon started.

"Oh my god!" She cried eureka. "The Black Cat! The Black Cat Bar!"

"The bar downtown?" Jon asked.

"Yeah, but the Black Cat is also a story by Poe. It's a rather gruesome tale of a man killing his wife and burying her in the walls, but her cat kept whining and he went insane. The cops found the cat had been walled up with the body. You see *The Black Cat* and *The Tell Tale Heart* are often linked together as a similar plot. Almost like twins, you know, two separate stories but with the same look and appearance."

"Courtney, hand me the file that came with the pictures," Jon said. "This is Bradley Henderson's file. He was one of the men who helped orchestrate Carol's death. He has a twin brother; Quinn Henderson."

"That would make sense," Courtney said. "The stories are twins, the men are twins."

"Why would Rob give this to us?" Jon asked.

Before she could answer, there was a knock at their door. Quickly gathering the pictures, Jon stuffed them in his top desk drawer.

"Come in," Jon called.

"Excuse me, sir," a police officer walked in. "But a Mr. Redorvsky is here to see you."

"Thank you... August, isn't it?" Jon asked the officer.

"Yes, sir," the officer replied smiling. "That's right."

"You're new, aren't you?" Jon asked.

"Just transferred," August answered.

"Good to have you on the team."

"Thank you, sir."

"And please show Mr. Redorvsky in."

———

"Hello?" Rob answered the phone.

"Can you talk?" Meredith asked.

"Hold on," he said. Looking around, he got up, and excused himself from the board room where he was having a meeting. Walking out to the breezeway, he sighed.

"Too many identities," he chuckled. "Miss you, baby."

"Miss you too," she answered. "More than you know. But I have news."

"What is it?" He asked.

"You were right," she answered. "I couldn't find Brad anywhere without blowing my cover."

"And?" he prompted.

"And… Steven is hot, you should've told me."

"He is my son. What part of *male model* didn't you understand?"

"The *Calvin Klein underwear* part."

"You made contact?"

"He actually did. Bought me a drink. Surprised me."

"Why do you think I picked you?" Rob asked. "I know what he likes. You have some very pleasing assets. And I look forward to uncovering them again."

"I look forward to letting you," she answered. "We talked for a little bit. He did say he was a spy," she laughed. "Guess he thought I was just another dumb blonde. But when I asked him back to my hotel room, he refused… so I'll have to find another way."

"Be careful, if he made Brad he could make you," Rob said.

"It might take longer than we planned."

"You know what's at stake here, Meredith, you need to keep Steven away from Jon."

"And I'll do my best," she promised. "Do you want me to keep looking for Brad?"

Rob paused. "I say we cut our losses and move on."

"But his brother? He'll not stop," she answered.

"That's not your concern. I'll deal with him," he replied.

"You know, I never understood why you, of all people wanted me."

"I know the history between you two, I witnessed it first hand," Rob said. "You have more cause than most to hate that family."

"Especially him," she replied.

"Keep your head down, it'll all be worth it. I've put plans in motion that cannot be undone. They still have no access to the money Riley stole last month."

"I only wish it was more, so we could've ruined him."

"All in good time," Rob said. "Look at me, it's taken me nearly twenty years to get back at Jon for what he did to me."

"You have a lot more patience than I do," she said.

He chuckled and heard someone call to him from the office behind him.

"I gotta go," he said to her.

"I'll check in later," she replied and hung up.

<hr />

"Mr. Redorvsky, please come in," Jon greeted the eighteen-year-old Viktor Viktorovich Redorvsky.

"Oh, please, call me Vitya. *Mr. Redorvsky* is my father," Viktor said.

"We appreciate you coming in," Jon replied. "This is my partner Detective Shields."

"Ma'am," Viktor nodded to her. Courtney eyed him trying to see the mafia heir in the clean-cut kid before her.

"You know why we asked you to come?" Courtney asked when Jon offered him a seat.

"When I got the news Greg was dead, I knew I had to come in and help somehow," Viktor said. "You see, Greg Hollywell was one of my best friends. He was the older brother I never had. Without him, I doubt I would be here right now. I seriously am in shock he's gone. I guess it hasn't sunk in yet."

"How did you meet him?" Courtney asked.

"Honestly, he caught me breaking into the offering box in the church," Viktor looked down. "He knew who I was, of course, my father's reputation is all over the Midwest, but he didn't call the police. He offered me something to drink, sat with me and asked me one question. Why? We ended up talking for hours. I didn't realize how much I needed someone else to talk to," his eyes locked with Jon.

"Else?" Jon asked.

"I have a friend but he's... he's my father's righthand man so it's tough to talk to him about things sometimes. I hate what my father does and what he stands for. Greg helped me so much."

"Vitya, Pastor Hollywell died on Friday, do you know where your father was that evening?" Jon asked.

"He was playing poker with his friends as usual," Viktor said.

"You saw him?" Courtney asked. Viktor nodded.

"I have to be there. It's one of my father's orders. He thinks it'll make me a man, whatever that means, probably because of the prostitutes he brings in..." he looked over at Jon and Courtney. "I wish I could help but I don't think my father had anything to with this."

"You and Hollywell were friends?" Courtney asked.

"Yes, he was my mentor, my tutor. He made me think there was a way out," Viktor said.

"Forgive this next question," Courtney went on.

"I know what you're going to ask," Viktor said. "And the answer is no. Greg is a... was a godly man. He treated me and the other young people he mentored with the utmost respect. He never took advantage of us. He was... god there's no word to describe him. He listened, helped and was just there. He made me believe I had a choice to not get involved with the family business. I feel so... lost without him."

"You always have someone you can talk to," Jon replied.

"Yeah, Sergei is... he's there if I need him," Viktor shook his head. "But we have to keep our friendship a secret from my father. He's ruthless and would look at Sergei like he betrayed him. I know my father, if he finds out I'm talking to the cops? He'll kill me," Viktor said. "The only way, now, for me to get out of the business is feet first."

"Couldn't you refuse?" Courtney asked.

"I tried that once," he replied. Holding up his right hand, Viktor showed his fingers, a little crooked. "When I told him I didn't want to go with him somewhere, Dad ordered his men to break my fingers as I had broken his heart... slowly." Courtney flinched. "I was 12," he said. Jon's jaw clenched. "You see why I want to get away? Greg and Sergei were always there for me. He was going to help me through college. He was tutoring me so I could pass my SATs. I was applying to La Salle. Greg had a friend there who was willing to pull some strings for a low life mobster whose daddy owned half of the Midwest," Viktor explained.

They were quiet for a moment, then Viktor spoke again. "Can I ask, how did he die?" Courtney looked over at Jon. "Did he suffer?" Viktor pressed.

"I'm afraid it wasn't instantaneous," Jon replied. Viktor looked down.

"When he didn't answer my calls the other night, I knew something was wrong. He always answered, even if it was two in the morning," Viktor said.

"We have no record of any such phone calls," Jon replied.

"You won't," Viktor explained. "At least, not from my personal phone. My father always takes it at the end of the day to see who I've been talking to. He's... very cautious. Greg would probably have had it under VR it's a different number. Sergei lets me use his phone after my father takes mine."

"Is there a number I can reach you? Should the need arise?" Jon asked.

"There's no way for you to call me without my father finding out. If you need to contact me, I go every Friday to Barney's on the Circle to get my dad's lunch among other things..." he sighed harshly. "I wish I could turn states' evidence against him."

"One step at a time," Jon replied. "First, let's get you safe.

Then you might be able to give some clues to some of our men inside and they will be able to take him down."

"Your men," Viktor said. "I'm afraid Dad knows who they are."

"What do you mean?" Jon asked.

"I mean my dad knows everything. They aren't the first ones to try and get him," he revealed. "Do you really think he had something to do with Greg's murder? I know he wasn't too happy that I was hanging out with him."

"We are following all lines of inquiry. Do you know of anyone in his group who would use a dramatic flair to their killings?" Jon asked.

"Dramatic flair?" Viktor asked. "No, my father hates that sort of thing. Was Greg killed dramatically?"

"Keep your ears open," Jon said. "See if you hear anyone talking about killing the devil."

"The devil?" Viktor asked confused. "Lieutenant, what is going on?"

"Greg was tied up in the belfry of the church, knocked unconscious, dressed in a devil costume and hanged. He was killed by the sound of the bells ringing 13 times," Jon explained quickly.

"You're serious?" He asked looking at Courtney. She locked eyes with him and nodded once. "What kind of sick—" Viktor couldn't continue.

"That's what we're trying to find out," Jon said.

"I'll keep an ear out, but honestly it sounds like something out of Edgar Allen Poe," he said. Courtney looked over at Jon. "My god, but I'll listen. Would it be all right if I talk to Sergei about this? He might know something. He'll talk to me. He doesn't want me in this life either."

"So long as he's trustworthy and won't tell your father you're speaking to the police," Jon said.

Viktor shook his head. "He won't. We're... close."

"Understood," Jon replied. "Listen, you are not alone. Here's my card. My cell number is on the back. If you need anything, please call me, even if it's just to talk. Okay?"

Viktor looked at him. "You can't give me that. You don't know what you're opening yourself up to."

"Viktor, listen, you call me if you need anything. Memorize my address here," Jon said showing him.

"You do realize who I am right?" Viktor asked.

"I have a good feeling about you, Viktor," Jon replied. "I want you to feel like you have a friend even though Greg is gone." Viktor smiled slightly. "And if there is anything else you can think of, anything at all that might help, let us know," Jon said.

"I will," Viktor replied. "Thank you, Lieutenant. Just be careful."

CHAPTER TWENTY-THREE

"Viktor Redorvsky?" Rob asked over the phone.

"What do you want? Who are you?" An older man's rough Russian accented voice came over the phone. "How did you get this number?"

"My name is Rob," he said. "I thought you would be interested to know where your son has been for the past hour and who he's been talking to."

"Don't you think we should have done a background check on Junior before you asked him over for tea?" Courtney asked her partner when they were finally alone. Jon looked down at his desk and tapped a folder. "You did already," she stated.

He smiled still not looking up. "Of course. Now we need to find the connection. And if I am the connection, how would Rob know Hollywell knew me? My family and I stopped going to that church nearly fifteen years ago. I need to place Rob and Hollywell in the same area at the same time."

"I bet it's something we're overlooking, something small," Courtney offered. "It will come out. It always does. Was there anything more in those pictures he left you?"

"Nothing," he answered. "I'm going across the street for some coffee, want one?"

"I'm good, thanks," she smiled. As soon as Jon left the office, she pulled out her phone and dialed a number. "Father Isaac? This is Detective Shields, Jonathan Greene's partner, I was wondering if I could speak with you about Pastor Hollywell's death?"

———————

"Thank you for meeting me on such short notice, Father," Courtney said sitting down in one of the chairs in Father Isaac's office at the church.

"Of course, I was very pleased to receive your call," Father Isaac answered. "I assume Jon is not coming?"

"No," she replied feeling her phone buzz at her hip. She knew Jon was wondering where she was, even though she left him a note and sent a text stating she would be back later.

"Probably for the best," Isaac nodded slowly. "Our parting was not amicable. I blame myself for it."

"May I ask," she started but stopped not wanting to pry into Jon's history, but it could be vital to the case.

"Ask why?" Father Isaac offered. Courtney nodded. "Carol, his wife, had just died and he was questioning God and I was of little help, I'm afraid. Everything I said to him he was tired of hearing. I could not give him a definitive answer to his burning question... why did God take her from him?" Isaac explained.

"I think that is a reasonable question given the circumstances," she defended.

"I agree, but I was less knowledgeable then and he didn't like my answers," he explained looking down for a moment, then locking eyes with her. "But I'm sure you didn't ask to meet with me just to discuss Jon's and my history. What can I help you with?"

"I hope you don't find this offensive, Father, but I am not

Lutheran, I grew up nondenominational. I want to make sure I am addressing you properly. Is *Father* the correct term?" She asked.

"For one of my age, my dear young lady, it is," Father Isaac smiled. "But you can call me Isaac if you want."

"Oh I don't think I could do that," Courtney said. She respected his age and position far too much.

"As you please," he smiled. "American Lutherans normally use the less formal title of Pastor but it all depends on the hierarchy. Jon understood this due to him being raised Catholic and I think that made him more comfortable around us as he was not protestant. My actual title is Priest which should be addressed as Father, but I do not stand on ceremony and do not like to correct those I am leading to the ultimate Father." He indicated the stained-glass mural behind her depicting Jesus on the cross. "But since you asked me, I will tell you *Father* is correct and it is *Pastor* for Greg Hollywell."

"Thank you," she smiled.

"Now, what would you like to know?"

"Pastor Hollywell. What can you tell me about him?" She asked.

"He was a good man, a bit headstrong in some areas but I had high hopes for him. One of the best men in my parish. He could reach the young men and women in our congregation unlike any other pastor I know. It was a gift," he explained. "He was a good man, a very good man."

"I did some digging and found a news article. Do you know about his past life?" she asked delicately.

"You mean his devastating accident that claimed the life of his fiancée and unborn child?" Father Isaac replied. "Or are you asking if I knew of his premarital relationship with the mother of his child?"

"A little of both I guess," she answered.

"We all have sinned and fallen short of the glory of God. I

am no judge. My place is to guide not condemn," Father Isaac replied.

"More people could learn that, Father," Courtney said. "Especially now."

"Well, my dear young lady, we must pray for them. Greg came to me a broken man. He blamed himself. As I know it, that horrible day in December 1995, a car lost control on the ice and hit Greg's car. He was not a pastor at the time, but a graduate psych student with an emphasis on child psychology at IU. He and his seven-month pregnant fiancée were traveling home to his parents' house in Fort Wayne when his car was hit, spun out of control, flipped over and landed upside down. Greg was in critical condition when the EMTs found him. His fiancée was dead when they arrived, and they couldn't save the baby.

"He was not a child of God at the time, but an atheist. His girlfriend took him to church a couple of times. During the accident and his subsequent recovery, the Chaplin visited him. He was a man tattooed and with his own dark past who explained it was not who you were but who you become. Greg was one of the most devout men I've ever met. We're all human. We all have weaknesses, but it is our response to those weaknesses that make us who we are. Please ask, what specifically did you want to know about Greg?"

"I was interested in getting to know more about him," she answered. "Tell me, Father, did you ever notice any strange visitors? Anyone asking to speak with Pastor Hollywell that wasn't, perhaps, known to you?"

"We always have visitors," he said. "Are you thinking it was someone he knew?"

"We have to explore every possibility," she answered. "Do you remember anything unusual that could have happened around the time of his death?"

"I'm sorry, Detective, with the numerous visitors we get

and the fact Greg's office is closer to the entrance than mine I'm sure there were times he would have handled more situations than I would have known about," he explained.

"I see," she sighed. "Well, thank you, Father. If you do think of anything please give me a call," she handed him her business card.

"I will," he stood and showed her to the door. As they walked he turned to her. "Detective, I don't mean to pry, but… is Jon happy?"

"I don't think anyone really knows, sir," she replied. "Jon keeps those things close to the chest."

"But surely *you* would know," he said.

"Me?" Courtney asked surprised.

"Well, being his fiancée," Isaac indicated her ring.

"Oh, no," she replied. "No. Ryan, I'm engaged to Ryan."

"Oh goodness, please forgive me, I didn't mean to—"

"No no, it's all right," she said waving him off. "Jon is just my partner."

"I see. Forgive me, I just wanted to make sure he was happy," Isaac said.

"I'm sure he is," Courtney answered. "But please let me tell him I spoke with you first. I wouldn't want him to find out and then be upset."

"Is he likely to be?" Father Isaac asked.

"Not that I followed a lead, but that it may have involved his past. He has very difficult feelings for that."

"Yes, yes, I know," he sighed. "Carol was a lovely woman… You know, you remind me of her."

"I have been told that," she admitted. "Her brother was our captain for a few years."

"Same lovely personality, same beauty, same good nature. I can see why he loves you."

"Ryan?" She asked not sure what he meant.

"Jon," he answered. Courtney locked eyes with his, her brows furrowed immediately. "Surely you've seen it. The way he looks at you."

"He's a wonderful man, but my heart belongs to Ryan," she replied.

"Does it?" he asked. "Sometimes we are blind to the things right in front of us."

"Father, I understand your concern, but Jon and I are merely good friends. He is a mentor to me. He doesn't love me in any way inappropriate and I am in love with Ryan."

"Of course, please forgive an old man. I talk too much and don't think enough," he said as he opened the front door for her. "Please give him my best when you do tell him. And if you need me again, I will be here."

"Thank you," Courtney said as she stepped out into the sunlight. Pulling on her sunglasses she mulled over what the pastor had said.

Chapter Twenty-Four

Steven wasn't due into HQ for another two weeks. Taking the opportunity to stay in a new town, he went for an early morning jog. Passing the soccer field, he saw Josh's team warming up for a game. Smirking, he headed over.

"You made it!" he heard Josh cry. Turning toward the voice, he opened his arms to the young boy as he raced toward him.

"Yeah, buddy," Steven smiled as Josh slammed into him wrapping his arms around his waist.

"Where have you been?" Josh asked.

"I've been working," Steven said. "But I'm here now."

"I'm glad you're here!"

"Me too, buddy," Steven grinned. "Go on, the coach is calling you back."

Steven walked on to the bleachers as Josh left, grabbed the towel off his shoulder and wiped his face and neck of sweat. Jade locked eyes with him and if looks could kill…

Sitting a couple seats away from her next to a couple about his age, Steven smiled at them.

"Morning," he greeted. "Your son playing in the game?"

The couple nodded and pointed him out. "Is yours?" the

husband asked.

"Not mine, but a friend's," he smiled. "He's a great kid."

"They're wonderful little terrors at this age, aren't they?" The wife said.

"Absolutely," Steven laughed. "But you know, even though it was forever ago, I still remember what it's like to be that age."

"Don't we all?" the husband chuckled.

"I thought I made myself perfectly clear," Jade said without looking at him.

Steven and the couple looked over at her. He waited to answer until she looked at him.

"I'm here for your son," he replied. "Don't get your panties in a bunch."

"How dare—" she started to say, then shut her mouth.

They stared at each other. Eventually the game started and everyone around them cheered as their players ran out. After an hour and a half, Josh scored the final goal winning the team the trophy.

"Okay," Jade said hugging her son. "This deserves something *very* special. What would you like? Anything. How about lunch and then ice cream?"

Josh nodded vigorously. "Craig too?" Josh asked.

"No," Jade said sternly locking eyes with Steven.

"Why not?" Josh asked.

"It's not something you need to worry about," she replied.

"It's grownup stuff, bud," Steven winked.

"Oh," he replied then turned to his mom. "Is it because you guys slept together?"

"Joshua Conner Lawton, what on earth?" Jade scolded.

"It's okay, mom," Josh answered. "Lots of people do it."

"Joshua, that is not something we should even be discussing. One, it is not the appropriate time or place and two," she lowered her voice. "How do you even know what *that* is?"

Steven was heartily trying to cover his laughter, gaining him an evil stare from Jade.

"One of the guys told me. He caught his parents at it and his dad explained it to him," Josh explained. "Is that why you're upset mom? Because you and Craig aren't sleeping together anymore?"

Steven laughed outright that time.

"It has nothing to do with that at all, Joshua," Jade said glaring at Steven. "And I don't want you talking about this to the boys, okay?"

"Why?" he asked looking from one to the other.

"Just don't, Joshua," she replied.

"Whatever," Josh replied.

"Joshua!" Jade disciplined.

"Fine, mom!" Josh grumbled. "But you said I could have anything I wanted, didn't you?"

She looked at Steven with her jaw set. "Yes, I did."

"Well," he answered. "Then I want Craig to come to lunch with us and ice cream."

Steven looked at Jade, a smug smile toyed his lips.

"Fine," she replied. "But that's it. Would you care to join us, Craig?"

Steven had heard that cover name said with disgust before, but nothing as blatantly obvious as her snide comment.

"I would," he replied grinning. "Thank you."

Jade hardly said two words to him as they had lunch. After they got ice cream, they sat outside together again.

"This was so fun!" Josh said. "I wish we could do it again sometime soon."

"I hope so too, buddy," Steven replied.

"Can Craig come to dinner tonight?" Josh asked his mother.

"No," Jade replied. "Actually, I think Craig has some work

he needs to do."

"Actually, I was just given a couple weeks off," Steven said. "So, I'm free. I wanted to do something fun. I was wondering if it would be okay if I took Josh to a movie sometime this week."

"Oh, can I, Mom? Can I?" Josh asked.

Jade gritted her teeth. Steven watched her. He didn't know why he was enjoying this so much, but he didn't want to stop.

"I don't think so," she answered.

"Oh come on, Mom!" Josh complained. "He's really a cool guy, if you'd just give him a chance!"

"Yeah, Jade," Steven said. "I'm a really cool guy, if you'd just give me a chance."

"Fine, dinner at six, bring the wine," she ordered.

CHAPTER TWENTY-FIVE

Sitting in his study, Jon combed through Bradley Henderson's file as he waited for his computer to remotely connect to the precinct. The file had not been altered in any way and Jon was trying to figure out why it was left for him. He was also waiting on the Warden of the prison to get back to him.

Rereading his own statement as the arresting officer, he remembered the sheer emotion he tried to hide. The men had conspired to kill his wife. For a moment, Jon's chest ached, and his eyes drifted to his favorite photo of Carol still resting on his desk.

Thirteen years had passed, but it felt like yesterday he had held her as she died. Breathing hurt as his chest constricted. Her smile captured so perfectly in the photo, forced him to close his eyes. The hardest part for him was knowing he would never see that smile again.

"Jonny," he heard her whisper to him. His eyes still closed he reveled in the memory of her running her fingers through his hair. "Aren't you coming to bed?"

"In a minute," he remembered saying. "I have to finish this. Keelan needs me."

"I need you," she replied, and he heard the smile in her

voice.

"Do you now?" he asked.

"Yes," she answered walking around and sliding slowly down on his lap. "And didn't you promise to take care of your wife?"

"I did," he replied.

"Well, she needs you," she said. "She aches for you."

He swallowed thickly. "Then I should look after her."

"Oh yes, you should," she leaned in to kiss him. Remembering the feeling of her kiss on his lips was fading with every day that passed. The thought of never remembering what it felt like to kiss her, to make love to her, to feel her beside him, caused his chest to constrict even more. Gasping for breath, he kept his eyes closed trying to remember what happened next.

She slipped the strings off her nightgown and let it fall away. Smiling, he remembered how he lifted her in his arms but they did not make it upstairs. Making love before the fireplace and sharing a bottle of wine afterwards, was a common memory but that time he remembered refusing more than a single glass as she told him something important.

"I love you, Jonny," she said.

"I love you," he replied.

"I need you to do something for me."

"I thought I just did," he teased. She stroked his face.

"And you did a very *very* good job. But, Jonny, I need to tell you. If anything were to ever happen to me, I want you to know, I would want you to be happy."

"Nothing is going to happen to you," he said kissing her neck. She pushed him away slightly.

"Jonny, please," she went on. "If something happens to me, know I love you but I want you to move on."

"Why are you talking like this?" he asked. She looked down. "Care," he lifted her chin to look at him. "What is it?"

"I don't know," she said. "I haven't been feeling very well

for the last few days. I guess I'm a little worried."

"What do you mean?"

"I've tried to hide it from you," she went on. "But I've been throwing up nearly every morning or whenever I eat something. I can't keep anything down. I... I'm scared."

Jon held her to him. "It's all right," he said. "We will figure out what's going on."

Remembering the next morning they were given the best news imaginable, Jon smiled and opened his eyes looking at the picture of his son sitting opposite the one of Carol. Tears had escaped his eyes and streaked down his cheeks but the tightness he felt eased as he focused on the life they had created.

Something dinged on his computer causing him to turn away from the photos and memories. His computer had finally connected to the police database. Taking a deep breath, he wiped the tears away and focused on searching for Bradley Henderson. Once Bradley's information came up, Jon looked through the various warrants, arrests, and evidence against him. But there was also a flag at the top left corner. Clicking on it, it opened a password protected file. Jon's brows furrowed.

Looking at who had protected the file, he was surprised when he saw Dave Weston, Acting Captain. Jon entered his own password for high level clearance. As soon as he hit enter, a red alert box popped up.

UNAUTHORIZED ACCESS

"What do you have to hide, Dave?" Jon breathed.

He was about to try another password when he heard a notification from his personal email. Clicking over to see what it was, he noticed a new message from Keelan O'Grady with an attachment.

Subject: *Riley's Diary Pages.*
Jon, I'm sorry this has taken a little longer than expected. I've

had some personal issues to sort through. I have attached the pages from Riley's diary.

Thanks for understanding,
Keelan

Personal Issues? Jon wondered. *What sort of personal issues?* His hand itched to call his friend but knowing he needed to read through the diary pages, he resisted, clicked on the attachment, and began reading through the photocopied pages.

Chapter Twenty-Six

Steven arrived at Jade's place right at six o'clock. Unlike the last time, he did not see anyone walking or any vans housing the FBI surveillance. Josh was excited to see him as usual, but Jade did not speak to him. After dinner, she took Josh upstairs to bed. When she returned, she did not invite him to have a drink.

"Can we talk about what happened?" he asked. She took the cups from the sofa table to the sink without looking at him.

"There's nothing to talk about," she answered. "We slept together and that was it. There's no reason to make it more than it was." Turning on the water to wash the cups, Steven saw her hand shake slightly.

"I want to explain," he said walking over to her. "I regret the last words I spoke to you. They were said in anger and I apologize. I know you don't want me here, you've made that clear, but I do not want to leave knowing I've made an enemy out of someone I respect. And I do respect you. I respect what you do for this country and what you do in the FBI. When I reported my Handler's activities to HQ they knew immediately who you were. You have a reputation. A damn good one. But no one knew you as anything but Jade. I would really like to know your real name."

"Not happening," she said.

"Please," he asked stepping closer and reaching toward her. She spun around grabbing a knife from the holder and holding it to his throat.

"Don't touch me," she ordered.

"Then talk to me," he said raising his hands in compliance.

"You back off first," she demanded.

Taking a step back, he asked, "what's your name?"

She stared at him for a moment. "Amber," she finally said. "Amber Lawton."

"Amber," he replied smiling. "Pleased to meet you. I'm Steven Anderson."

"I don't care. You may have charmed my son, but I know exactly what and who you are, Craig Stevens," she sneered. "Now get the hell out of my house and my life. If I never see your sorry ass again it would be too soon."

"God, woman, shut up for a moment and just listen?" Steven demanded.

"Excuse me?" her voice was low. "Get out!"

"I was on an assignment, obviously you were too," he continued without moving. "My job is to infiltrate terrorist cells by getting the women in them to trust me."

"And you do that by sex?" she sneered.

"Most of the time, yeah," he shrugged. "It's all about a connection, building trust. That whole thing about me being sympathetic to the terrorist, wanting to know the whole story, that's not me, that's the cover."

"And you expect me to believe you? After what you said and did?" she demanded.

"You want proof?" Steven stated the question.

"That'd be nice," she replied.

"Fine," he pulled his shirt off and pointed to the bullet scar just above his heart she had seen a couple days ago. "Here's your proof," he went on. "My girlfriend, Chrissy was killed on nine-eleven. I was on the phone with her when the tower crashed down on top of her. I was on leave from the CIA for a couple weeks. I had just gotten back from Afghanistan after a six-month long mission. I begged her to stay with me that morning, an engagement ring burning a hole in my pocket.

"I had fallen back asleep after she left, and her phone call woke me. She was in the North Tower. I begged her to get out of there, but she said she was on the one hundred and second floor. There was no way out. While I was on the phone with her, I got the Company wide call. *All hands on deck, leave cancelled, everyone needed.* I called my handler begging him to help her. You wanna know what he told me? He said, since I wasn't married to her she was not under the Company's protection, he couldn't or *wouldn't* do anything. I still remember the scream she gave when she realized the tower was coming down..." he cut off feeling his throat constrict.

"After that, I quit the CIA and joined the Army. I served two tours and was shot by a ten-year-old boy while I tried to help his family out of an evacuation site. He turned on my men who were coming to my aid and blew them up along with his baby sister. I can still taste their blood and brains in my mouth. I am still haunted by it and them. I was knocked unconscious by the blast and my hearing was temporarily gone. When I woke up in the hospital, I was told I would never be fit for active military duty again. Spinal compression. Therapy took months for me to even be able to walk again. I was approached by my handler to see if I wanted back in.

"I was reinstated in the CIA and I have been there ever since. And you know what, I'm good at it. I have done things I'm not proud of, sure, we all have, but the most important thing is that the terrorists I come face-to-face with, are either put away or I kill them. So, you want proof of my loyalty? Look me in the eyes and see my men who died in that blast. See my girlfriend's face and hear her scream when the towers collapsed on top of her. Listen to the last thing I heard her say to me was the building was coming down and she loved me. The CIA did *nothing* to save her and yet, I am still working with them because I love this country."

Amber stared at him but did not speak for a long time.

"I'm so sorry," she finally said. He scoffed as he twisted his shirt in his hands.

"Yeah, me too," he answered. Just as he was about to put his shirt back on, she took a step toward him and ran her fingers across his chest resting them on the scar. They locked eyes and Steven grabbed her to him, kissing her firmly. Throwing her arms around his neck as he picked her up, she wrapped her legs around his waist and kissed him back.

CHAPTER TWENTY-SEVEN

Walking into Dave's office that next morning, Jon shut the door behind him. Dave looked up and stopped his conversation with Officer Callen.

"Jon," he smiled pleasantly. "Good morning, what can I do for you?"

"Callen, I need the room," Jon replied.

Callen looked back at Dave who held up his hand telling him to wait.

"Callen and I are in the middle of a conversation, Jon. What do you need?" Dave asked.

"All right, fine," Jon pulled out the file Rob had left for him. He also presented a print out of the alert message he had received. "I want to know why I don't have clearance to open this file. I was the arresting officer in this case. I should have unlimited access to the information surrounding Bradley and Quinn Henderson. You come in here, pretending to be helpful and all the while you're hiding things from me. From *me*! Not only am I your friend, I am the lieutenant of this division. Now I want to know why."

Dave looked at the file, then back at Callen.

"Give us a minute?" He asked.

Callen nodded and left the room. Once they were alone, Dave looked at the file then back at Jon.

"Where did you get this?" Dave asked.

"Does it matter?" Jon asked. "The important thing is that I have it and when I tried to open the secondary file, it was protected. What are you hiding from me?"

"Bradley and his brother Quinn escaped from prison two weeks ago," Dave said after a pause.

"What? Why wasn't I informed?" Jon demanded.

"Because we were trying to get them both to turn evidence over for a reduced sentence. Bradley did give us some information worthy of a deal but during a prison transfer, they escaped," Dave explained.

"These men killed my wife and shot me. You don't think that was worth mentioning to me? Even as a friend?" Jon asked.

"I'm not your friend when it comes to this, Jon," Dave answered.

"Then as their arresting officer, I have a right to know," Jon replied.

"We thought you were too close to this case. We needed to distance this from you," Dave explained.

"We? Who's we?" Jon asked.

Dave did not answer, he merely stared at him.

"My god," Jon finally said. "What does Homeland Security want with them?"

Dave flinched when Jon said it out loud. "Keep it down."

"Oh, that's right," Jon replied loudly. "You don't want anyone out there knowing that you're not one of them. That you never have been."

Callen opened the door and walked back in. Dave held up a hand telling him to stop.

"It's all right, Callen," Dave replied.

"Callen?" Jon looked back at him. "You're a part of this too?" Callen did not respond. "How many others?"

"Right now, it's only Callen and me," Dave said.

"Oh grand," Jon replied sarcastically. "You knew about this?"

Again, Callen said nothing.

"Jon," Dave walked around his desk. "You have to agree, you are too close to this one. Mat let you be the arresting officer to give you some kind of revenge. Well, I'm pulling you from this case."

"Why?" Jon challenged.

"I don't have to answer that, you know why," Dave said.

"What did the Henderson's tell you?" Jon asked. Dave looked at him. "Tell me!"

Sighing, Dave continued.

"They said there was someone else behind the whole thing. That the anonymous tipster who called in to the precinct that morning and wanted you and Carol to go, was the one who organized the crime. Carol's death and your injury were all part of the game. With that evidence, we have discretely reopened Carol's cold case."

"Why are you interested in Carol's death? Why her case?" Jon asked.

"That I cannot answer, please understand. I swear to tell you when the case is over," he said. "So, now, why don't you take the day? Go home," Dave offered. Jon shook his head. "That wasn't a suggestion."

Sighing, Jon continued. "Fine, but I'm taking some work home."

"Understood," Dave replied.

Watching Jon leave the room, Callen walked to his boss with his arms crossed over his chest.

"Don't you think you should have told him the truth?"

Callen asked.

"And have him die going after him?" Dave asked. "No, it's better he doesn't know."

"Still, O'Malley isn't someone to sweep under the rug," Callen said.

"That's not what I'm doing," Dave replied. "But Jon cannot know he is back in town. If he finds out, trust me, you do not want to be around when that happens. I know what he did to him."

"But still, Boss," Callen said. "I trust you, god knows you have never given me reason not to, but if this is to do with his past, he should know."

"Old sins cast long shadows, Callen," Dave replied. "And trust me, Jonathan Greene has some old sins and they cast some pretty bad shadows. It's better this way. Now get on the phone with the director, I want to talk to him about Brent."

"Yes, sir," Callen answered.

Courtney walked into the Black Cat Bar with her best friend Chelsea. Heading up to the bar, they ordered two glasses of white wine as Courtney's eyes scanned the room. Chelsea picked out a table near the middle of the room and danced her way to the chair. The band was playing, making it difficult to hear but the women cheered and drank.

"Shots?" Chelsea yelled over the music.

"Maybe later," Courtney replied.

"So," she gulped her wine. "What are we doing here?"

"Just having a good girl night, we've been too busy and it's been too long," she answered.

"Uh-huh," Chelsea leaned in. "You know I'm your best friend, right?"

"Yeah of course," Courtney answered.

"And so it follows that, other than Ryan, I'm the person who knows you the best," she replied. "What are we *really* doing here?"

Courtney laughed and looked down. "Okay, you caught me. I do have a reason for coming here."

She reached into her handbag and pulled out the picture of the Black Cat Bar Rob had sent to Jon.

"What's that?" Chelsea asked.

"It's a picture someone sent Jon and I think it's part of our case," she replied.

"And we're here because Jon got a picture of this bar in the mail?"

"We're working an angle."

"You mean, *you're* working an angle," Chelsea said. "Why isn't Jon here with you?"

"If I'm going to chat up some guys, I don't think having a gorgeous, imposing, and father-like man around would be best," Courtney replied.

"Mm, there's nothing father-like about that sexy man," Chelsea drank her wine. Courtney just laughed. "So you brought along your best friend to smoke this guy out?"

"Something like that," she replied. "I am hoping if we drop the name Rob, someone will let something slip."

"Rob, huh?" Chelsea asked. Courtney nodded. "Well, then," Chelsea stood, went to the stage and flirted with the lead singer of the band. Courtney watched from her seat as the singer helped Chelsea up on the stage. She stood in front of the mic. "Today is my best-friend-in-the-whole-wide-world's birthday!" she lied. "And because of that, shots are on me! Court, this is from Rob, he says he loves you and he can't wait to see you! Bottom's up!" Chelsea cheered and drank down the shot she had.

Courtney watched the faces in the room. Those who were drunk were just happy to see a girl in a mini-skirt on the stage. Those who were sociably drinking were happy for the free shot. But there was one man who was staring straight at Courtney. His eyes never left her. He was older, early 40s, with light brown hair. He hadn't touched his beer since Chelsea started speaking. Seeing Courtney watching him, he lowered his eyes, pulled out a ten-dollar bill and set it on the counter. He slipped off the bar stool and headed toward the door.

"So, that should get some reactions," Chelsea said coming back over and sitting down.

"Sorry, Chels hold that thought," she replied standing and quickly following the guy out of the bar.

CHAPTER TWENTY-EIGHT

Jon and Scott sat together in the living room, reading as the music of Chopin played in the background. The quiet evening was one they shared nearly every week, if their schedules permitted. But that evening there was a knock at the front door. Putting his book down, Jon went to see who it was.

"Viktor?" Jon breathed as he opened the door quickly. The boy turned toward him, face bloodied, lip busted, eye swollen shut, cheek so badly bruised Jon knew it was broken. Tears streamed down Viktor's cheeks.

"I'm so sorry," he whimpered. "I didn't know where else to go."

"Come in," Jon opened the door wider and reached for him. Looking past him to the black SUV down the driveway, it drove off before Jon said anything more.

Taking Jon's hand, Viktor walked stiffly inside.

"Who is it, Dad?" Scott walked around from the living room. He saw Viktor and froze.

"It's all right, Scott," Jon said looking at his son. "Let's get you to the living room, Viktor." Slowly, they walked into the other room and Jon helped him to his chair. "What happened to you?"

Jon asked.

"My father found out I was talking to the cops," he said through gritted teeth. "I think a rib is broken. It's hard to breathe."

"Scott, call Ryan," Jon ordered.

"Dad…" Scott cautioned.

"Just do it," Jon replied. Scott walked out of the room pulling out his phone.

"I'm sorry," Viktor apologized watching Scott. "I didn't mean to put you in a bad situation."

"You haven't, my son is just cautious," Jon replied crouching low to help him take off his jacket. Viktor cried out when he moved his arm. "Tell me what happened."

"My father," he flinched. "Didn't appreciate me going to the cops."

"How the hell did he find out?" Jon demanded.

"He always finds out," Viktor shrugged. "This is tame, I've had worse from him."

"How did you get here?" Jon asked rushing to the kitchen to get a wet paper towel.

"Sergei drove me," he said. "He won't tell anyone."

"It's good you have him," Jon replied. "But why didn't he stop them from doing this?"

"He couldn't," Viktor looked at Jon like he was crazy. "If he stepped in, dad would have known about us…"

Jon nodded but gently wiped the blood from his lip and cheek.

Scott walked back in the room. "Ryan's on his way," he said.

"Who's Ryan?" Viktor stammered looking at Jon.

"My nephew," Jon replied. "He's a doctor. He'll help you."

"Dad," Scott called. "Can I talk to you for a second?"

Jon nodded then turned to Viktor pressing an icepack into his hands. "Just relax. You're safe here. I'll be right back."

Following Scott into his study, Jon waited for his son's myriad of questions. And he did not disappoint.

"What the hell going on?" Scott questioned. "Do you know who that is? That's Viktor Redorvsky's son. The –"

"Head of the Russian mob, yes I know," Jon replied.

"You just happen to be BFFs with a known mobster?" Scott asked.

"That boy lost his best friend and mentor when Pastor Hollywell was killed. He came to the precinct at our request to see if he knew anything that could help find Greg Hollywell's murderer. It is because we asked him to come that he's in there right now," Jon explained.

"Dad, I know you love helping people and you've taught me to do the same, but there are only so many stray kittens you can take in until one of them scratches you. Viktor Redorvsky is a kitten you do not want to mess with."

"Scott, I told him he could come by at any time. If he ever needed help to ask. Do you expect me to kick him out, now? You see the state he is in."

"And how long until his dad comes around?" Scott asked rhetorically. "How did he get here? How do we know the person who dropped him off isn't back there right now getting everyone together?"

"Viktor says the man who dropped him off cares about him. I'm fairly certain he means that in a… unique way. I doubt anyone who loves someone would do what you're suggesting."

"And that's fine, I don't care about his personal life but how do we know we're safe? I admire you, you know that, but you just can't teach old dogs new tricks." Scott said. "It's bred in them."

"Not him. I appreciate your concern, son and I agree with you, but I truly believe all is well. Trust me."

"I do," Scott sighed. "What are you going to do?"

"Well first, I'm going to have Ryan take a look at him.

Then, I'm going to get him something to eat and a place to stay for the night," Jon said.

"I don't feel right about this, Dad," Scott replied.

Jon put a hand on his son's shoulder. "I need you to trust me."

"It's not you I don't trust."

"Maybe you should go to Kim's place. Wait until he's gone."

"Hell, no," Scott said. "I know you don't give a damn about yourself, so someone has to watch your back."

Surprisingly, Jon nodded but leaned in and lowered his voice. "I'm leaving the gun cabinet unlocked tonight. If you need to, take one with you to your room."

Scott agreed. "He wants to get out of the life, Scottie. I know what that's like. When I was neck deep in the IRA I wanted out too. I had someone who helped me. Now it's time to pay it forward."

"Okay, why doesn't he turn states evidence against him. He could go into witness protection. It would be a lot safer for all involved," Scott offered.

"Don't you think his father has men in that program?" Jon questioned. "They'll find him."

"Is he gonna be one of your projects?"

"Maybe, but right now could you get the door?" Jon answered seeing Ryan's jeep pull in. Scott nodded and they both left the study.

Jon walked back to be with his houseguest as Scott met Ryan and explained what was going on.

"I shouldn't have come," Viktor looked up. "I'm so sorry. I shouldn't have put you in this situation. I'll call Sergei to pick me up."

"You're fine," Jon replied. "My nephew is going to take care of you and you'll stay here tonight."

"No," he said shaking his head adamantly. "I can't do that to you. What if my dad finds out? You'll be dead. No, you've been so kind to me. I'll head out soon." Jon crouched down beside him.

"Hey, easy," Jon soothed. "It's all right. You are safe, nothing will happen."

"Why are you so nice to me?" Viktor asked. "I don't deserve it."

"I wasn't unlike you at your age," Jon said. "I was a rebel and I was able to change and get away. I guess I see a little of me in you."

"Was your father a mob boss who beat you within an inch of your life simply for discipline or because he felt like it?" Viktor asked.

"I said a *little*," he winked.

Viktor laughed lightly, but he flinched with pain.

"Uncle Jon?"

"Come on in, Ryan," Jon called. Ryan walked in, followed by Scott. "I'll leave you two. You can trust him," Jon placed a comforting hand on Viktor's shoulder.

Ryan stepped forward.

"Hello, Viktor, My name's Ryan. Can you tell me what hurts?" Ryan set his bag down on the couch and Jon left the room.

"What's the verdict?" Jon asked as Ryan walked into his study half an hour later.

"He really needs to go to the hospital, but he refuses," Ryan said.

"He can't go, Ryan," Jon explained. "He barely got away alive. Do you honestly think his father wouldn't try and finish the job if he was at the hospital after coming here?"

"No, but... he agreed I tell you. He has a concussion. Without an x-ray I can't be certain but it looks like two broken ribs, his nose is broken, and he has a hairline fracture of his right cheek bone."

"Is *that* all?" Scott quipped.

"I've done what I can, but it's not good, there could be internal bleeding," Ryan said. "There's only so much I can do without the proper equipment."

"I can't go," Viktor said. Ryan turned quickly.

"What are you doing?" Ryan demanded. "You shouldn't have moved! I told you!"

"I had to," Viktor answered.

"What is it?" Jon asked heading to him.

"You have been so kind to me and how do I repay you?" Viktor asked. "By putting you all in danger. I should go home."

"He will kill you," Jon stated.

"Better me than any of my friends," Viktor shrugged. "Greg taught me that it's better to give of your own life than to take someone else's."

Scott got up before Jon could speak.

"Viktor," Scott began. "You owe no man your life. Let us help you. Greg taught me it is better to help your fellow man than to pass by on the other side of the road without a glance. Stay the night, regroup, let my dad figure out what to do," Scott went on. "He's the best man I know. He will come through for you. And, for what it's worth, I will help you too." Jon smiled with pride at his son. Scott looked over at Jon and continued. "I didn't understand his motives at first, but now I do. And I will help in any way I can."

"Thanks," Viktor said in a small voice.

"Any way you can, huh?" Jon asked, breaking the serious tone of the moment. Scott looked over at him.

"Yeah," he shrugged.

"Good, then you can order dinner," Jon winked.

CHAPTER TWENTY-NINE

"Hey," Courtney called rushing down the sidewalk to the man who had left the bar. "Do I know you?"

He stopped and turned around. "No," he answered and walked away again.

"Hey," she yelled. "Don't walk away from me. I'm not done talking to you. You were staring at me."

"You regularly follow men out of a bar who have been staring at you?" He turned to face her. His eyes were so dark it would have frightened a normal person, but Courtney was in cop mode and her gun was burning a hole in the back of her pants.

"Only those I've seen before," she replied, showing the picture. "Thought you might want to know who you're dealing with." Courtney saw the moment he recognized himself in the picture coming out of the bar. Cursing, he thrust a hand through his hair. "What does he have over you? Talk and I'll be lenient."

"I'm done talking to you, lady," he said turning to leave.

"Hey! The name's Detective," she pulled out her gun and aimed it at him. "And I'm taking you in. I think you know the drill. Don't try and run, these stilettos are killers and I would really enjoy shooting you, just ask the guy who broke into my apartment."

Knowing she would make good on her threat, he raised his hands in surrender.

"Thank you for helping me," Viktor said as Jon walked back to the living room with a glass of water for him. Scott and Ryan had called it a night and went up to their rooms leaving Jon and Viktor alone.

"It's my pleasure," Jon replied.

"I'm just so worried about you and anyone who helps me. My father will hunt me down like a dog. I'm dead either way. If he knew I was talking to the cops," he shuddered. "It'd be slow."

"You're talking to a friend," Jon smiled slightly resuming his seat near him. "I'm not a cop right now."

"He won't see a difference," Viktor said.

"I'm not the only friend you have," Jon reminded him. "Tell me about Sergei."

Viktor looked up at him, his brows furrowed. "Why?"

Jon shrugged. "I want to know about you and you seem pretty close."

"We are," he admitted. "Sergei has always been there for me."

"How old is he?"

"Thirty-two," he answered.

"Is he the one who dropped you off here earlier?"

Viktor nodded. "He never laid a hand on me," he said. "But he couldn't stop them without my dad knowing something was going on."

"And what is going on, Viktor?" Jon asked gently.

Viktor locked eyes with him for a long moment but said nothing. Finally, he shrugged. "I don't know. He got me to my room after they left me but I told him I needed to get away. He wanted to help. He hates me being in this life. I told him I had someone who could help me and he offered immediately to drive me. I swear he won't tell anyone."

"I don't care about that. I only care about your safety," Jon said. "What does Sergei do for your father?"

"He's his right hand. He's to take over the business when dad retires."

"Was he born into it?" Jon asked.

"Back in Russia. He was an orphan. My dad found him on the streets when he was ten. He told me the story once after he had a few too many beers. He was a child. My father took him in and eventually forged papers to pass him off as his nephew, though they aren't related. When my father moved to America, Sergei was eighteen. I was born a few years before. We all moved here and then my mother left."

"What happened to your mother, Viktor?" Jon asked gently.

"Please call me Vitya, all my friends do," he said.

"Vitya," Jon agreed. "What happened to your mother?"

"She died. At least, that's what they told me," Viktor said. "Sergei told me the truth later. She had run off with one of my father's men. Father tracked them down to the Caribbean and put a bullet in both their heads. That's what he does to those who try to leave."

"He will not touch you," Jon promised.

"How can you promise that?" Viktor asked

"Because I have some powerful friends I've already spoken to about you. They will help keep you safe, if you want it," Jon said.

"What do you mean?" He asked.

"I knew Greg Hollywell too. He was a good friend to Scott when he went through a tough time after his mother died. I can see what he saw in you. I have a lot of friends at different universities. I would be happy to call any of them and pull some strings to get you in. You mentioned La Salle, do you want to go to a Catholic university?"

"I don't really have a religion. I picked La Salle for two reasons, one, Greg knew someone there and two, it was far away from my father," Viktor explained. "My grades were getting better since I had Greg's help. But now…"

"You wanted to go out of state?" Jon asked. Viktor nodded. "What were you interested in studying?"

Viktor shrugged. "I've always wanted to go into business but a legitimate business."

"How do you feel about Ireland?" Jon asked.

"I've never been," he answered.

"If you'd be interested, I know several people at Trinity College in Dublin. And if you would need a place to stay or a job, I have a place near there. Would you allow me?" Viktor didn't answer. "You could reinvent your life. Change your name, get away."

"He'd never stop hunting for me," Viktor finally said.

"What if Viktor Viktorovich Redorvsky died?" Jon asked. "And you became someone else?"

"I'd be looking over my shoulder my whole life," Viktor said.

"Not if we could get you away from here," Jon replied. "Would you like me to contact my friends at Trinity and see about getting you in? You would have to take all the tests and fill out the application, but I can at least help a little. I have some friends who could help you fill it out. You're smart. You'll get in."

"Do you honestly think it would work?" Viktor asked.

"Your father may have some powerful friends, but I have more," Jon answered. "I will take care of everything. But I need to know you'd be on board with this."

"I'd do anything to get away from him," Viktor said. "But…"

"Sergei," Jon offered. Viktor nodded. "From what you've told me, he seems to want what's best for you. I imagine he would

166

back you."

"I'm sure he would," Viktor said. "But... I would miss him."

"We miss anyone in our lives who mean something to us and we're away from them for any length of time," Jon replied. "Do you love him?" Viktor's eyes grew wide, but he didn't look away from Jon when he nodded. "Then I imagine he loves you too and would want what's best for you," Jon went on. "Talk to him, see what he thinks and let me take care of the rest. Do you trust me?" Viktor nodded again. "You will need to play their game and keep your head down until we can get everything ready."

"That means I will have to break the law," Viktor said.

"If you ever get arrested for something," Jon started. "You don't call a lawyer, you call me."

"You'd do that for me?" Viktor asked.

"Yes, I would," he answered simply.

"Why?" Viktor asked.

"Because some people are good. Also, I'm a father, and my son was your age once. We weren't talking at that time because of his mother's death. My wife was pregnant when she was killed and, though I have a feeling it was a girl, it could easily have been another boy. You remind me of what could have been."

"I'm sorry for your loss," Viktor said softly.

"Thank you," Jon replied taking a drink of his whiskey. "Now, how about you get some rest, we'll talk more in the morning, okay?"

"Okay, thank you," Viktor said. Before they said anything more, Jon's phone rang.

"Sorry, I need to take this," Jon said. Viktor nodded and watched him walk down the hallway answering the call. "You did what?" he heard Jon yell after a moment. "You didn't tell me! No, no, I'm beyond angry, Courtney. What the hell were you thinking? I don't care if you had back up and Chelsea does not count as backup. Jaysus, do you know what could have happened to you? I don't give a damn if you caught the guy or not, I'm your partner you should have told me. No, I'm on my way in."

After he hung up the phone, Jon walked back into the living room.

"Vitya, I'm sorry but I need to go in to the precinct, will you be okay here for a couple of hours?" Jon asked. Viktor nodded. "Good. Scott, Ryan!" Jon called up. The lads were at the landing before Jon said anything else.

"What's up dad?" Scott panted as if he had woken suddenly and in a panic.

"I need to go into the office, Viktor's going to stay here. I'll try and be back as quickly as possible," Jon explained.

"What's happened, Uncle Jon?" Ryan asked.

"Your fiancée has gone off on her own and collared one of our main suspects. I need to go in," he explained. Ryan rushed down the stairs.

"Is she okay?" Ryan demanded standing on the last step.

"Yeah, yeah, but she went without telling me and only had Chelsea as back up," he replied. "She's fine. I'll be back soon. Viktor, there's guest rooms in the basement all made up and ready. You're welcome to stay where you are if you don't want to move."

"I don't want you going up or down the stairs without me, Viktor," Ryan said. "I'll help you. Be careful, Uncle Jon."

Jon nodded and grabbed his keys off the ledge, heading out to his car.

Chapter Thirty

"I called Jon," Courtney said to Dave as she walked into the adjoining room. "Quinn Henderson isn't talking. When's the prisoner transportation coming?"

"Not until tomorrow," Dave replied.

"We could make a deal with him. Get more information, figure out who is behind this. How did he get out?"

"I don't make deals with cop killers," Dave stated staring at Quinn Henderson through the one-way mirror. "We need to find his brother."

"Bradley right?" Courtney asked.

Dave nodded. "They're inseparable. Wherever Bradley is you can bet Quinn knows."

"And if he doesn't?" She asked.

"I have feelers out," Dave revealed. "We'll find them."

"What if they lawyer up?"

"They're convicted criminals, escaped felons."

"Granted, but with all the shit being thrown at the police right now, we need to make sure this is by the book. The last thing this department needs is more bad press after the captain's fiasco. You know the feelings toward the police are pretty bad right now.

What do you suggest?"

"If he asks for a lawyer, we'll get him one," Dave replied. "But until then, you read him his Miranda Rights, didn't you?"

"Of course," she answered.

"Then we're fine. When's Jon getting in?"

"Knowing him? He's probably downstairs already."

"Try in the room," Jon's voice came from the doorway.

Courtney and Dave turned to him. "Are you going to complain about me going on my own again? Or are you going to be my partner?" Courtney asked.

"I'm still not happy about it, but I know why you did it," Jon said walking up to them. "I want to talk to him, Dave. See if I can get anything out of him."

"I don't think that would be the best option," Dave replied.

"I'm not asking permission," Jon said turning to go.

"Jon," Dave called to him. Jon froze but did not turn. "Don't mess this up. Keep your anger for what he did to Carol in check."

"You think you know me," Jon started. "But there is a side of me you have never seen."

"May 20, 1968, Belfast," Dave said. Courtney watched Jon's back tense. "I know everything about you, and I'm ordering you to keep your anger in check."

"May 20, 1968? Belfast? What is that?" Courtney asked when she and Dave were alone.

"He knows," he replied.

"What is he going to do?"

"Give Quinn what he wants," Dave said watching Jon walk into the interrogation room.

"Quinn Henderson," they heard Jon say over the intercom. "It's been a while."

"Not long enough," Quinn sneered as Jon sat opposite him.

"You look good for a dead man," Jon said.

"So do you," he answered.

"Oh, I'm alive and well, but you…" Jon opened the file in front of him. "You have a lot of people after you. I can see why you wanted to escape, but man… caught by a woman? That doesn't sound like you. Slipping up? Getting lazy after ten years? I thought they fed you well in prison."

"Yeah? I'm not the only one coming after you, you know."

"No? Well that's good, I'll line them all up in the cells next to you. Bet they'll love that new haircut of yours. Makes you look… well, fresh. Speaking of, how's your brother?" Jon looked up at him, closing the file.

Quinn's lip twitched. "He's fine," he answered.

"Is he?" Jon asked.

"Why?" Quinn demanded. "Do you have him?" Jon didn't say anything. "I swear if you hurt him, I will kill you just like I did your precious wife," he spat.

"That all depends on you," Jon replied coldly. "He's already cut a deal with the DA. How else do you think we knew where to find you?"

"Your partner showed me a picture," Quinn replied. "That's how she found me."

"And where do you think we got that picture?" Jon asked.

"Brad would never do that," Quinn stated. Jon didn't say anything. "Unless you lied to him."

Jon leaned back in the seat and crossed his arms over his chest.

"Here's what we're willing to offer, you give up Rob and we'll put a good word in for you with the DA and see about getting your sentences reduced."

"We're twenty-five to life," Quinn said. "Do you honestly think parole at twenty years would be worth it?"

"You killed a cop," Jon replied calmly. "You're lucky you're not on death row."

"You know he told me you would use my brother against me," Quinn rebuttaled. "I want to see him, now."

"Can't let that happen," Jon shook his head.

"Why? Because you don't have him?" Quinn demanded.

"He's a bit... well, tied up at the moment. He fell down and hurt himself, he's a little banged up," Jon said.

Quinn gripped the table. "You know," he breathed heavily. "Rob told me he would have enjoyed spending more time with your precious wife. He said it was pity to destroy such beauty. That's why he wanted the wounds to be as slow as possible. And he enjoyed seeing your face as you held her. He said it was the best moment of his life to see you suffer. Did she say goodbye? Tell you she loved you? Look after Scott. You've done a piss poor job at that, now that Rob — well, he has something special in store for *him*. It did surprise him how slow you were to move on. Does Ryan know about how you feel about your partner?"

Jon kicked Quinn's chair out from under him and drew his gun.

"You tell me where he is!" Jon yelled aiming his gun at Quinn. "Where is he?"

Courtney and Dave burst into the room both their guns drawn.

"Stand down," Dave yelled at Jon.

"Not until he tells me where Rob is!" Jon shouted.

"I'm ordering you to stand down, Lieutenant," Dave commanded.

"Jon, put your gun away," Courtney begged. "Please."

"No," Jon stated.

Dave aimed his gun at Jon's back. "Don't make me do this."

Jon stared down at Quinn, his gun still aimed at his head. The pin drop silence was deafening. Finally, Jon lowered his gun and Quinn took a breath.

"He said you wouldn't have the balls to shoot me. You can't

even avenge your wife," Quinn said.

Jon raised his gun again.

"No!" Courtney screeched as Jon fired. The moments of silence stretched on as Courtney, Dave and several other cops who had come running into the room, took in the scene. Quinn looked at the floor beside his left ear where Jon fired.

Crouching low, Jon whispered, "you tell Rob that I will find him, and when I do, that shot will be between his eyes." He straightened and walked over to Courtney and Dave. "I'm done," Jon said handing Courtney his gun and Dave his badge.

————

Courtney followed Jon to their office and found him standing at the window looking out to the stars above. She stood near to him but said nothing.

"I miss Ireland," he finally said. "All the stars, the beauty, my family. I am always so relaxed when I go home. I don't want to be here anymore. I don't know how this is going to play out, Courtney. But I've done too much, seen too much. I don't think I can go on." She didn't say anything, only slipped her hand in his.

"Everyone has a breaking point and I think I've reached mine," he went on. "That wasn't as much of an act as I would have liked for it to be. I'm afraid I would have shot him had you not screamed at me. That is a man I haven't been in a very long time. Not since Carol…"

"Tell me about her," she finally said. "You never really talk about her. Tell me about your wife."

He sighed deeply. "She was the most incredible woman I've ever known. I was a… I guess the term nowadays is *bad boy* when I met her. But she was able to show me who I wanted to be. She gave me the strength to put my past behind me and to forget what I've… what I've done."

"What have you done?" Courtney probed gently.

"I can't," he murmured.

173

"Tell me," she pressed.

He was quiet for a moment then a sigh emitted from his lips.

"When I was a young man, I joined the IRA. I believed in the mission and freedom for all of Ireland. I still do. Did you know it wasn't the Catholics who started the war? History commonly mistakes that. Protestants opened fire on a Catholic school, killing children. That is what started it. I hate religious battles, but they happen often. I told my leader I wouldn't kill innocent people, but they told me I would not be killing innocents but *protecting* innocent people... they had a way of explaining things away... So, I did as they asked. On May 20, 1968, I planted a bomb in the basement of a building. I watched from across the street as a bus load of school kids pull up," sighing, he broke off and closed his eyes for a moment.

"I tried to rush across the street, but my partner stopped me and said if I did, it would give the whole team away. I didn't care. I knew the lads didn't know there would be kids, there wasn't supposed to be anyone there. They had made sure the building would be empty... I knew they wouldn't want that to happen.

"I convinced my partner to help me. We ran in to try and get the kids out... they laughed at us. I went down to the basement to try and disarm the bomb, but I couldn't. When I came back up, my partner, Jimmy was his name, he told me to get the kids out and he would take care of it. Just as the last of the kids were getting out of the building, I turned to see Jimmy carrying the bomb up the stairs. I told him to drop it and run. He said he couldn't disarm it but he would try and get to the roof. I couldn't stop him. Just as he started up the stairs, I ran out with the last of the kids and when I looked back, the building exploded. Jimmy hadn't made it out.

"I knew had I not let them convince me to plant that bomb, Jimmy would still be alive. I left the IRA that day without a word. It took them a while to find me as we all went by different names.

Carol knew, Carol always knew what I had done. She helped me see myself as she saw me. The man she wanted and knew I could become. I've killed people for other people's causes. Sanctioned or not, it's wrong. But Carol helped me understand it is in the past and it cannot harm me unless I let it. She always told me, tomorrow was a new day. She helped me focus on who I wanted to become. I wanted to be someone my son could look up to and honor. I wanted my friends to think of me as someone who would always be there for them. Since she died, I've tried to still be the man she knew I could be, but recently, I don't know. I guess I've been letting her go more and more since Beth. I'm living in the moment and not looking to the future. But I'm becoming the man I was again, and I hate it. I'm not that man anymore, but, like a ghost it's haunting me and making me relive my old sins."

"Let me tell you something, Jon," Courtney began. "You are the best man I know. When I look at you, I don't see a killer, I don't see a man with a colorful past. I see the man Carol knew you could be. You are that man, Jon. And I know she couldn't be happier with you. She knows you're hurting, she knows you miss her. She knows you're fighting it still. But I think she also sees the man you are. And I know, if she were still alive, she would be so proud of you. She loves you, Jonny." Jon froze and looked at her. "Sorry, *Jon*," Courtney shook her head. "I don't know why I said that. I never call you that."

"No," he breathed, "Carol did."

"There, you see?" She answered. "Maybe it's time for you to stop wishing for her back, stop longing for the past and look ahead to the future. She would want you happy."

"I was reminded of that fact just the other day," he replied closing his eyes for a moment.

"One thing, though, I know she would not have wanted you to leave a job half finished," she said. "Now I will talk to Dave and see what can be done. You can retire when this case is over. Go home. I'll meet you there. We can go over the evidence then."

———✳———

"What is it, August?" Rob answered the phone.

"Jon's breaking," the Sergeant on duty said on the other end. "You should've seen what just went down over here."

"You're calling from the precinct?" Rob demanded.

"Well, yeah," he answered. "Where else?"

"You fool!" Rob said harshly. "Don't you think they're monitoring?"

"I'm calling from my cell," August answered.

"It doesn't matter," he scolded and hung up quickly.

CHAPTER THIRTY-ONE

Jon woke that next morning, his whole-body aching. Reaching out for Beth, he opened his eyes when his hands hit empty sheets. Only then did he realize she never came over the night before. Grabbing his phone off the nightstand, he sent his girlfriend a flirty good morning text.

Sitting up, he rolled his neck and flinched when he felt stiffness on the left side. Beth sent him back a text that made him laugh out loud. Once dressed, he trotted down the stairs, overhearing voices in the kitchen. Ryan was at the stove, Scott was grabbing some plates from the overhead cabinet and Viktor was sitting at the kitchen bar. Scott saw Jon first.

"Hey!" Scott smiled. Ryan and Viktor looked over at him.

"Hiya," Jon yawned.

"You look like shit, da'," Scott replied.

"Cheers," Jon answered sarcastically.

"Good morning, Lieutenant. I hope you had an all right evening," Viktor said.

"Ehm," he answered sitting next to him as Scott flipped the switch on Jon's espresso machine. "Not the greatest, and it's *Jon*, not Lieutenant."

"What time did you get in, Uncle Jon?" Ryan asked concentrating on the omelet in the pan.

"About eleven," Jon replied gratefully accepting a glass of orange juice from his son.

"Everything all right?" Ryan asked.

"Courtney called you, didn't she?" Jon asked. Ryan shrugged evasively. "I'm fine. Really."

"Oh, Beth called earlier, said she figured you were sleeping and didn't want to wake you," Scott said. "She asked you to call her whenever you get a chance."

"Already texted her good morning," Jon answered.

"Can't go a minute without texting the girlfriend, eh?" Scott teased passing his father the espresso after it had brewed.

"A good morning text is like a good morning kiss," Jon replied. "It makes their day better. You know, romantic stuff."

"Romantic, shit," Scott laughed. "Thank God my woman is above that."

"Trust me, send her a good morning text," Jon said. "It will win you brownie points."

"I don't need brownie points," Scott winked. "She wants me all the time. Can't get enough actually."

"TMI, son," Jon laughed.

"You have a girlfriend?" Viktor asked Jon.

"Girlfriend?" Scott barked a laugh. "Yeah, he's got a girlfriend; my future mother-in-law."

Viktor grimaced.

"Now, now, in all fairness, we were together long before you and Kim," Jon said to Scott.

"Yeah but still," Scott shrugged. "It's gross, man."

"Oh, tanks very much," Jon teased back, his Irish accent showing through.

"Omelet's up," Ryan called. Scott held out a plate to him. "That's Vitya's."

"Thanks," Viktor replied. "So, you and your partner, Detective Shields aren't a couple?"

Ryan looked over at them both. "What?" he asked curiously.

"It's well known in our society Jon and his partner are more than just partners," Viktor said.

Ryan raised an eyebrow and looked over at Jon. "Is it?" He asked.

"Now, Ryan, you know partners spend a lot of time together and when there is a partnership of two people of the opposite sex, rumors are bound to spread," Jon explained.

"Huh," Ryan grunted.

"I'm sorry," Viktor said. "Did I say something wrong?"

"No," Jon shook his head.

"Just let me know people believe my uncle and my fiancée are together," Ryan teased.

"Your fiancée?" Viktor asked surprised. Ryan nodded. "Oh my god, I am so sorry," he said. "I didn't mean—"

"It's okay," Ryan interrupted. "I know there are rumors. But trust me, she's happy with me."

"Just keep making the omelets, Ryan," Jon said. "I'll have one with the works."

———————

As Jon dressed for work, he called Beth. Pulling on his tie as the phone rang, he smiled when he heard her voice.

"Hi, handsome," Beth said as she answered.

"Hey, baby," he said. "What are you doing?"

"Oh nothing, just packing for the over-nighter in Cincinnati tonight," she replied. "And thinking about you."

"Oh?" He asked. "And what are you thinking about?"

"How much I want to hear your voice and have a repeat of the hot tub from the other night."

"Yeah," he breathed. "We need to do that again, soon."

"I miss you."

"I miss you too. Let me know when you get there."

"I will," she answered. "Save some wine for me."

"Keep the side of the bed warm for me."

"I might, or I just might find me a hot guy."

"Oh?" he chuckled. "Could you find anyone hotter?"

"Never," she giggled.

"That's what I thought," he grinned. "Be careful, baby. A lot of stuff is happening right now."

"I have my twenty-two in the glove compartment," she said.

"Good," he replied. "Good luck, and call me when you get into town."

"I will. I love you, Jon," she said.

"I love you too, Beth," he replied. "Now go do what you do best."

CHAPTER THIRTY-TWO

At Courtney's urging, Jon arrived at the precinct and headed up the elevator to his office. When the elevator doors opened, he heard the commotion of several police officers surrounding a man who was demanding to see him.

"What is going on here?" Jon asked.

"Jon! Oh, thank god!" the man said when he saw him. He broke through the line of cops to get to him.

"Jason? What on earth are you doing here?" Jon asked surprised to see his godson.

"It's Anna," Jason said, shaking.

"What about Anna?" Jon asked.

Jason pulled out his phone to show Jon a text. "I got this today, she was supposed to be at school. I was driving to work when I saw her walking up our street. She seemed almost in a trance. She told me a nice man had given her an ice cream cone and let her go home. Then I got this text."

Jon looked at it and motioned him to follow to his office.

"Jon," Dave said at the door of his office. "A moment."

"I'll be right back," Jon told Jason then followed Dave into his office.

"You may need this if you're planning on coming in here," Dave said handing him his badge and gun back.

"Thank you," Jon replied.

"That was one hell of a performance," Dave stated. "Make sure that's all it was."

"Understood," Jon answered.

"Also, I have some bad news. Quinn was transported after his lawyer showed up. He's not here any more."

"What? When? Why didn't you do something?"

"My hands were tied, you know that," Dave quipped.

"Now, go and talk to Courtney."

Courtney appeared at the adjoining door. "Talk to Courtney about what?" She asked.

"Something is going on with my godson," Jon explained but turned back to Dave. "We're not done talking about this. I want to know where he is."

"I'll keep tabs on him," Dave promised.

Jon opened the door of his and Courtney's office and beckoned Jason inside.

"Courtney, Jason; Jason, Courtney," Jon introduced quickly. Jason looked at her and nodded. Jon sat next to him. "Where is Anna now?" Jon asked.

"Mom just got back from Florida so I took her there then came straight here," Jason explained accepting Jon's coffee with shaking hands.

"Where's Sally?" Jon asked.

"She's with her new boyfriend somewhere in the Caribbean," he spat. "I tried to call her but it went straight to voicemail."

"Anna was staying with you?" Jon asked.

"Yes, what does this have to do with finding the man who almost abducted my little girl?" Jason demanded.

"Trust me we're going to figure out what happened, Jaye.

Now do you think Anna got a good enough look at him to give us a sketch?" Jon asked.

"I'm not letting her do anything. The best thing is for her to just forget this whole thing," Jason said. "Are you gonna help catch him or not?"

"Jason, I know you're scared, but you're not giving us anything to go on. You're tying our hands. Now how did Anna get to school today?"

"The bus, but I stayed with her at the stop until she got on and the bus drove off." Jason explained.

"Is it usual for her to take the bus?" Jon asked.

"Yes," he answered.

"Have you met the bus driver before?"

"No, Sally usually takes care of that."

"Sally is?" Courtney prompted.

"My ex-wife," he answered.

"How far away from the house was she when you found her?" Jon went on.

"About a block away."

"Did you see anything strange?"

Jason looked at Jon. "You mean besides my daughter walking along the street when she supposed to be at school? No."

Jon asked to see the phone again and read the text.

Unknown: She is such a beautiful girl, I'm glad nothing happened to her. The rue morgue can be very dangerous.

Jon handed Courtney the phone. He didn't have to look at her to know her entire body stiffened. They locked eyes and Jon nodded slightly.

"I'll be right back, okay, Jaye?" Jon said as he and Courtney walked out of the office and shut the door behind them. "That means something to you, doesn't it?"

"But before I tell you, let me ask, what is the little girl's full name?" She asked.

"Anna, umm…" He thought a moment. "Anna… Oh what is her middle name… Belle, that's it. Sally is obsessed with Disney. Anna Belle Leigh." Courtney closed her eyes slightly. Even Jon stopped for a moment. "I never thought of that," Jon sighed.

"You know that one then?" she asked.

"It's familiar," he replied.

"Jon, rue morgue, *Annabelle Lee*, prefect, the *Black Cat*, the *Devil in the Belfry*, the *Tell Tale Heart* you know what I'm going to say…"

"Poe," he confirmed.

"I was a lit major before I switched to criminal justice, Poe was my specialty," she explained. "I still have my old notes and stuff in one of my desk drawers. I'll show you when Jason leaves."

"Chess terms now Poe, how does he know?" Jon challenged.

"Great question," she replied. "Have you swept for bugs?"

"Not recently," Jon admitted. "But I will."

"Today," she stated.

"Today," he confirmed. "But a more pressing issue is how do we tell my godson his daughter was taken for two reasons, one, because her name matches a poem from Edgar Allen Poe and two, because this person who is obsessed with Poe will stop at nothing to get to me?"

"The truth is always best," Courtney replied.

"You're right," Jon answered. "Let me do this alone."

She nodded and watched Jon head to their office. Courtney went to the break room and grabbed some water. Just as she walked out to speak with Officer Callen, Jon's office door opened, and Jason stalked out, a furious look on his face.

"Jason," Jon's voice bellowed after him.

"You stay away from me!" Jason yelled.

"Jason!" Jon roared again.

"You stay the hell away from my family," Jason ordered. "If

my daughter is hurt in any way, if there was one hair ripped out of her head, I will come for you."

"Officer Callen, could you escort Mr. Leigh from the premise, please." Courtney asked. Callen nodded, got up and pulled Jason away.

"I swear, Jon, if she is hurt, you are dead," Jason yelled.

"Arrest that man for threatening an officer of the law," Dave's voice came next as he opened the door to his office.

"No, Dave," Jon said. "No, he's just got a lot on his mind, he didn't mean it."

"You stay away from me!" Jason yelled as Callen pulled him completely out of the room.

"One of our best has been threatened because of something that was out of his control," Dave addressed the room of officers. "He needs our support in this, not your pity or your scorn."

Courtney went up to her partner.

"He's taking everything from me," Jon said shaking. "If he's trying to break me, he's succeeding."

Courtney hid her smile as she got him back into the office.

"Oscar worthy, Jon," She said.

Jon turned to her smiling. "Thank you." Dave walked into the room from their adjoining door. "Was it too much?"

"I just know you too well," she replied. "So, you do think there's a mole?"

"We have our suspicions," Dave said. "We're monitoring all calls in and out of the desk phones."

"What did you see?" Courtney asked.

"Not sure," Dave answered. "But last night something seemed off for us both."

"Off how?" Courtney asked.

"When I left the interrogation room," Jon began. "Dave and I both saw something between Henderson and August, the new sergeant."

"So, you're monitoring all calls to try and trap him?" Courtney surmised. "But what happened with Jason? Did you tell him and he agreed to play along?"

"Yes, I was originally going to use you as the one who yells and storms out, but with Jason here, it gave me a chance to hold on to my partner for a little while longer," Jon explained.

"And Jason's daughter?" Courtney asked.

"Anna is fine, a bit shaken but unharmed," Jon answered. "Everything he said here did happen. I told Jason about this Rob character and he asked what he could do. I told him my plan to make the mole think I've been broken, he agreed. Now if it is August, he can tell Rob I've been isolated. Soon you will have to put on that same performance. Hopefully, without the almost getting arrested part."

"We could, it's an option," Dave shrugged. "I had to make it realistic."

"Now we can get down to business. Courtney and I are going to my place to sweep it for bugs, can you keep the monitor going here and let us know what happens?" Jon asked.

"Will do," Dave answered.

"Good, thanks," Jon said. "Now let's get to work. Jason left me the text message and the phone number the text came from. Our computers could be hacked, both of ours. So, let's head to the store and get another one," Jon got his jacket. "Be sure to bring the notes you wanted me to see, Courtney."

August watched Callen escort Jason Leigh out of the precinct from his cubicle near the break room. Seeing Dave's eyes scan the crowd, August took his desk phone and called Rob.

"What is it now?" Rob answered.

"You'll never guess what just happened," August said excitedly.

"Did I hire a former cop or an old biddy?" Rob asked. "I

don't care what just happened. When you have something to report then call me."

"Things have been happening here," he said.

"What sort of things?" Rob asked.

"That little girl you picked up this morning? Her father just showed up and freaked out on Jon," August explained. "He had to be escorted out of the precinct."

"You are not calling me from your desk phone, are you?" Rob asked.

"It's the only phone I had handy at this moment," he replied. "Besides the acting captain is watching us all like a hawk."

"And why do you think that is?" Rob demanded. "Dammit, August, they've made you. Get out of there now!"

CHAPTER THIRTY-THREE

"I can't believe you just bought a $3,000 laptop," Courtney said as they drove.

Jon shrugged. "I needed a new one and one I was sure couldn't be bugged."

"I'm pretty tech savvy but I didn't understand half of what that guy was saying," she said.

"Well, you wanted to look around so don't blame me if you missed the first bit," Jon teased.

"And I'm very grateful you bought me that series. I've been looking for it for a while," she smiled.

"Anything for my girl," he winked. "And I have some news I wasn't able to tell you earlier," he started. "I got a text from Viktor while the sales guy was talking to me. He said he spoke to Sergei and he reminded him Hollywell has a surveillance camera set up in his office behind some books in the bookcase just in case someone raised suspicion about him. Viktor remembered seeing it there one day and mentioning it to Sergei."

"Who is this Sergei?" she asked. "He's mentioned him before."

"Redorvsky's senior man," Jon replied. "And Viktor is in

love with him."

Courtney raised an eyebrow. "Okay. So, we pull the surveillance footage from that camera and see what shows up."

"Maybe it caught something," Jon replied. "Rob could have showed up one day. Maybe get a face with the name."

"Jon, I need to tell you something, and I need you to promise you'll look at this rationally and not like I betrayed you somehow," she said.

"You went to go talk to Father Isaac the other day when I went for coffee," he supplied.

"Did he tell you?"

"No," Jon answered. "It's exactly what I expected you to do. You're a good cop, Courtney. You knew I wouldn't go and we had some questions. You had some questions you didn't think I would be able to answer regarding Pastor Hollywell."

"Not that you couldn't answer them," she said quickly.

"No, I wouldn't want to remember," Jon replied. "If you *didn't* go to see him, I'd be surprised. Did you learn anything interesting?"

"Not really, he didn't have any information relevant to the case," she answered. "Just that he was a good man. He did tell me Hollywell wasn't always a pastor. He had a fiancée who was carrying his child."

"They both were killed in a car accident," Jon finished. "He told the parents that story when he was ordained into the church."

"Okay, well, I thought maybe Isaac knew something or maybe saw something, but he didn't," Courtney said. "I still don't understand the Poe connection. I know Rob/Paul is obsessed with Poe but why use his stories?"

"Probably because he degrades everyone he meets. He's a rapist and a murderer. He saw a way to tear down someone who has spent his life trying to lift others up. That's what he does. Pastor Hollywell was the perfect victim for him."

They were both silent for a moment before Courtney took a deep breath.

"So, where are we going now?" She asked. "Back to the precinct or to the church?"

"Neither."

"Then where?"

"Somewhere we can't be bugged."

———◦◦◦———

"Lieutenant Greene, Detective Shields, good afternoon," the receptionist smiled as they walked into Scott's offices.

"Hiya, April," Jon smiled back. "Is he free?"

"Let me double check, sir, he just had a meeting with the partners a little over an hour ago but he may be out now," she picked up the phone and dialed an extension. "Ah, sir, your father and Detective Shields are here to see you... all right... thank you, sir," she hung up the phone and looked at Jon. "He says to have you go on back."

"Cheers," Jon smiled. Several of the lawyers greeted them as they walked to Scott's corner office. When a blonde-haired man wearing a tailor-made suit, walked out of another office in front of them, he grinned.

"Jon," Alex greeted. "Courtney, hey guys."

"Howya, Alex," Jon replied extending his hand to his son's best friend.

"It's been a long time, how are you?" Alex asked.

"Pretty good, you?" Jon replied.

"Oh, you know..." he teased. "Someone got himself shot and left all the work to Tom and me."

"Oh yeah," Jon laughed. "Heard about that. Looks like you guys managed to keep the ship afloat."

"One tries one's best," Alex winked. "How're you doing, Courtney?"

"Great, Alex it's good to see you," she answered.

"You too," he said. "How's Chelsea?"

"She's good," Courtney laughed. "Asked after you the other day."

"Yeah? Well, tell her I said hey, would ya?" he asked. "Maybe we could catch a movie and dinner sometime."

"I will let her know, but," Courtney started. "The way to Chelsea's heart is a brewery tour."

"Seriously?" He quirked a smirk. Courtney nodded. "Okay, thanks."

"You gonna keep them all to yourself?" Courtney jumped when she heard a voice behind her. "Oops, sorry, didn't mean to startle you," the man put a hand on her shoulder. She turned to see Tom Roberts, Scott's firm's third partner standing behind her.

"It's all right," she replied as a grin spread across her face. Tom was the quintessential silver fox and Courtney always enjoyed seeing him. Tall, slim but defined through his navy-blue suit, tan shoes, blue eyes, clean shaven with salt and pepper hair. Almost too late, Courtney realized she was staring. "Didn't hear you."

"Sorry, I snuck up on you," he apologized.

"How you doing, Tom?" Jon asked.

"Well, thanks," Tom replied shaking Jon's hand. "It's good to see you."

"Don't you guys think you could've let my dad get to me before ambushing him?" Scott walked out of his office with Kim at his side. Jon turned to his son, noticing he was far too pale and the sling was irritating him.

"You know how much cooler your dad is," Alex teased.

"Ha. Ha," Scott replied sarcastically. "Come on into my office, guys, let these two jokers get back to work which I pay them to do."

"Our clients pay us, ya nut," Alex laughed.

Before Scott could answer, he clutched Jon's arm tighter and thanked the discreet support Jon offered with a hand on his back. Out of the corner of his eye, he saw Jon look over at Kim. She nodded and went into his office ahead of them. Once Jon got his son to his desk chair, Kim came around with an ice pack and placed it on his shoulder.

"Did you take your meds this morning?" Jon asked concerned when his son groaned in pain.

Scott nodded, though his eyes were closed, and he had turned another shade paler.

"I'll be all right in a minute. This spasm is pretty painful," Scott said through clenched teeth.

"You're doing too much," Kim said soothing his hair. "You need your rest."

"I'll be all right," he answered.

"No, you won't be. Now, I'm your father, and you promised you would listen to me," Jon said firmly. "You need to take some more time off. Your body needs to heal."

"I know you're my dad," Scott said looking up at Jon. "And you only want what's best for me. I know you still blame yourself for this even though it was my fault, but Dad, trust me when I say; I'm 29 years old. I can take care of myself. I know I haven't exactly proven that in the past, but I will stop if it gets to be too much, I promise. Now, I know you're concerned about me, but I also know if you wanted to know how I was doing, you could have called my fiancée who, I'm sure, would have loved to give every detail about how she thinks I'm doing too much..." he side glanced Kim beside him. "So, there must have been a reason you're here."

"Well, yes, there is a reason. However, being that this is an open investigation, I can't talk a lot about it. Mainly, we have a Poe problem."

"I'm guessing you mean the author and not using it as some euphemism," Scott said.

"Yes, the author," Jon replied. "A lot of the recent investigations have had Poe elements and themes. You know about

Hollywell's murder, but there are other things, things I can't discuss."

"This has something to do with Rob, right?" Scott asked.

"Yes, we think so, but we need to work somewhere where we won't have Rob knowing what we're doing." Jon explained.

"We think there's a mole at our offices, so we needed somewhere to work. My apartment could be bugged and well…we know both our places are an easy target…" Courtney said.

"Feel free to use any of the conference rooms," Scott offered. "Kim, could you go with them and then let April know to reassign any meetings from that room to another?" Scott asked.

"Sure," Kim answered.

"I'd go, baby, but," he started.

"Rest," she kissed his forehead and stroked his cheek. "I'll take care of it. I'll be right back. Do not get out of that chair."

"What if I have to go to the restroom?" Scott complained.

"You know what I did last time," Kim answered. Scott smirked.

"I do," he called after them. "And I might just have you do it again."

Jon laughed hearing the playfulness in his son's voice.

"At least he's in good spirits," Jon said. "But he seems awfully pale," he said.

"I know," Kim answered. "I've been trying to help him as much as I can, but he's stubborn."

"Your mother would say something about *like father, like son*," Jon admitted.

"Yes, she would." Kim laughed.

"And she'd be right," Courtney added.

"Hey, enough out of you," Jon nudged his partner with his shoulder gently.

"Will this one work?" Kim asked indicating a conference room. "It's the only one that locks and it's pretty much sound proof."

"Perfect," Jon thanked her.

"I have a few appointments today, but I'll be around if you need me," she said.

"Is Scott going home half-day today?" Jon asked.

"Probably not," Kim answered pursing her lips together. "I keep trying but he won't go. I have a meeting at 3:30 and another at 4:45 so I won't be able to take him home."

"I could do it," Tom came up and offered. "I'd be happy to drop him off at home."

"Thank you," Jon replied. "Let me see how we end up here and I'll let you know."

"Sure, sure," Tom answered. "He's getting better, Jon, really he is."

"Then why do I feel like he's not?" Jon mumbled when he and Courtney were alone.

"Come on, partner," Courtney said. "We got this. Let's finish so you can go be a dad."

CHAPTER THIRTY-FOUR

"Jon," Courtney called to him. "We got a ping."

Jon turned from the window back to her, leaned down to watch the computer as the indicator blinked on the screen.

"Who is it?" Jon asked. "Whose number?"

"Indianapolis," she said clicking through and scanning the information. "Says it is registered to an August Dupin..." her voice trailed off as she leaned back.

"The sergeant?" Jon asked. "I knew it. I have to call Dave."

"Not just the sergeant, Jon," Courtney opened the internet tab and typed into the search bar. "Here, listen. 'However, above all of Poe's literary creations,'" she read. "'One stands out; his one character that transcends science and common sense. The one to whom several scholars attribute being the first and, coincidently the least well known among mystery fans. The character, wrapped in mystery much like his creator, sets the stage for some of literature's most well-known and beloved detectives; Sherlock Holmes, Hercule Poirot, and Sam Spade. These characters can all trace their styles back to one: Edgar Allen Poe's, C. Auguste Dupin.'" Courtney leaned back and explained. "My lit professor wrote this, he did his dissertation on Dupin."

"But why that specific one? Didn't Poe have multiple police and other people in his stories to choose from?" Jon asked.

"Because C. Auguste Dupin makes his first appearance in *The Murders in the Rue Morgue*," Courtney said.

"'It's dangerous on the rue morgue...'" Jon quoted from the text sent to Jason. "I've got to freshen up on my Poe."

"Damn, he's good," Jon breathed as he read from the copy of Poe he had just purchased from the bookstore.

"I love him. I was going to go to grad school in Baltimore where he died," Courtney replied sipping her bookstore latte.

"That's a little macabre," Jon answered not looking up.

"And being a cop isn't?" Courtney asked running a finger along the white lid. "You know, many experts credit Poe as the first cop procedural writer? His death is also a complete mystery. He was found dying in an alleyway the cause of death is still unknown." Jon was chuckling. "What?" She asked.

He shrugged. "The theories range from poison, to a heart attack, to tuberculosis," Jon supplied.

"You know all about this, don't you?" Somehow, she wasn't surprised.

"I *am* dating a bestselling mystery writer whose favorite style is detective procedural stories," he answered. "It may have come up once or twice."

"You mean during pillow talk?" Courtney rolled her eyes.

"Sometimes," he teased.

"What do you want to do now?" she asked taking another sip.

"Well," Jon checked his watch. "There's not much more to do today," he stated.

"Do you want to get the surveillance footage from Hollywell?"

"Yeah," he huffed.

"Want me to go get it?"

"Am I that transparent?" he asked.

"To some and not all the time," she replied. "I'll go get it, run home to shower, change and meet you back at your place by seven."

"Be careful," he said.

"I will," she replied. "Drop me off at my car?"

They drove the short distance to the precinct and Jon watched her get into her car, wave and drive out of the garage. As Jon waited for cross traffic to clear, he noticed a black sedan at a metered spot. When he pulled out the sedan followed him.

Glancing in the rearview mirror a few times, he cursed the heavy tinted windows of the car behind him. When he reached the entry of his subdivision, he braked and turned on his turn signal. The car behind him stopped but kept driving straight on College Avenue when Jon turned. Breathing a sigh of relief, his cell phone rang his son's ringtone.

"Hey, Scottie," he answered.

"Hey, Da'," Scott replied. Jon smirked there were only a handful of occasions Scott called him that with an Irish accent.

"How's Iollan?" Jon asked.

"How did you know I talked to him?" Scott asked.

"Because I can read minds," Jon teased. "And you also called me da'."

Scott chuckled. "Right, well, he's doing well, called to ask me how to propose," Scott relayed.

"Since you have such vast knowledge on the subject," Jon laughed.

"Exactly," Scott agreed. "But he's planning on proposing in Italy."

"Fancy," Jon replied.

"Right? I feel badly, Kim got a hospital room and a guy high on morphine," Scott laughed. Jon heard her muffled voice in the background and the slight echo of a kiss.

"Gross, you two," Jon replied. Scott laughed but Jon could hear the underlining pain in his voice. "How are you feeling?" Jon asked.

"Still in some pain. Kim's driving me to Ryan's place. He wanted to keep an eye on me again tonight. He said since it was my first full day back he wants to make sure I didn't overdo it. Kim told me Beth is in Cincinnati. You'll have the house all to yourself tonight."

"Better get used to that," he said.

"Yeah, yeah, whatever, you have more company now than you did in all my thirty years," Scott laughed.

"That's a different type of company."

"Talk about gross."

"I'm home now," Jon answered not keeping the grin from his voice. "Courtney's coming over. I'm gonna go for a swim before she gets here."

"Kay, be careful," Scott said. "It's freezing out."

"I'll be fine. Let me know when you get to Ryan's," Jon asked.

"Will do," Scott replied. "Have a good night, dad. Love ya."

Jon turned off the car and grabbed his new computer. Walking in through the garage, he texted Courtney to tell her to let herself in using the garage code and if he wasn't there to check in the pool when, "what the hell!" he started as a gigantic black raven flew directly at him. It cawed constantly. Jon ducked and dodged as it flew at him. Opening the back door, he tried to shoo it out, but it wouldn't go.

Following the bird to the front door, Jon opened the storm door and held it as the bird flew around. Just as it dived for him, he moved aside, and it flew out.

Resting his back against the front door, panting, his eyes fell on a piece of paper crumpled near the front stair. He grabbed it and read.

Quoth the Raven… Nevermore.

———————

Courtney got out of the shower and wrapped her towel-robe around her. Music played on her iPod system as she got ready to go to Jon's house. Her phone chimed, and she looked down at the text.

Jon: When you get here let yourself in, you know the garage code. If I'm not inside, check out in the pool. See you soon. Wine or tea?

She laughed and quickly sent a text.

Courtney: Hey, Romeo, got your speedo? I'll sell tickets to the freak show lol And wine sounds great! See you soon!

As she pulled on her jeans and packed her sweatpants, she sang along to a song on her iPod. Finishing up, she made sure she had the surveillance tape and headed out to the main living area of her apartment.

She stopped dead in her tracks. Her eyes fixed on the item on her kitchen bar.

CHAPTER THIRTY-FIVE

Courtney could barely move, but slowly she walked toward the kitchen bar, knowing beyond a shadow of a doubt the dark bottle had not been there earlier. Swallowing, she read the label.

AMONTILLADO

She licked her suddenly dry lips and looked down at the note in front of it.

My dear Fortunato, you are luckily met... here is the Amontillado.

"*The Cask of Amontillado...*" she breathed. Springing into action, she grabbed her spare gun again and walked around her apartment looking everywhere someone could hide. When she knew she was alone, she fell onto her couch and grabbed her phone. This was the second time someone had gotten into her home. She needed to get a dog.

"Jon," she said into the phone. "You won't believe what just happened."

"Oh, I think I will," his voice had an edge to it. "But tell me."

"Are you listening to me, Tom?" Tom Roberts, Scott's law firm partner, finally turned back to his wife as they sat at the table. "Sorry, honey, what?" He questioned.

"I was talking about Jack's school. Did you hear a word I said?" she asked.

"I'm sorry, I've been distracted. I just..." he sighed.

"What's wrong?" she questioned. "That's the sixth time tonight you've checked your phone."

He reached over the table to take her hand.

"I'm sorry," he said softly. "I guess this whole business with Scott getting shot has my nerves on edge."

"I couldn't believe it when I heard," she answered stroking his knuckles. "How's he doing?"

"He's a little... forgive the pun... a little gun-shy."

"With good reason," she replied. "But don't let that bother you."

"I've known him for nearly ten years," he answered. "I feel like a second father to him."

"I know, I still remember his divorce case. You came home and told me you hated seeing the young suffer so much. You vowed to win his case and get... how did you say it?"

"I said, I will get that lying, cheating harlot off his back if it's the last thing I do," he replied.

"And you did, Meredith has never bothered him since. You should take pride in that."

"I do. I know the history between them, I witnessed it first hand," he yawned. "Sorry."

"It's all right," she answered. "You're bound to be a little drained doing all the work. You've been out past midnight everyday this whole month. How's Alex doing?"

"He's a joker as usual," he said. "I swear, sometimes I feel I'm the only one who doesn't get his jokes."

"Well, that's what happens when we get older," she laughed. "But you still like your job, right? You don't regret leaving Chicago?"

"And the slave master of a boss I left behind? Oh, no," he answered. "I still remember when Scott offered me the partner position at his law firm. It was like a dream come true."

"Well," she raised her wine glass. "You're *my* dream come true."

He leaned over to kiss her and clinked his glass to hers. "Listen, maybe you should take the kids to the lake house," he said after taking a sip.

"Why?" She asked.

"Well," he started. "You said yourself I'm a little distracted. Coming home late, working at all hours of the night. I wouldn't want my behavior to worry them."

"You're a lawyer, honey," she replied. "I think they're used to it."

Chuckling, he reached across and clutched her hand. "I guess you're right, but I would feel better if I knew you were safe…"

She squeezed his hand. "If you think it's for the best," she said. "Just promise me you'll be safe."

"With you to come home to, how can I not be?" He asked.

"I'm glad you decided to listen to reason and stay over," Jon stated as he made up Ryan's old room.

"Well, I knew I couldn't sleep in that place alone tonight," Courtney said. "In fact, I'm thinking about moving apartments."

"After everything you've been through with them, yeah I'd say it's time. I'd be happy to help you move."

"Thank you," Courtney said. "For tonight, it was either your place or a hotel."

"My place is cheaper," Jon replied.

"True," she answered. "I called mom and dad and told them

to keep an eye out."

"Where are they?"

"Wine country," she revealed. "They'll be back on Sunday."

"Good," Jon finished making the bed and turned to her. "Wine is poured, we can check out the surveillance video. But I haven't had a chance to shower yet so I'm gonna do that now. You have your gun?" Jon asked. She nodded. "I'm a yell away."

"Me too," she answered. "I'm gonna just stay up here. I don't want to be alone downstairs."

"I'm closer here," he smiled. "I'll come and get you when I'm done." She nodded and picked up the remote. "Lock this door after I leave. I'll call to you before I knock."

After hearing her lock the door, he walked back to his room. As the water struck his chest inside the shower, he stared at the marble wall. *How had Rob gotten into their homes? Why Poe? What was the end game?* Questions was all he had. Huffing a sigh, he didn't realize the water had turned cold until that moment. Soaping up and rinsing quickly, he was just about to get out when he heard something outside the door.

"Courtney?" He called. "Is that you?"

There was no answer. Turning the water off, he took a towel and wrapped it around his waist. Slowly stepping out of the shower, he reached for his gun on the counter beside the sink.

"Courtney?" He called again. "Scott?"

Still, there was no answer. Reaching for the door knob, he slowly turned it and yanked the door open, pointing his gun. The person in the room screeched.

"Beth?" he exclaimed, seeing his girlfriend lying on his bed waiting for him. "What the hell?"

"Oh my god, Jon! I'm sorry!" she scrambled off the bed.

"What are you doing here?" he demanded.

"I just wanted to come home, I have some great news to share! I – What are you doing with that gun? Is it something to do with the case? Honey, I'm sorry, I was just wanting to surprise you. Is everything okay? You're scaring me. I've never seen you come out of the shower with a gun before. Is there something wrong?"

"Why the hell didn't you call me?" he questioned.

"I wanted to surprise you!" she cried. "I had some good news! I just wanted to share."

"It's okay, it's okay, honey, come here," he sighed and opened his arms to her. She stepped into him and hugged him tightly. "I'm sorry, love, it's okay."

"You scared me, Jon," she said pulling away slightly. "Is there something wrong? Is it the case?"

"Jon?" Courtney raced in, gun drawn. Beth looked over at Courtney.

"What?" Beth breathed looking at Courtney.

"Stand down, it's Beth," Jon stated.

"Oh, okay," Courtney replied lowering her gun. "I'll be outside."

Jon looked at Beth once Courtney had left and held her head in his hands. "Look at me, love. Everything is okay. But we're on lock down."

Beth's eyes grew large as she looked at him. "Okay," she replied with a single nod and a strength she didn't feel. "We'll talk later."

Jon's eyes went to the bottle of expensive champagne in the ice bucket on the nightstand with two glasses.

"Oh, honey," he sighed and pulled her into him. "I'm sorry. What's your good news?"

She shook her head. "Later," she promised. "I need to know what's going on."

CHAPTER THIRTY-SIX

Courtney put in the surveillance video on Jon's computer. After an hour seeing Hollywell sitting at his desk doing paperwork, Courtney got up.

"As riveting as this is, I could use some popcorn," she said. Jon chuckled. "Want some?"

"Please," he answered. "In the pantry."

"I know," she teased.

"Ooh, with some garlic salt?" Jon asked.

"How long have I known you?" Courtney replied. "I think I know how you like your popcorn."

Jon chuckled but turned back to his computer screen, covering a yawn.

Heading into the kitchen, Courtney saw Beth at the table typing on her laptop. She looked up when Courtney walked in.

"Beth, I'm sorry, I didn't mean to startle you earlier," Courtney said.

"Oh sweetie, it's okay, I understand now," Beth replied. "I just didn't know what happened. I'm not used to my boyfriend pulling a gun on me."

Courtney laughed. "I bet," she motioned to the pantry. "I

was just getting some popcorn," she said.

"Oh, sweetie, I'm so sorry. I should have gotten you guys something!" Beth said sliding off the high-top chair.

"Oh no! Please! Let me make it up to you. I'll make something," Courtney replied.

"Are you sure?"

"Yeah, Jon told me you had some good news to share," she said disappearing into the pantry for a moment to get the stove top popcorn Jon always had stocked. "I'm sorry it was ruined."

"Oh, no worries, sweetheart," Beth replied when Courtney headed to the stove. "I'll tell him later tonight."

"What was it you wanted to tell me?" Jon asked Beth as they lay together on his bed. When the surveillance camera did not show anything for the hours they watched, Jon called it a night.

"Oh, I just wanted to tell you about the conversation I had with my agent as I drove home," she admitted.

"I like that you call it home," Jon replied kissing her hair. She snuggled deeper into his arms. "What did she say?"

"Well," she started. "It just so happens my publisher and TimeLine Studios have agreed on a contract to pick up my book *Old Sins* for a blockbuster movie, there's even talks of A list actors," she revealed.

"What?" Jon breathed moving to look at her. "Seriously?" She nodded. "Honey, that's amazing! Congratulations!"

"It is exciting news."

"Very!" Jon said kissing her. "Oh baby, that's wonderful! Hey, we need that champagne."

Beth grinned and nodded emphatically as Jon slid out of the bed and tiptoed downstairs. Finding the bottle, he grabbed the two glasses and went upstairs. Thinking how similar the cork would sound to a gunshot, he knocked on Courtney's room and let her know.

After popping the cork and clinking their glasses together, they drank, finishing the bottle before making love.

———◦◦———

Jon slowly woke with Beth resting snugly against him, her hand on his chest. It was barely six o'clock in the morning. Carefully peeling away from her and pulling on a shirt, he walked down the front stairs. Just as he was going into the kitchen to get some coffee, movement in his study caught his eye.

"Courtney?" He called, looking toward the closed smoky glass double doors.

"Hey, good morning," she greeted him, walking around from the kitchen, drying her hands. "I was just making some pancakes. What are you doing up so early?"

Jon reached for his gun hidden behind him and Courtney froze. Gesturing toward the door, Courtney nodded and backed him up as he approached.

Opening it quickly, he came face to face with a dead man.

"Hiya, Jon," Riley said, standing in front of him. He smiled as blood seeped out of his mouth and between his teeth. Jon watched as a deep burgundy blood stain appeared on Riley's white shirt.

———◦◦———

Jon awoke in a cold sweat, sitting straight up in bed, breathing heavily.

"Jon?" He heard Beth call beside him. "What's wrong?" She asked wrapping her arms around him.

"A bad dream," he heaved. "Just a dream."

She rubbed his arm and rested her chin on his shoulder. "I'm sorry, baby. Do you want to talk about it?"

"No, sorry, not really," he shook his head as she stroked his hair.

"Lie back down," she coaxed, wrapping her arms around him. Knowing there was no possibility he would be able to fall back asleep, he waited until she relaxed beside him and slowly slid out of bed.

Walking down the stairs noiselessly, he keyed in the security code deactivating the lower level and went over to the bar. Pulling out a bottle of his favorite Irish whiskey, he poured a double and sat in his chair in the living room, grabbing his book of Poe from the coffee table.

It was about ten minutes later when he heard movement on the stairs and saw Courtney sneaking down with her gun. When she saw him, she relaxed.

"I hoped that was you," she said softly, leaving her gun on the coffee table that lined one of the sofas. "I heard someone go down the stairs and saw your door open. It's only one in the morning, are you okay?"

"I'm fine," he said. "Just couldn't sleep. Do you want something?"

"What have you got there?" She asked gesturing to the glass beside him.

"Green Spot," he answered taking another drink.

"Any good?"

"Very, if you like whiskey."

"Could I try some?"

Jon looked over the rim of his glass and smirked. "Sure," he answered. Pouring another glass and a little more for himself, he brought it back to the living room. "Sláinte," he toasted and clinked his glass to hers.

"Cheers," she replied.

They drank and Jon watched as she closed her eyes reveling in the taste of the whiskey on her tongue.

"So good," she replied after she swallowed.

"That's my girl," Jon teased giving her a slow wink. They were quiet for a little while, but Courtney finally broke the silence.

"What are you reading?"

"*The Masque of the Red Death*," he said not looking up.

"Ooh, that is one of my favorites," she replied.

"I'm starting to understand you a bit more," Jon looked over to her.

"And it only took you two years," she teased back. He chuckled but did not respond. "I made a list, by the way," she went on, pulling out a piece of paper from her pajama short's pocket.

"List of what?" Jon asked.

"List of which stories we've encountered so far," she explained.

"Read them off to me?" He asked. "Slowly, let me find it in the book."

"*Annabel Lee*, it's a poem," she started. Jon flipped to it and skimmed the poem.

"Damn," he sighed. "That's..." he breathed out. Immediately, Courtney's heart sank. *Annabel Lee* was a poem written to a dead lover.

"Oh, Jon, I am so sorry," she started. "I shouldn't have asked you to read that."

"It's fine," Jon waved her off. "Next?"

"*The Tell Tale Heart*," she said knowing he would prefer to keep his emotions to himself.

"I read this in Primary School," he said after skimming. "I'd forgotten it was Poe. Next?"

"*The Black Cat*," she answered. He read and nodded. Without prompting she continued. "*The Murders in the Rue Morgue. The Cask of Amontillado. To One in Paradise. The Purloined Letter. The Raven. The Devil in the Belfry.*"

"So," Jon started closing the book. "Main question, how does he stay one step ahead of us?"

"You think he has eyes on us?" She asked.

"Or ears," Jon replied.

"Do you really think this is Rob or," she looked over her

shoulder before leaning in and whispering. "Paul masking his identity by using Poe?"

"Who else could it be?"

Before Courtney could answer, Jon's cell phone rang a blocked number. Courtney started recording on her phone and nodded. Jon answered it and put it on speaker before the other person spoke.

"Very clever of you, Jon," the voice on the other end said.

Courtney got up and walked around behind his chair, so her phone would pick up on the voices.

"Who are you?" Jon asked.

"I'm sure Riley mentioned me," the voice said. "If not, I know you've figured out most of it."

"Do I address you as Rob? Or Paul?" Jon asked.

"Depends on how much you want to sleep in your own bed tonight, Jon. How is my wife?" He asked.

"She's enjoying a real man," Jon replied.

"Oh yes, I've been listening to how much she's *enjoying* you," he chuckled.

"Glad it was good for you," Jon said. "So, what do you want?"

"To play," Rob answered.

"All this because you want to play?" Jon pressed.

"Of course, that *and* the fall of the house of Greene," he said. Courtney's grip on Jon's shoulder increased. "That's right, Courtney," Rob continued, without pause. "Sacrilege to you, I'm sure, but a play on words to me."

"I'm curious, what do you want to come from my ruin? What's your end goal?" Jon asked.

"Let's just say... I enjoy watching you get yours." Rob said. "But don't worry, it'll all be all right soon."

Beth's shrill scream came from the front stairs and echoed through the house.

"Beth?" Jon roared, racing to her. Courtney immediately followed him and saw Beth shaking on the last stair. "Baby, what's wrong?" Jon demanded. She didn't speak, her body shook uncontrollably. "Honey, talk to me," Jon tried to reach out to her; she looked up sharply at him, screamed and rushed around the corner to his study, hiding. Peeking out around the door, she kept hidden behind the glass.

"Jon, wait," Courtney said putting a hand on his chest. "Just hang on, okay? Let me try." He nodded but his hands clenched at his sides. Courtney walked slowly over to her as one would approach a skittish cat. "Beth," she said softly. "It's me Courtney. Can you hear me?" Beth peaked out again and locked eyes with her. "Hi," she smiled at her. "You are safe. Nothing will hurt you. You know Jon would never let anyone or anything harm you. He loves you."

Her eyes grew wide. "Jon doesn't love me," Beth started. "He hates me."

"What?" Jon breathed. Courtney didn't turn but raised her hand and waved him to be quiet.

"What do you mean? Why do you think Jon hates you?" Courtney inquired.

"Because of Steven," Beth's voice was soft, as if telling a secret.

"What about Steven?" Courtney asked.

"He doesn't know," she whispered.

"Know what?" Courtney prompted.

"He thinks he's his, but he's not," Beth replied. "He's Paul's."

"Who is Paul?" she asked.

Beth shook her head and put a finger to her lips.

"Father and mother want me to be with him," Beth said. "They don't care. They know but they didn't want to help me."

"Know what?" Courtney asked.

"Paul…"

"What about Paul?"

"He forced me," she confessed. "My parents wanted me with him and when it happened… I wanted to go to the police, but they wouldn't let me. Paul hit me and they did nothing. I can't tell Jon. But I still love him. Paul tried to hurt Steven when he demanded to know if he was his or not. I told him Steven was Jon's son. He hurt me again that night but at least he didn't hurt my son."

"Where is Paul now?" Courtney asked.

"You shouldn't be here," Beth said. "He'll be home soon."

"No, he won't," Courtney said. "Jon is here."

"Jon?" Beth panicked. "No, don't let him see me." She hid further behind the door.

"Hey," Courtney soothed. "Everything is okay," Courtney waved Jon forward without taking her eyes off Beth. "Jon is here and he wants to tell you something."

Beth's eyes went to Jon, standing behind Courtney.

"I love you, Beth," he said. "I always have and I always will. Steven may not be mine, but he is yours and I love him like my own son. Paul will never hurt you again. You have my word."

Beth blinked a couple times then her eyes cleared.

"Jon?" She asked, back to her regular self.

"Hey," he breathed a sigh of relief and reached for her. She raced into his arms.

"I'm sorry," she said.

"No, you have nothing to be sorry for," he answered hugging her tighter. "You're safe."

"That voice," she finally got out. "That voice is evil."

"I know," Jon replied.

"I know that voice," Beth declared.

"Baby, I hate to ask you this but who is it?" Jon asked.

She buried her head into his chest and clutched his back.

"Paul," she mumbled. "It was Paul."

Jon and Courtney looked at each other.

"Are you sure?" Jon asked, pulling slightly away from her and looking into her blue eyes.

"Hoh, yes," she breathed. "Not only will I never forget that voice, but… that's what he would say to me during…" she looked down swallowing hard. "It was his favorite phrase."

Jon clutched Beth protectively and turned to Courtney. "Could you put on some tea, please?" he asked.

Courtney nodded and headed for the kitchen.

"I think I might need something a little stronger than tea," Beth admitted. Jon nodded once and went to the bar to pour a small drink for Beth.

"Here, baby," he said handing her the glass as she sat on the couch with Courtney. She swallowed a full gulp, shuddering as the liquor hit the back of her throat.

"Jon," she started. "What did I say?"

"It's okay," he replied.

"I didn't mean it, whatever I said," she clutched his hand. "I love you."

"I know," he answered. "You know I love you?" She nodded. "Baby, this case… it's hard to explain," he continued. "You know I would do anything for you and anything to protect you, but the case revolves around Paul. He's back."

Beth's eyes grew wide as she stared at him then her eyes rolled back in her head and Courtney grabbed the glass as Beth's body collapsed into Jon.

"Call Ryan!" Jon ordered picking Beth up and cradling her to him. Courtney grabbed her phone dialing her fiancé's number as Jon carried Beth upstairs.

"Courtney?" Ryan's voice was groggy. "What's wrong?"

"Ryan, we need you, now," she said. "It's Beth."

CHAPTER THIRTY-SEVEN

"Jon," Courtney walked into Jon's room seeing him holding Beth. "Ryan's here."

Ryan stepped around her and Scott walked in behind his cousin. "What's going on?" Scott demanded.

"Jon?" Beth questioned groggily.

"I'm right here," Jon promised.

"I've got her, Uncle Jon," Ryan said peeling Beth away from Jon. "It's all right, let me take a look, Beth."

"I'm so embarrassed," Beth stated pressing the heel of her hand against her forehead.

"Don't be," Ryan soothed. "Now, tell me, do you have a headache anywhere?"

"Just behind my eyes," she confirmed.

"She just collapsed, Ryan," Jon stated heatedly.

"It's all right," Ryan answered turning to his uncle then looked back at Scott. "I'll take care of this. I need to check her vitals."

Scott pulled on Jon's arm. "Dad, come on, let's go downstairs. Let's let Ryan work."

"I won't leave her," Jon argued.

"You don't have to," Ryan said. "But now there is nothing you can do. I'm gonna give her something to help her sleep, but until then."

"She's collapsed, Ryan!" Jon yelled.

"Jon," she whimpered. "Please. I'm okay."

"Do you trust me?" Ryan asked. Jon's eyes went from his nephew to his girlfriend then back. Finally, he nodded. "Then let me do my job."

Eventually Jon leaned down and kissed Beth's forehead.

"I'm here," Jon whispered.

"I know," she replied. "I promise, I'm okay."

"I love you," he pressed his lips to hers but pulled away before she said anything.

He headed out of the room, followed by Courtney and Scott but, he paused at the stairs.

"Not the walls," Scott cautioned. Courtney looked at him then followed his eyes to Jon's clenched hand. "Punching bag downstairs. Come on." Scott edged him on. Courtney followed silently behind.

Once down in the basement, Scott pulled out the boxing gloves hanging on the rack and tossed them to his dad. Courtney stepped forward when she saw Scott take position behind the punching bag.

"He won't, not with your shoulder," she said. "Let me." Scott nodded and stepped back. "Come on, old man," Courtney started, grabbing the punching bag. "Show me what you got."

Jon looked at her then at the bag. He taped up but refused the gloves. Against his better judgment, he began punching. After about half an hour, Jon's shirt was plastered to his chest and back with sweat. He stopped for a second and walked away.

"That all you got, old man?" Courtney taunted.

"Stop," Jon replied.

"You aren't done, are you? I was just starting to feel

something," Courtney said.

"Enough," Jon snapped. They were all silent for a moment then Jon turned back. "The fall of the house of Greene."

"Usher," Courtney clarified.

"The singer?" Scott asked.

"Poe," Jon replied. "What's that one about?"

***

"*The Fall of the House of Usher* is a very unsettling work," Courtney started as they sat in the living room, the book opened to the story. Scott went into the kitchen to make something to eat. "A man is traveling through the countryside and comes across a mansion. The mansion is owned by the Usher family. The current owner had a sister who died tragically due to an illness, I believe. The brother buried her in the family crypt, but it was a sleeping illness and when she awoke inside her coffin, she would yell and scream that she had been buried alive but the brother would not open the crypt because he thought it was her ghost come back to kill him.

"The sister did finally get out. She had gone insane and killed her brother. The innocent traveler runs out of the house to his horse. There was a mighty earthquake and when he turned to look back at the house, it had split in two and left in ruins. Without both siblings, there was no house. But the story goes," Courtney continued. "Nothing could destroy the family more than their own flesh and blood. The Usher family could not be conquered from without only from within."

"He wants to destroy my family from within," Jon surmised. "So he's attacking people who mean something to me. Mat, Scott, Ryan, Beth, you, Kim, Keelan, even Pastor Hollywell meant something. Every person he has used or attacked has, in his mind, torn me down more and more."

"One other thing bothered me, Jon," Courtney said. "How did he know to call us right then? You remember what Paul said?

'Very clever of you, Jon'. Why would he say that?"

"Obviously, he was listening to us, but how?" Jon wondered. They both pulled out their phones.

"I'm going to email the recording I took of the conversation to both of us," she said before turning off her phone and pulling out the SIM card.

"If anyone needs to get a hold of me they can call me on Beth's phone or the landline in the study," Jon said following suit.

"Do you think that'll do it?" She asked.

"For a man who could get in and out of this house and yours without anyone noticing, god only knows," Jon rubbed his jaw. "But I think for right now..." he broke off, his eyes fixed behind her. Courtney turned to follow his gaze. Their eyes rested on the intercom system in the wall. Jon stood and walked over to it. "There is one of these in every room," he went on, pulling out his Swiss Army Knife and unscrewing the plate. "He would have perfect ears on us, throughout the house." Jon finished as he pulled off the covering to look inside.

"Where's the master?" She asked.

"There's a box outside beside the air conditioner," he answered. "Jesus, I'm such an eejit," he said. "Why didn't I see this before? I'll call the electrician in the morning and have them remove the box and get me another one *inside* the house."

She nodded, her eyes going to Scott who walked in from the kitchen.

"I made some tea and sandwiches," Scott said. "How's the hand?"

"Fine," Jon replied looking down. His hands were sore and an angry red from punching, but it felt good to let out some anger. Scott yawned but set the tea tray down on the table.

"Wanna tell me what's going on?" he asked.

"Yes, but then I need to make a phone call," Jon said.

Steven thought he was dreaming until he felt Amber move beside him. Opening his eyes, he realized the buzzing sound was not a dream and looked over as his phone lit up on the nightstand.

"Steve?" she moaned.

"Sorry," he replied. Grabbing his cell phone, he checked the name. "Hello?" he answered, not knowing if he had seen the name right.

"Hey," Jon breathed. "Steven, I need to talk to you. Do you have a moment?"

Jon's voice worried him. "What's wrong?" Steven asked, sitting up and swinging his legs over the edge of the bed.

"It's your mom," Jon replied.

"What about Mom?" Steven demanded. Amber sat up and touched his back. He looked over at her but said nothing.

"She's okay, but we have had an issue with the case," Jon revealed.

"What sort of issue?" Steven demanded. Amber wrapped her arms around his shoulders.

"Do you remember when Riley said something about Rob?" Jon asked.

"Yes," Steven replied.

"Well, we figured out who he is," Jon said.

"And?" Steven prompted.

"It's Paul Anderson," Jon replied.

Steven's whole body tingled as his heart sped up and his blood pressure skyrocketed. He felt dizzy for a moment then his mouth went dry and started to tingle like he had gotten up too fast and was about to black out for a moment. Grounding himself in Amber's soft caress on his chest, he cleared his throat.

"Where's Mom? What's going on with her?" he demanded.

"She's here with me, but when she found out, she collapsed," Jon explained. "Steve, I'm sorry, but I'm worried about her and I promised to tell you what was going on."

Jon hung up with Steven and looked up to see Courtney leaning against the doorway.

"How long have you been there?" he asked.

"Not too long," Courtney said. "Ryan sent me. He says he gave Beth something to help her sleep. Her vitals are good."

"Oh, thank god," he sighed, standing.

"Jon," she stopped him. "You need to talk about what's going on."

"What do you mean?" he asked.

"You're keeping it all inside," she went on. "You know you can talk to me, right?"

"Courtney, I appreciate your concern, but this is how I am," he started. "You should know it by now."

"I do," she replied. "But I also know you need to not hold things in so much. There are people who love you and want to be there for you." He stopped and looked at her. She held his gaze for a short time then looked down. "All I'm saying is, you need to let someone in, and that is not Beth right now," Courtney went on. Then, emboldened for some reason or other she stepped forward and placed a hand on his chest. "Talk to me. Let me in. I'm here."

Jon gently took her hand off his chest and kissed her fingers.

"Thank you," he said softly. "But no."

Courtney removed her hand from his and stepped aside.

"I'm sure you want to see her," she replied.

Without another word, he headed to the stairs, pausing only for a fraction of a second near his partner.

Courtney took a shuttering breath and wrapped her arms around herself. She didn't know what had made her say and do those things, all she knew was she should never have touched him so intimately. Her eyes traveled to Carol's picture on Jon's desk then Scott's voice from behind her spoke low.

"Is there something going on that I don't know about?"

She turned quickly toward him. "No, of course not," Courtney said. "I'm his partner. I'm concerned about him."

"Just be sure that's all it is," Scott replied. "There's more than just you involved in this."

"I do know that, Scott," she answered.

"Do you?" Scott questioned. "Because it sure as hell doesn't look like it."

"I'm trying to give my partner some support," she replied.

"Just be sure that's all you're giving," Scott countered.

"I don't know who you think you are," she spat. "But I am not a child to be scolded by the son of my partner."

"Dear god!" Scott hissed. "I saw you! What were you thinking? You sure as hell weren't thinking of your fiancé!"

"I refuse to justify myself to you, Scott!" Courtney rebuttaled.

"Is something wrong here?" Ryan's voice from the stair interrupted them. They both looked over at him and Scott sighed harshly.

"No," he huffed. "I was just talking to Courtney about the case."

"Which I have told him I cannot speak about current open cases," Courtney supplied.

"Okay," Ryan looked from one to the other. "Uncle Jon is with Beth. I'm gonna get some coffee. Are you sure everything is okay?"

"It's fine," Courtney replied looking over at Scott. "I'll get you that coffee."

———

"Steven, what's wrong?" Amber asked when he hung up the phone.

"Jon just told me some very disturbing news. My family needs me right now," he said.

"Then you should go," Amber answered kissing his shoulder.

"I need to," he said. "I need to be there."

"Absolutely," she replied. "I hope it'll be okay."

"I don't know. My biological father is someone I wouldn't wish on my enemy and he's fixated on Jon and my mom."

"If you need me or anyone, call me."

"I will, thank you," he leaned back to kiss her gently. "I'm sorry, not exactly how I expected to spend our weekend."

"It's okay, really," she answered rubbing the sides of his torso.

"I wanted to stay in bed with you all weekend," he whispered.

"Silly, don't you remember? We've stayed in bed nearly every day," she said.

"Oh yeah," he teased. "*That's* where I've been." She laughed and kissed him again. When he finally pulled back, he headed to his duffle bag and began packing his things. "Tell Josh I'll see him soon?"

"I will, be careful," she said. "And let me know you're okay?"

"I promise," he turned to leave. "Oh, and Amber?" He turned. "I love you." He left before she could react.

CHAPTER THIRTY-EIGHT

Steven pulled into Jon's driveway an hour later. There were lights on in two rooms. He caught movement in the front room and soon heard piano music. Pulling out his cell phone, he dialed a number before he got out.

"You called," Amber answered, a smile in her surprised voice.

"I told you I would," he replied.

"I know, just didn't know if you actually were going to."

"You surprised?"

"Pleasantly."

"I made it to Jon's house."

"Good, but you know, you left so fast I didn't get a chance to reply to you," she started. "Did you really mean what you said? Do you really love me?"

"I know it sounds strange. I mean we've only known each other for a couple weeks," he said. "But... yeah."

"Huh," she murmured. "Well, that's convenient."

"Convenient?" He asked.

"Yeah, it's been a while since I have been in love with someone, I've almost forgotten how it feels. I've never been one to fall in love quickly, but you make me feel things I've never felt before. You love my son which is the most important thing to me. So yeah, it's convenient because oddly, I'm in love with you too."

Steven released the breath he was unconsciously holding. "Wow," was all he could say.

"Yeah," she answered her voice low and sultry. "Wow. Now, go and do what you do best."

"Best?" he teased.

"Well… second best," he could hear the grin in her voice.

"That's better," he replied. "Tell Josh I'm sorry I'll miss his game today, but I promise to be there Sunday. Okay?"

"I'll tell him you'll do your best to be there," she said. "I know you're not the usual guy, but I just don't want him to get his hopes up."

"I understand," he replied. "But short of ending up in the hospital, nothing will stop me from being there."

"And I love you for that," she said. He smiled. "Now," she continued. "Go help your family then come home to me. I need you, Casanova."

Chuckling, he told her he loved her and hung up. As he got out of the car, his eyes subtly scanned the area. Nothing seemed unusual, but then again, in Jon's subdivision, any noise would be unusual. It was too quiet for Steven. He loved the sound of kids playing, BBQ's in the backyard, cars driving by, people biking and walking in springtime. A quiet subdivision, in Steven's mind, held secrets and it was his job to unearth secrets.

He walked up to the front door of the house and rang the doorbell. The piano music stopped and a few moments later Scott opened the door.

"Steven," Scott questioned. "What the hell are you doing here, man?" Offering his hand, he pulled Steven in for a back slapping hug.

"Got a call from Jon a little while ago, sounded like he

might need all the help he can get," Steven answered.

"Come on in," Scott stepped aside. "How've you been?"

"Good," he answered. "Just working."

Steven and Scott stood eye to eye at a few inches over six feet. Similar in build, Steven had Scott by a few extra pounds of muscle, mostly in his chest and back.

"How's the shoulder?" Steven asked.

"Better, doc says I still have a ways to go but at least it's healing," he answered. "Everyone's over here right now. Kim just got here a little while ago. She's up with your mom."

"How's she doing?" Steven asked.

"She was awake, but Ryan gave her something to help her sleep," Scott explained.

"I'd like to go see her," Steven said.

"Sure," Scott replied. "Can I get you anything?"

"A water would be great," Steven thanked him.

"Steve?" Jon's voice on the stair drew their attention. "I thought that was you." He walked down and embraced him. "What are you doing here?"

"Thought I'd lend my expertise," he said. "I was on leave, and I thought I might be an asset."

"Always," Jon answered. "Seems like there's a lot I've missed. Everything go okay?"

Steven breathed a laugh. "Long story."

"Well, tell me later," Jon offered. "I know your mom would like to know you're here."

"Is she awake?" Steven asked as he and Jon headed up.

"No," Jon replied. "Ryan made sure she was able to sleep."

They reached the doorway and Steven peered in. Kim sat beside the bed with their mother's hand in hers.

"Steve?" she breathed when she looked up.

"Hey, baby sis," he replied. She got up and raced to him. Enveloping her into a hug, Steven held her tightly.

"I'm so glad you're here," she mumbled into his chest.

"Me too. Where's Mark?" he asked after their middle brother.

"I called him, but he didn't answer. I left a message."

"He might be at work," Steven said.

"No, he was supposed to be off this weekend. But he might have a date or something."

Steven nodded and pulled her away from him for a moment. He gazed deeply into her eyes. She looked haggard. "Hey, we'll get through this."

"I know," she nodded. "It's just when I think of what he did to her."

"Don't," he stopped her. "Come on, baby sis, you can't do that to yourself."

"I know, I know," she replied. "Just to see her in so much pain."

Scott cleared his throat by the door. Steven turned.

"Sorry, I got you some water, Steven," Scott said.

"Thank you," he replied taking it. "I'll call Mark, he usually answers for me, since he knows when I call it's usually something important." He tried to make his sister laugh but it fell on deaf ears. Pulling his phone out, he speed dialed their brother.

"What the hell is going on?" Mark's voice came over the phone. "I've gotten ten texts and three calls from Kim."

"Where are you?"

Mark didn't answer for a second. "Out," he finally said.

"It's three in the morning. Get to Jon's place," Steven answered. "It's mom. She's okay but it looks like our father is back."

Mark went silent for a long moment. Steven pulled the phone away from his ear to check and make sure he hadn't lost the call.

"Mark?" Steven asked.

"Yeah," Mark finally said. "Yeah, I'm still here. What's

going on?"

"Get your ass over here and we'll tell you," he said. "I'm going to help Jon. Mom and Kim need you."

"Are they okay?" Mark asked.

"Yes, mom fainted earlier but she's okay. Ryan gave her a sedative."

"Let me talk to him," Mark, a doctor by trade, demanded. Steven saw Ryan walk into the room and offered the phone after saying who wanted to speak to him. Ryan turned and spoke to Mark in hushed tones.

"I don't want to leave her, but I think now you're both here, I'll go down and talk to Courtney," Jon said. Steven watched Scott sigh and look away. He made a mental note to deal with that later. Ryan walked back over and handed the phone back to Steven.

"Yeah?" Steven said into the receiver.

"I'll be over in a little bit, but Ryan's prognosis is good," Mark replied. "Just give me some time."

"Tell your date sorry and get a taxi," Steven barked.

Mark said nothing again for a while. "I'll be there in twenty minutes."

"Good. I'm going to transfer some money into our joint account, could you bring over some carry out? Where are you?"

"Downtown," Mark said.

"What restaurant?"

"I'll pick up something." Without another word, Mark hung up.

"Dammit," Steven knew something was up with his brother, but Mark wouldn't tell him. He wasn't the secretive type. Huffing a sigh, Steven clicked over to their joint account app and transfer a hundred dollars. Wherever Mark was, Steven hoped he would hurry.

———

"How is she?" Courtney asked.

"Asleep, thankfully," Jon replied entering his study, seeing her behind his desk.

"I told Ryan to try and catch some sleep too, he's upstairs," she said.

"Yeah he came in and talked to Mark on the phone. He's on his way," Jon took a deep breath and sighed. "Any news from Dave?"

"Nothing yet," she replied.

"Okay," Jon sighed again. Rolling his neck, Courtney grimaced when it cracked. "Waiting... I hate waiting."

"Wanna get some sleep? It's late."

"No, I'm not tired," Jon stated. "You go if you want."

"No, I'm with you, partner. Let's go through some more of the surveillance tape," Courtney offered. Jon nodded and turned to his computer. After half an hour, Courtney's eyes were getting heavy and she eventually lowered her head to Jon's shoulder. Dozing, Courtney closed her eyes for just a minute. The next thing she remembered was Jon's sudden movement. Jerking awake, she looked at him. His eyes were fixed on the screen. Eyeing the time, she couldn't believe she'd been asleep for nearly another hour and Steven was sitting on Jon's other side crinkled to go wrappers compressed into a ball on the desk. A very nice smelling bagel wrapped up and on a plate in front of her.

"Hello?" she looked at Steven, his light blue eyes rested on her. "Steven, right?"

He nodded but said nothing. Jon had leaned forward and rested his elbow on the desk and the lower half of his face pressed into the cleft of his forefinger and thumb.

"You're sure?" where the words out of Jon's mouth as he looked over at Steven. Steven nodded again. "There's our connection."

"Fill me in?" she asked reaching for Jon's mug of coffee and taking a sip. Raising an eyebrow, Jon watched her.

"Please help yourself," he teased.

"Thanks," she grinned sleepily.

"Well, when you fell asleep on me, I needed someone to keep *me* up," Jon said. Courtney winced and mouthed *sorry*. "Steven's been sitting with me for a little while and nothing happened but a few more of Pastor Hollywell's students coming and going. Then just out of the camera angle a man came to his door. Hollywell looked confused but stood and walked to the entryway. He stood there for a little while as they spoke. Finally, the man came into the room fully and sat down. Of course, we didn't get a good look at his face, but he was shorter than Hollywell, about six foot and what would you say, Steven? Older?"

"Mid-to-late-sixties, I'd say," Steven replied. "Just from his gait and posture."

"And average build," Jon went on.

"That just described my philosophy professor at Butler," she said. "And economy professor, oh and my theory prof. So how do we know that it's what's-his-face?"

"Because of this," Steven leaned forward, hit a couple keys. The screen zoomed in and pixelated for a moment then cleared. Courtney could see a distinctive, and rather large scar on the man's right wrist.

"What does that prove?" she asked.

"Paul Anderson had a tattoo of a raven in flight over a gravestone with the inscription *lo! Death has reared himself a throne* above it," Steven explained. Courtney swallowed the coffee swirling around in her mouth. "And it's clear this scar was his way of trying to remove it."

"I guess we can't get a close up on his face, huh?" Courtney asked.

"It's not like we don't know what he looks like," Jon replied.

"I don't," she said.

"And he could have changed his appearance to make him

harder to find," Steven offered.

They were quiet for a moment then Courtney took in a deep breath. "Jon," she started. "There was something about that man that seemed familiar—"

"Steven," Jon interrupted her without a glance. "Do you really think his play is to be found?"

"If it were me? No, unless," Steven started. "He's found a way to hide who he really is."

"Jon," Courtney called.

"New life, new appearance, new identity," Jon went on, not hearing Courtney.

"Jon," she tried again.

"That explains how he's able to get information. He's been with us the whole time," Jon said. "We need to compile a list of all the men we know who are close to us and the right age, build, and height. There's a couple things you can't change with surgery, your height and any physical defects you might have."

"Paul Anderson has one leg longer than the other," Steven said. "It's only slight but it makes his walk very unique."

"And that poem?" Jon asked.

"It's Poe," Steven replied.

"Clearly," Jon said turning to Courtney. "But which one?"

"*The City in the Sea*," Steven said. "Trust me, I know every detail about that hand. I saw the tattoo up close and personal every time it swiped across my face."

Jon's phone rang before they could respond. Courtney raised an eyebrow, it was about two hours ago Jon had removed the SIM card and didn't want to take any calls.

Answering quickly, Jon said two words to the person on the other end then looked at Courtney. Putting the phone on speaker, he went on. "Say that again, Dave?"

"We caught someone calling out from here," Dave said. "Someone used their desk phone and it's an interesting conversation. Jon, you'll wanna hear this."

CHAPTER THIRTY-NINE

Stopping at the checkpoint, Jon rolled his window down to speak to the uniformed officer walking up.

"Morning, Lieutenant," he said. "You're in early."

"Morning," Jon answered handing him Courtney's and his security card. "Just wanting to get an early start on the case."

"Of course," he keyed in a couple things on his screen. "And how are you, Detective?" The officer asked, peering in to see Courtney.

"After my cups of coffee? I'm fantastic," she replied. The officer chuckled and handed back the IDs.

"My son is also with us," Jon indicated the backseat. Steven rolled down the window.

The man raised an eyebrow when he saw Steven. "I'm his adopted son," Steven explained. "Steven Anderson," he extended his government ID.

"Dave Weston is expecting us," Jon clarified.

"Of course, sir," he answered taking Steven's ID and examining it. Entering the information into his handheld computer, his eyes widened when Steven's security clearance flashed on the screen. Dazed, he handed Steven's ID back to him, swallowed and waved them through. "Have a good day, Special Agent."

"Thank you," Steven replied putting his ID away.

"Special Agent?" Courtney asked, her suspicious mind rearing its head. "What is it you do, Steven?"

"I'm with the government," Steven dodged.

"Clearly, but which branch?" She asked.

"The Executive," he answered. She dropped it, he was only going to dodge her questions. Both FBI and CIA were part of the executive branch of government.

"That's not what I meant," she mumbled.

"You okay?" Jon asked her.

"Yeah," she forced a smile.

"Sure?" He pressed.

"Steven, why are you here now?" she asked.

"Thought I'd lend a hand," Steven replied.

"But isn't it your dad who's doing this?" she asked.

The car went silent. Even Jon's grip on the steering wheel tightened.

After what seemed like ages, Steven spoke. "Paul Anderson is my father, but he was never my dad."

"Are you taught how to do that? Or does it just come naturally?" Courtney asked checking the harshness in her tone. Jon's jaw ticked but he did not look over at her.

"What?" Steven asked noticing the bite in her words.

"The ability to answer a question without actually answering the question," she said striving to be pleasant.

Steven shrugged. "It's a gift," he said.

───────

Stepping off the elevator, Jon led the way through security and toward Dave's office. Jon knocked and heard Dave call for them to come in.

"Ah, Jon, Courtney," Dave smiled. Leaning over his desk,

he had been looking at something on the computer. "Good of you to come in so quickly."

"Dave, allow me to introduce Steven, Beth's eldest son," Jon said. Dave glanced back at Jon for a second recognizing the name, then turned to Steven and shook his hand.

"Jon's mentioned you a few times," Dave said.

"So I gathered," Steven answered. "I asked Jon if I could lend a hand with this. I may be able to give a positive ID for the killer."

"Well, that's very good of you, but I don't think we should involve a civilian in police business at this time," Dave said. "Once an arrest is made then—"

He hadn't finished his sentence before Steven had pulled out his wallet and extended a card.

"Please, call that number, and use this when prompted," he gestured to the card that looked like a credit card. Dave stared at him. "I'm afraid you both," Steven turned to Jon and Courtney. "Will have to leave the room."

Jon nodded and took Courtney out of the office. Steven shut the door after them.

"What's wrong?" Jon demanded once they were alone.

"What do you mean?" She asked.

"Oh, come on, it's me you're talking to," Jon replied. "Don't think I didn't notice the jab you made earlier."

"What jab?" she asked genuinely confused.

"About him being Paul Anderson's son," Jon clarified.

"Well, isn't he?" she asked.

"Anderson may have fathered him, but he is no father," Jon replied.

"And you are not his father either, Jon," Courtney said. "So why are you defending him?"

"That man could very easily be my son," Jon answered.

"But he's not, Jon," she replied. "And you should really start looking at this more professionally and not so emotionally."

"Emotionally?" Jon hissed.

"So much so you're practically compromised in this investigation," she replied.

"*I'm* emotionally compromised?" he demanded. "What about earlier? What were you if not emotionally compromised?"

"I've never made my feelings for you a secret," she stated.

The door opened and Dave stepped out. "Everything all right?" he asked.

"Fine," Jon answered tightly.

"Good, well you can come back in now," Dave said.

Courtney entered the room without another look at her partner. Steven stood and offered Courtney the chair. Refusing, she took the chair opposite. Jon stalked in and stood between them, arms crossed and body tense.

"Special Agent Anderson has been cleared by HQ and will be joining both of you in the field," Dave explained.

Jon nodded once. Courtney took a deep silent breath. Knowing she had crossed the line with her partner a few times the last couple days, it would be best to remain silent. For now. But Steven's motives for suddenly wanting to be a part of the case still bothered her. From what Ryan had told her, Steven was never involved in Jon's life. And now that his biological father is behind everything, Steven wanted to join the investigation? Something didn't sit right with her. A dark thought entered her mind. Could he be insinuating himself into the investigation and feeding information back to his father? Could he be part of it all? Not knowing him well enough, she couldn't answer either question, but the thoughts were there and were there to stay.

"I asked you in because I wanted you both to hear a conversation we recorded on one of the desk phones," Dave explained picking up a file on his desk. He reached over and handed it to Courtney. Jon looked over her shoulder and Steven leaned in to take a look as well. Even though Steven wasn't very close to her, Courtney could still feel his heat and a chill went down her back. There was something about him she did not like. Maybe it was because he was so mysterious or maybe she was attracted to him. She couldn't explain it, but she didn't like it. Without letting her mind wonder, she looked down at the file in her lap.

"Officer August Dupin," Dave said indicating the personnel file he just handed to her.

"Wait," Steven looked up. "Like Dupin, Poe's detective? May I?" He asked Courtney. She handed him the file.

Dave glanced up at Jon. "I'm afraid my knowledge of Poe is limited," Dave answered. "I'm more of a Dickens fan."

"Dupin is lead investigator in several of Poe's mysteries," Steven explained.

"*The Murders in the Rue Morgue* and *The Purloined Letter,* among others," Courtney went on.

"There was also some suspicion when we saw the look between Henderson and him. Dupin was the name of the owner of the cell phone that sent Jason the text message," Jon replied. "Courtney and I had been following him for a little while."

"Well, he's not fiction," Dave indicated the file. "And whoever he is, he's on the run. Callen was listening to the phone recordings and heard a conversation between Dupin and another man. Since that phone call, he left the precinct, and no one has heard from him since."

"Do you have an address for him?" Jon asked.

"It was empty," Dave explained. "I had Callen lead some uniforms over there last night."

"Last night?" Jon asked. "Why was I not informed?"

"I was going to bring him in and lean on him myself, first," Dave explained.

"Quick question," Steven interjected. "Why is there no photo on file?"

"The lock to my filing cabinet has been jimmied but it looks like the photo was the only thing taken," Dave explained.

"And is there surveillance in this room?" Steven asked.

"No," Dave answered. "I cannot have that for various reasons."

"Why didn't he take the whole file?" Courtney asked.

"Obviously he didn't want to draw attention to himself. Come on, I taught you that," Jon bit. "If the entire file was taken then that would peak our interest. If, however he only took a portion of it, well none's the wiser." Courtney looked up at her partner.

"Is everything all right between you two?" Dave asked.

"Fine," they both said at the same time.

"What about family?" Steven went on. "Do we have an address for them?"

"Only what's in the file, it says his parents died a few years ago. Honestly, I'm not even sure what's in there is true," Dave said.

"*Mostly* true," Steven answered focused on the file.

"What do you mean?" Dave asked.

"A cover story is only good if you can remember it under the most incredible amount of pressure," Steven began. "That's how it works. You use elements of your own life so you don't have to remember specific details. For example, Jon, what's your middle name?"

"Mitchell," Jon replied.

"Okay, so as an example, if you were going undercover, you would use a name you knew belonged to you, something you would recognize and answer to if you were focused on something else. You might go under the name Mitchell Johnson, something familiar. You would be an English teacher from New York, unmarried with a son named Charles. You would be first generation American, probably depending on how you wanted to play it, you'd say you were from either England or Spain. You wouldn't use Ireland because it might be too easy to look you up.

"So, if we're looking at our UNSUB here, we reverse the process. I would look for a man with a similar name, say Lupin or Newpin who lives in a five-mile radius of 1609 North College Avenue. This man would be a recluse with an extensive knowledge of Poe, but is it something newly acquired for this job or is it a lifelong pursuit? I would check the local libraries including any college campuses nearby for anyone who has checked out a book of Poe or a Poe thesis more than twice in the last two months. That will give us a baseline. This man would have to have an extensive knowledge of police procedure in order to pass unnoticed by anyone around him, but enough notoriety that the man pulling the strings would have heard of him and been able to contact him.

"So, I would look for any recently fired cop with a grudge – something that made headlines. Maybe dirty but could also be that he took the heat for something he didn't do. He wouldn't have been from around here, there could be too many who might've known or recognized him. Somewhere close but not in the general metropolitan area. Also, he knows how to cover his tracks, but he's not used to all the new software that can track him. He's probably middle aged or slightly younger with basic military training. He follows orders and knows how to hide."

"How do you..." Dave started.

"Trust me," Steven went on. "Cover stories are my job. I'd be dead if I didn't know this. You're looking for a late 40s to mid-50s ex-military turned cop who was recently relieved of duty for something that created headlines. His name is very similar to Dupin. He is an only child, no history of violence. He keeps himself to himself and lives in a five-mile radius of 1609 North College Avenue. Now if I could hear the recording of the conversation, I will be able to give you more information."

"Sure," Dave answered. As the phone conversation played, they all listened carefully to the voices. When Rob stated the police had made him, Steven nodded.

"That was definitely Paul Anderson," Steven looked up at Jon. "I'll never forget that voice. Thank you, Captain, that helped me formulate the man in my mind. I can now say he is definitely in his 40s to 50s and he's originally from Oklahoma."

"How on earth could you know something like that?" Courtney challenged.

"I could hear his accent. He was doing a passable job of masking it, but you can definitely hear it in the e's and the o's," Steven explained. "I can further profile if you would allow me to sit at his desk."

"Callen," Dave called. Once Officer Callen opened the door, Dave continued. "Take Special Agent Anderson and Detective Shields to August Dupin's desk."

Callen nodded and opened the door wider. Steven handed the file back to Dave.

"Thank you," Steven said as he followed Callen out the door.

"Go with him," Jon ordered Courtney.

"I'd like to stay with my partner, if that would be okay," she said curtly.

"No, go," Jon replied.

"Jon, I'm sorry, no. I know he's your son and all, but come on, he's not *assisting* at all. He's driving the damn car."

"He's given us our first big lead on this, Courtney," Jon replied. "I'm willing to let him drive a little."

"How do we know he's not in on it?" She asked. "How do we know he's not making it all up?"

Jon's face was hard as stone. "What are you implying?"

"I'm telling you to use your head. Think about it logically. He's not involved in your life, he's never around. Then you become best buddies and he's suddenly involved in everything. We find out it's his father who is doing all this and you call him. Magically, he appears with no problem from his superiors? He asks to be a part of this investigation, then takes lead by giving us a profile of a man that is a little too Sherlockian for me. How do we know he's really giving us a positive description? He could be making the whole thing up to distract us, all while calling daddy and letting him know our progress. You heard him, cover stories are his job. What if this whole thing is just that… one big cover story and he is here to throw us off his father's track."

"*I'm* his father," Jon replied in a low voice.

"Yes, Jon, I know you want to be, but you're not blood. You taught me blood is thicker than water, and you told me to keep an open mind when it came to Poe. I'm telling you to do the same. Don't let your feelings for someone cloud your judgment."

"Like you do?" Jon demanded.

"That has nothing to do with my judgment in a case," she replied. "But it has everything to do with this man, who you claim to be pearly white. Do you even know what he does for a living? How do we know he's not just like his father?"

"The next time you want to make an accusation about his loyalty to me, I want you to remember this – We would be dead right now if it weren't for Steven. He saved our lives by killing Riley last month," Jon said.

"But he didn't have to *kill* him," Courtney went on. "That's the whole point. Why kill a man if he has nothing to hide?"

"Because he was going to kill us," Jon replied. "Are you saying you wouldn't have done the same thing?"

"I'm saying let's hold off on jumping into bed with him until we know all the facts," Courtney said.

"Courtney," Jon warned. "Stop now."

"No, Jon, I'm sorry but someone has to be the voice of reason here. You have to see this whole thing could possibly be orchestrated by Rob or Paul or whatever the hell his name is, to bring you down. 'The fall of the house of Greene', remember? We thought he could use Scott to hurt you, but what if it's Steven? It's *been* Steven all along? Think about it. It makes sense. Riley wasn't going to kill you, he was just waiting for Steven to show up and prove his loyalty to you. It was all a front. He was trying to get you to trust him which it's clear you do, more than your own partner. Steven killed Riley so no one could reveal his secret. Don't fall into his trap, Jon."

There was silence for a few seconds, then, "Courtney," Jon said low. "Get out."

"What?" She breathed.

"Get out, now," he finally turned to her. Courtney knew in that instant she had pushed it too far. Jon's eyes were like emeralds, hard, dark and unforgiving. She couldn't think. She couldn't speak. All she saw was the look in his eyes. A look she hadn't seen since they had first met. Standing up straighter, she took a deep unsteady breath.

"I'm sorry," she began.

"Now," Jon ordered.

She started toward him and paused. Reaching up, she kissed his cheek and leaned into his ear.

"For the love of god, Jon," she whispered. "Just know the house of Usher could not be destroyed from without. It could only be destroyed from within. Know that what I say was said because I want to protect you. I love you," she breathed. Jon closed his eyes, but the rest of his body was tense until she left the room.

CHAPTER FORTY

Jon and Steven visited the three main libraries downtown, all showing various students had checked out the books at roughly the same time. Jon concluded one of the universities must have had a class focusing on Poe. There was however, one name that appeared multiple times. Passing the information off to Dave, they headed home to check on Beth.

As Jon pulled into his driveway, Steven turned to him.

"Did something happen with Courtney?" Steven asked.

"What do you mean?" Jon replied.

"I mean I saw her leave the office and head to the elevator. She seemed upset. Is it something to do with me?" Steven questioned.

"It's nothing," Jon stated cutting off the conversation as he got out of the car.

After Jon checked on Beth, he stayed in his study. Scott had taken some tea to him and tried to talk to him, but Jon was as curt with him as he had been with Steven in the car. When Scott walked back into the living room, Steven looked up.

"Did he say anything?" Steven asked.

Scott shook his head. "No, what exactly happened?"

"I really don't know," Steven sighed.

Ryan came into the room. "Have you heard from Courtney?" he asked. Steven noticed his cell phone in his hand.

"Not since earlier," he replied. "Why?"

"She's not answering her phone or replying to my texts," Ryan said. "What happened?"

"All I know is she left shortly after we got to the precinct," Steven replied. "I haven't heard anything more."

Ryan sighed harshly and thrust his fingers through his hair. "I wish she would talk to me," Ryan grumbled.

———————

Later that evening, Jon left the study once when Beth came down the stairs. She thanked everyone but wanted to know where Courtney was. Jon's jaw ticked and he left the room shortly after, heading upstairs. They all heard the bathroom door slam and the shower turn on.

"Oh goodness," Beth said, looking up at the ceiling. "What's wrong with him?" Sitting next to Mark, she smiled when he took her hand in his and held it gently.

"I think I might have an idea," Steven replied. "Since you're all here I'll explain what happened today. Ryan, I'm sorry, some of this might be tough to hear, but it is the absolute truth."

Steven explained Courtney's cold attitude toward him and Jon's reaction to her accusations.

"I completely understand Courtney's wariness," Steven finished. "I only wish she would have spoken to me. I know it looks questionable, but I truly have a legitimate reason behind it."

"That goes with what I saw last night," Scott said. "Courtney had her hand on Dad's chest and the look in her eyes... well, let's just say it wasn't innocent."

"Look if you're going to talk about my fiancée at least do it with some decorum," Ryan stood.

"Shame on you both," Kim looked from her brother to Scott. "How could you talk about her like this? She has always been there for us. I refuse to listen to any more of this."

"We're not making this up, baby," Scott defended. "I truly believe she's in love with dad." His eyes went to Beth, who did not react then to Ryan, who was staring at him. "Did you hear me?"

"Have you been living under a rock?" Ryan asked.

"That really is old news, Scott," Beth answered.

"You knew?" Scott demanded.

"Of course we knew," Beth said. "Ryan and I have spoken a lot about it. But we both agree they are adults and they have other commitments. Do you honestly think two people, two *attractive* people of the opposite sex who work together twenty-four-seven, will *not* develop feelings for each other?"

"But..." Scott started. "He's old enough to be her father!"

"So?" Beth shrugged.

"It's gross," Scott replied.

"To you," Ryan answered. "Do you not remember the age difference with my sister and brother-in-law?"

"Ten years, right?" Scott asked.

"That's what they tell everyone," Ryan replied. "In fact, it's more like fifteen."

"And Jon doesn't look his age," Mark offered. "I could understand it. Not that I encourage it." He squeezed his mother's hand. "He hurts you, I'll kill him... well, Steven will kill him, I'll dispose of the body."

"I love you, sweetheart, but don't even tease about something like that," Beth patted her son's hand. Turning back to Scott, she continued. "Why does it surprise you to find this out, Scott?"

"Because I didn't know it was a thing," Scott said. "How can you both be okay with this?"

"Because they have never given us cause to not be," Beth replied. Ryan nodded.

"So, what's up with Jon?" Steven asked. "Why is he like this?"

"I've only seen him like this twice," Beth explained. "The first time, he was working on a case of a serial killer. The second, he and Mat had gotten into a huge fight. After what you told me, I think he and Courtney had what we writer's call a *lover's spat*."

"About me?" Steven asked.

"I don't know," she answered. "Possibly."

"I wish she would have talked to me," Steven scrubbed a hand down his stubbled jaw.

"Don't worry," Beth said. "I'll figure it out. Jon's pretty easy to read, though he doesn't think he is. Ryan, you keep trying Courtney."

Ryan nodded and they all heard the water shut off and the door to the bathroom open.

"I'll go see what's wrong," Beth said standing.

"You sure you're up to it, mom?" Mark asked.

"I'm fine, sweetie," she replied and headed up the stairs.

Kim's eyes went to Scott's and she shook her head.

"What?" he asked.

"How could you judge her when you have no idea what's going on?" she asked.

"Because he's my dad," Scott replied. "My loyalty is to him. Not her."

"And me?" she asked.

"Of course it's to you," he said. "But we weren't talking about you."

"She's my best friend, Scott," she replied. "She's gonna be my maid of honor, she's practically my sister."

"But she's not," Scott said. Kim shook her head and sighed harshly.

"I don't understand you," she replied turning and heading down to the basement.

"Kim," Scott called after her. Cursing under his breath, he got up and followed her.

"Ryan, really I'm sorry," Steven said.

"It's fine, I'll handle it," Ryan replied tapping into his phone. "The guest rooms are made up, you guys can pick where you wanna crash."

Steven turned to his brother when they were alone. "Now wanna tell me what's going on with you?"

"What are you talking about?" Mark asked.

"Where were you?"

"Oh, shit, sorry, Daddy, didn't realize I needed to check in with you after I hit eighteen," Mark mocked.

"You're keeping something from me and with our father showing back up, I need to know everything, Mark."

"You think I have anything to do with him?" Mark hissed.

"No, of course not, but I don't want to be blindsided with something that could have been preventable if I knew everything."

"You aren't a god, Steven, much to the contrary of popular opinion. I don't have to tell you jack shit."

"What is wrong with you?" Steven demanded. "You're never like this."

"Oh, so now Courtney is out of the way you want to attack me?" Mark stood.

"That's not what-"

"Go to hell," Mark spat, stalking out of the room.

———

"I seriously don't know what's going on with him," Steven said to Amber as they Skyped each other. "He's never like this and I don't know what's wrong."

Amber thought a moment, then shrugged. "Have you thought maybe he's gone through a bad breakup or maybe he's just upset about something at work?"

"He hasn't dated anyone seriously for a long time. And I doubt he would not tell me. He tells me everything. We're best friends."

"But he's been secretive recently?" Amber asked.

"And bitter," Steven supplied.

"Maybe he's just going through something and doesn't know how to tell you. It could be nothing and it could be something major. The only thing you can do is be there for him and when he tells you, have an open mind."

"Beautiful and brilliant," Steven said. "Are you taken?" He teased.

"Yeah, unfortunately for you, my guy treats me like a queen."

"As well he should," Steven grinned. "I miss you."

"I miss you too," she replied.

"Is Josh there?" he asked.

"He had to stay late at practice. I'm about to head out and pick him up."

"What time is it anyway? Shit, four o'clock? My internal clock is all messed up," he flopped on his back on the mattress of one of the guestrooms in the basement.

"That's what getting up at two in the morning will do to you," she said. "Get some sleep. I'll call you around dinner time. I know he'll want to say goodnight."

"Please do," Steven answered. "I love you."

"Love you too," she kissed the screen. "I'll see you soon."

Steven signed off and lay on his back. He was exhausted. Getting up at two in the morning and dealing with his mother's, brother's and sister's emotional rollercoasters had worn him thin. Wanting to catch a couple hours sleep so he could be awake and talk to Josh when he called, he settled down into the luxurious bedding. Closing his eyes, he let out a sigh and felt his body relax.

"Steven?" his eyes popped open when he heard his brother's voice. Looking toward the door, he saw Mark pop his head in. "Shit sorry, I didn't realize you were asleep."

"I'm not," Steven replied turning on the light on the bedside table. "Come in, what's up?"

Mark shuffled into the room and sat on the edge of the bed. "I wanted to apologize for what I said earlier. I'm sorry. You are right, there's something going on, but I need to work through it on my own."

"You can tell me anything, you know that, brother?" Steven said.

Mark nodded. "With our father coming back into our lives, and Kim getting married and all the other shit I'm dealing with... at work, it's just a lot for me to handle and I took it out on you. I'm sorry."

"Hey, forgiven always," Steven slapped him on the shoulder. "But when you want to talk, I'm here."

"I appreciate that," Mark said. "Sorry again," he stood and headed for the door.

"Mark," Steven called him back. "You know I'll always protect you against our father, right?"

"You always have," Mark said. "But I'm not a kid anymore."

"I know, but with him, we all have some unfinished business."

"It won't be unfinished for long. As soon as you kill him, it'll be finished for all of us."

"You think I'm going to kill him?" Steven asked.

"I hope you do," Mark answered. "He's hurt mom and Kim for too long. I don't want him hanging over us anymore. I want us all to have a clean break and start fresh. The only way is to not drag it out through the courts. He needs to die."

"Agreed," Steven replied. "But try convincing Jon of that."

"He doesn't need to know everything," Mark locked eyes

with Steven and though he knew Mark was trying to tell him something, the look vanished before he was able to decipher it. "Have a good nap. I'm going to lie down too before I head in for the night shift."

"Aren't you off this weekend?" Steven asked. Mark froze at the door.

"Oh, yeah," his voice was tight. "I forgot for a second. I guess I should stay."

"You don't have to, if you need to go meet someone. Just be careful," Steven cautioned.

"Yeah, will do, for sure," Mark nodded. But before anymore was said, Mark left the room and headed up the stairs. Steven leaned back in the bed and intertwined his fingers behind his head. Needing some sleep before he tackled the next big thing on his list, namely coming up with a plan to kill his father, he needed to sleep. Turning off the light on the bedside table, the room was bathed in darkness and he slowly drifted off to sleep.

Jon lay awake. Courtney's words were haunting him as were his actions. God, he hated himself for sending her away. *Just know the house of Usher could not be destroyed from without. It could only be destroyed from within.* He sighed. How could he have been so stupid? *I love you.* It didn't come as a surprise, he always knew it, but what did surprise him was, she actually said it. He sighed again, and Beth moved beside him.

"What is it?" She asked.

"Nothing," he answered not looking over at her. He kissed her hair. "I'm sorry I woke you, go back to sleep."

"Jon," she said. "I've been up. I know something is bothering you. Tell me."

"Courtney and I had a… disagreement," he explained.

She shifted, leaning up on her elbow to look down at him.

"Oh?" She asked. "What about?"

"No need to worry you," he said. "I'll be all right, go on back to sleep."

"Tell me," she said again. "Is it to do with Steven?"

"She made a ridiculous accusation about him," Jon started.

"What kind of accusation?"

"It doesn't matter, because it's not true."

"Tell me," she pressed.

Jon sighed. "Steven profiled the man we're looking for in seconds. Courtney… well, she had been acting strangely all day, but she accused him of being part of it; like he was in collaboration with Paul Anderson, or something. She even said he killed Riley so he couldn't tell on him, that they planned the whole thing to take me down," Jon explained.

"Baby," Beth started. "That's exactly how I would have written it."

Jon's brow furrowed and he looked up at her. "What?" he asked.

"Maybe it's my mystery writer mind, but her theory works. Motive, opportunity, close to the detective involved, the last suspect to ever cross your mind, it's a great cover."

"You don't honestly think Steven—" he started.

"No, I don't," she interrupted. "But I *know* Steven, so do you. Courtney doesn't and for someone who doesn't know him, his profile would worry any good detective. What did you say to her when she told you her suspicions?"

"I… I told her to leave," Jon replied.

"You did what?" She demanded.

"I didn't want to talk to her," Jon justified. "And I was very angry. I didn't want to take it out on her."

"You call her and apologize," Beth ordered. "Dear god, Jon, she's your partner!"

"She should never have attacked someone I consider a son," Jon said.

"Jon, I know, you know, everyone knows Steven is not yours," Beth said. "I've always known. He looks too much like Paul. I am so thankful you want to be a father to my children, but do not let your love for them, for me, cloud your judgment. Your partner is there to keep you level-headed and you sent her away. Did she tell you she loved you?" Jon swallowed but slowly nodded. "Oh god, Jon, call her," she said.

"In the morning, I promise, it's past midnight," he said looking at his phone.

"At least send her a text," Beth told him. "For me."

Grabbing his phone, Jon typed out a text to his partner.

Jon woke in a cold sweat. He did not remember all of the dream, all he did remember was he was in an old dilapidated mansion and someone was banging inside a crypt calling his name. Suppressing a shiver that raced up his back, Jon grabbed his phone to look at the time.

3:28am

Courtney 1m ago

Missed Call

Dialing her number, he called her back. The phone rang until her voicemail picked up.

"Hey, it's me, partner, I'm sorry," he began. "Call me back, we need to talk. I'm sorry, Courtney really. You're right, I should have listened to you. I know Steven, you don't. But I should never have sent you away. Just call me back, okay?"

When Courtney hadn't called him back within an hour he slowly fell back asleep.

Chapter Forty-One

There was a knock at Jon's bedroom door exactly at eight o'clock that next morning. When Steven opened the door and walked in, Jon leaned up.

"Steven?" Jon asked. "Are you all right?"

"I needed to tell you I'm leaving," Steven said softly not wanting to wake his mom.

"What do you mean?" Jon asked.

"I mean, I know something happened between you and Courtney and I know it had to do with me so the best way is to remove the issue," he gestured to himself. "I need to leave anyway. I'm expected somewhere tomorrow."

"Look, it was my fault," Jon stated. "Let's go down and have some coffee, we need to talk. Let me explain what's going on."

"All right, but I do have somewhere I need to be Sunday," Steven said.

"Grand," Jon replied slowly sliding away from Beth. "But let's talk first, okay?"

———

Steven handed Jon a cup of coffee as they sat down at the

kitchen table.

"So, where do you need to be Sunday?" Jon asked.

"Well, I wanted to tell you but we got pretty busy," Steven replied.

"Shoot," Jon said.

"I've… met someone."

"Someone like…" Jon prompted.

"Her name is Amber," Steven said. "She's an FBI agent."

"How did you meet?"

"On the job," Steven explained. "She was undercover trying to infiltrate the cell I was assigned to dissolve. Actually, *she* was my mark," Steven explained. "We turned out to be on the same side and after a rough start we really hit it off. She has a kid, Josh. He's seven and precocious."

"Sounds like someone I know," Jon laughed. "How do you feel about her?"

"I'm in love with her," Steven admitted.

"Woah," Jon said leaning back. "Really? That was quick."

"I know. Trust me. But I've not felt this way since Chrissie," Steven said. "But she makes me feel alive, complete, happy."

"That's great!" Jon smiled. "I'm very happy for you."

"Thanks," Steven replied. "It's been a while… for both of us, but it's been going great."

"I'd like to meet her," Jon said.

"Yeah, that would be… nice," Steven replied. "I'd like you all to meet her. And you'll love Josh, he's a great kid."

"He sounds it," Jon answered. "Where do you need to be Sunday? Something with them?"

"Yeah, he's on a little league soccer team," Steven explained. "And it's the championship game."

"That's always a good time," Jon replied. They were silent for a little while drinking their coffee when Steven finally turned to him.

"What do you think Paul's play is?"

"I wish I knew," Jon answered. "I know he wants me to see my life torn down around me. I know he doesn't like it that your mom and I are together. I think he has fixated on me for so long that he needs the thrill of the chase. He needs to see me suffer."

"And Riley?"

"Riley wanted revenge for a slight he believed was my fault," Jon explained. "He wanted me to acknowledge him as the future steward and I wouldn't do it. He wasn't the right one. But I have nothing that's going to convince a jury."

Steven leaned back. "You're actually thinking of what will convince a jury?"

"I'm a cop, Steven, of course I'm thinking of what will convince a jury. As much as I would love your approach, it's not how I do things." Jon replied.

"Clearly," Steven answered. "You know my approach solves the problem a lot faster *and* saves the taxpayers money. But most importantly it saves my mother the heartache and humiliation of a trial. I thought you would have wanted to spare her that."

"Of course I want her spared," Jon replied. "But she knows this is what I do."

"It's not what I do," Steven rebuttaled. "So you'd better hope you get to him before I do."

They both heard the soft knock on the front door and froze.

"Where are the lads?" Jon whispered.

"Scott and Kim went to his therapy appointment. Ryan went to Courtney's to see if he could talk to her. Mark had to meet someone," Steven replied. Jon nodded.

Slowly standing, he headed for the door, opened it and saw a plain white envelop laying in-between the storm door and the main door.

Jon picked it up with Steven right behind him, his gun in

his hand. Jon nodded to him and Steven pocketed his thirty-eight. With a deep breath, Jon opened the envelope.

"Oh god," Jon stammered. Steven watched him. "They have her." Jon turned the photo around and Steven saw a picture of Courtney, unconscious, bound and gagged sitting in a chair, a red fresh bruise forming on her forehead with a few drops of dried blood at her mouth. The photo was time and date stamped at 4:32am that morning.

"What does the back say?" Steven asked. Jon flipped it over and read.

"*Who entereth herein, a conqueror hath bin; who slayeth the dragon, the Shield he shall win.* Ready to play?'" Jon read.

"Where's your book of Poe?" Steven asked calmly.

"On the table," Jon replied. He was shaking, from fear or anger, he didn't know. "This is all my fault," Jon went on. "I should have called her. If I had, she would be safe right now. God only knows what he has done to her."

"Nothing yet," Steven answered still flipping through the book.

"She called me around three this morning. If only I had answered it, she could have been here with us last night," Jon stated. "I'm such a fool. I swear if he has hurt her, I kill him slowly."

"Are you done?" Steven looked up at him.

"What?" Jon questioned.

Steven walked slowly over to him as he spoke. "If there is one thing I've learned in my nearly fifteen years as a spy, it's if you blame yourself for every little thing that goes wrong, nothing will ever be done. The longer you take wallowing, the less time we have to save her before something *does* happen. Take ten seconds for your pity party then shut up and get to work." Jon nodded once. "Now," Steven continued. "Does this look familiar?" He passed the book over to Jon, his finger marking the page.

"*The Fall of the House of Usher*, again?" Jon stated as he read the same quote from the picture. "It wasn't you or Scott they were going to use against me, it was Courtney all along." Jon's phone rang Ryan's ringtone. "Morning, Ry, what's up?" Jon tried to sound like his usual self.

"Where are you?" Ryan was panicked.

"At home, why?" Jon asked.

"Have you heard from Courtney?" Ryan demanded.

Jon looked over at Steven. "No, why?"

"We were supposed to meet for breakfast today. She was upset about something last night. She finally texted me early this morning. She didn't say much just that she wanted to meet over breakfast. She didn't show. I tried calling her cell and it rang out. I'm here at her place and the apartment is trashed." Ryan was terrified, Jon could hear it in his voice.

"We're on our way, stay there," Jon said.

"Who's we?"

"Steven and me," Jon explained.

"Hurry, please, Uncle Jon," Ryan begged.

"We're leaving now, ten minutes," Jon said hanging up. Steven's eyes were glued on something just over Jon's shoulder. Turning, Jon saw Beth, wrapped in a housecoat, standing in the doorway. She had heard the whole thing.

"He has her, doesn't he?" she asked, calmly.

"We don't know," Jon answered.

"Don't sugar coat it, Jon," she replied.

"Yes," he finally said. "He has her."

Beth took a deep breath and nodded. "What can I do?"

"Come with us?" Jon offered.

She shook her head. "I'll only get in the way."

"Then stay here, safe, and keep calling her, maybe we'll get lucky," he asked.

"I can do that," she agreed. "Let me know what's happening, please."

Jon nodded, kissed her head then looked her straight in the eye.

"Set the alarm when we leave," Jon said. "Take one of the guns from the cabinet and do not let anyone in."

She nodded. "Jon," she called him back. "Kill that bastard once and for all."

CHAPTER
FORTY-TWO

A thousand and one scenarios were running through Jon's head as he and Steven drove to Courtney's apartment. The only thing keeping him sane, was he knew Courtney could take care of herself. He had seen her take down some of the best in sparring, he had even lost to her once, but she cheated. That memory lifted one side of his lip, but it was quickly replaced by the memory of her bindings. If Paul had her bound... he stopped his thoughts before they made him sick.

Pulling up to Courtney's apartment, Ryan met them at the front door, his dirty blonde hair tousled, his blue eyes bloodshot.

"What's going on?" he demanded. "Where is she? Why isn't she home?"

"You know the case we're working on. Edgar Allen Poe works were used to taunt us and Courtney was the last clue," Jon showed him the picture he had received earlier that morning.

Ryan's jaw clenched, his fingers curled into a fist around the photo and his arms shook.

"You!" He yelled at Steven. "This is all your fault! Had you never come here none of this would have happened!" Ryan barreled into Steven knocking him to the ground. "It's because you put doubt into her head she left! If she's hurt, I'll kill you!"

Steven captured Ryan's hands and twisted. Crying out, the next second Ryan was pinned beneath Steven.

"Calm down," Steven ordered.

"Get off me!" Ryan shouted.

"Ryan, stop this now," Jon commanded. "This will not help her."

"Oh my god," Ryan screeched. "What has he done to her?"

"Nothing yet," Steven said. "Trust me, I profile people for a living. He doesn't want her, he wants Jon. She is just a method of getting to him. Paul Anderson wants to take *Jon* down and he knows the only way to do that is through those he loves."

"But why Courtney?" Ryan demanded.

"Two reasons, her name matches a poem, and she's in love with Jon," Steven said.

"My fiancée has been kidnapped because *you* left her alone and vulnerable," Ryan yelled at Jon. "And you claim to love her!"

"Courtney is not going to benefit from me blaming myself. I swear to you, I will get her back. No matter what. I would give my life for her," Jon said. Ryan looked up at Steven still pinning him down and then back at Jon. He nodded once and Steven let him up. As soon as he stood, Ryan swung at Jon catching his jaw. He pulled back after the first strike.

"That's for my future wife," Ryan said.

"Understood," Jon replied wiping the little trickle of the blood off his lip. "Now, let's go up?" Jon asked indicating Courtney's apartment.

Courtney was dazed but she slowly became conscious. Blinking her eyes slowly, she suddenly became aware that she was not in her apartment. The last thing she remembered was shooting someone who barged in and then she felt pain. *Where am I?* Her head pounded and her eyes were blurry. Raising her hand, she touched her forehead, only to feel a large knot.

"Well, look who's awake," she heard a woman's voice. Turning, she saw a statuesque blonde woman walk into the room with a platter of food. "Rob's compliments." She indicated the sandwich. "Wouldn't want you passing out from lack of food, now would we?"

"Who are you?" Courtney asked.

The woman laughed. "I'm no one to you," she answered. "Eat, or the dogs will."

"Dogs?" she asked.

"Most men are, don't you think?" she replied. "Oh, and Rob told me to tell you *impia tortorum longos hic turba furores.* I'm sure I butchered it, but hey Latin was never my forte." She walked out of the room as Courtney's stomach fell. She knew that quote well and it made her sick.

Jon, Ryan and Steven stood in Courtney's apartment staring at the mess before them.

"Look for anything that might tell us when and where," Jon finally said just before his phone rang. Seeing Dave's name come up, Jon answered it and put it on speaker. "Dave?" Jon asked.

"Jon, we have a problem," Dave replied.

"What?"

"They just found August Dupin's body in the canal," Dave revealed. "He was shot with a thirty-eight, police issue."

"We have an officer down, Dave," Jon replied.

"Well, Dupin may have worked for us for a little while but I hardly think *officer down* really works in this case," Dave said.

"No, I mean Courtney," Jon replied.

"What do you mean Courtney?" Dave demanded. As her former trainer, Dave had a vested interest in her.

"I mean, she's missing, presumed kidnapped by Paul Anderson," Jon said.

"Why the hell haven't you called this in?" Dave bellowed. "Where is she?"

"We're looking into it," Jon replied.

"Tell me everything."

"I don't have time right now."

"Uncle Jon," Ryan called from the master bedroom. "You better come look at this."

"I gotta go, Dave," Jon said. "Keep it quiet until you hear from us again."

"To hell with that, I'm putting the entire force out to look for her," Dave replied hanging up.

Ryan indicated the master bath and immediately Jon saw what had Ryan worried. Blood splatter was on the wash basin and a pool of blood was on the floor. Jon bent low to look at the side of the counter.

"Why is there so much blood?" Ryan asked.

"Because she shot August Dupin here," Jon explained. "One of the men we've been investigating in this."

"Good," Ryan sneered.

Steven picked up Courtney's cell phone from the counter with a handkerchief.

"Looks like mom's been trying to call her just like you asked. But the last number Courtney dialed was your cell, Jon," Steven said, looking through the phone. "There's an unfinished unsent text message too. Looks like it was to you, Ryan."

"What does it say?" Ryan asked.

"It's more a message to Jon," Steven explained. "'If you get this,'" Steven started reading. "'Tell Jon I think I know who Rob/Paul is. It's someone we overlooked. I'm sorry I accused Steven. I'll tell you more at break—' that's when it cuts off."

Jon asked to look at the phone and scrolled through the photo gallery.

"The most recent photos are from yesterday. She took some

pictures of Scott's office building. Just the outside. But it looks like she was trying to get a picture of a man walking out."

"Who?" Ryan asked.

"I have no idea," Jon replied. "He always has his face hidden. But she followed him. Took some pictures of his car," Jon explained.

"Do you have a license plate number?" Steven asked pulling out his phone.

"Partial Indiana plate: EAP12... something," Jon squinted.

Steven nodded as he typed something into his phone.

"I'm having the best tech run it for me, should have the answer in less than fifteen—" Steven was cut off by Jon's phone ringing Beth's ringtone.

"Hey, Baby," Jon answered.

"Hello, Sweetie," Jon froze when he heard Paul's voice from the other end.

"Paul," Jon said. Steven stepped forward, for the first time in a while showing an emotion; worry. At Steven's urging, Jon put the phone on speaker.

"Bravo," Paul replied. "Isn't this nice, I know who you are, you know— almost— who I am. Courtney was close though. I saw her following me. I had to stop her. Oh, and we've both slept with the same woman. We're just all one big happy family, aren't we?"

"Where's Beth?" Jon pressed.

"She's with me," Paul replied. "You don't really think a little thing like the house alarm would stop me, did you? I got in once before."

Steven's stomach twisted. He walked away for a brief moment to control his emotions.

"What do you want?" Jon asked watching Steven.

"I told you already, Jonny," Paul's voice was dripping with sarcasm. "I want to play."

"So you take Courtney and Beth?" Jon asked.

"Well…" Paul started. "You left them vulnerable. You left them wide open for me to take. Just like you did your wife. You know, you really should protect your queen better, she is the most powerful piece. God knows I've taken pains to hide mine."

"Let's get together and play sometime," Jon replied.

"Oh, but we are playing and isn't playing with life sized pieces so much more fun?" Paul asked. "You have the next move, Jon. Play carefully. Wouldn't want to take *another* queen away from you."

"You bastard," Jon breathed.

"Ooh," Paul said. "*That* struck a nerve. Did you finally figure it out, Jonny Boy?"

"You're the one behind Carol's death!" Jon yelled.

"I always wondered if you remembered me," Paul chuckled.

For a moment, Jon remembered the brief few seconds thirteen years ago, after his wife had died. Just before he passed out, he vaguely remembered brown Italian leather shoes approaching him. And for the first time, he remembered a voice. *"Shh, it'll all be all right soon."*

"Now you have two choices, Jon," Paul went on. "Save the woman you love or the woman who loves you… your lover or your partner… which one will you choose? Ooh, I'm excited to know. I'll even be so kind as to give you a clue as to where we are. You have the clue for Courtney… here's Beth's… 'far in the forest, dim and old, for her may some tall vault unfold-and winged panels fluttering back,' have you got all that?" Paul asked. Jon didn't answer. "Ryan, dear you might have to answer for him. Does he have all that?"

"Yes," Ryan said clenching his fist so tightly his hand shook.

"Good, you boys have three hours," Paul answered. "Good luck."

"You have to give me more time," Jon said.

"Oh, but I can't, they'll both be dead in three hours. Trust me, no time to save them both. Who will it be? I look forward to knowing," Paul hung up.

"Who is it going to be, Jon?" Steven asked finally. "Who will you save?"

Jon looked from Steven to Ryan.

"How can you even hesitate?" Ryan demanded.

"Ryan, I—" Jon started.

"No, no, you swore to me you would do anything to save her. How can you even hesitate?" Ryan asked.

"Circumstances have changed, Ryan," Jon said. "I need time to think. I might be able to save them both."

"You don't have time, you heard him. Three hours! That's it! We don't have time for might!" Ryan yelled.

Steven had picked up Courtney's book of Poe off the coffee table.

"Listen to me, Ryan," Jon said. "I want this man dead more than you know, but before I can have what I want, I have to find Beth and Courtney. Now he has given me a deadline. I know Courtney. She can take care of herself. Beth on the other hand, not so much when it comes to him."

"So, you're choosing Beth?" Ryan challenged. "You're abandoning Courtney *again!*"

"I'm not abandoning anyone," Jon replied. "I know Courtney can get out of this. She would want me to save Beth."

"Don't you dare speak for her, you have no *idea* what she would want," Ryan yelled.

Jon tried to calm his nephew, but Ryan yanked his uncle's hand off his shoulder.

"I'm sorry you think that," Jon answered.

"If you do this," Ryan took a step closer to him. "You're dead to me."

Jon paused a moment. "Then this is what he wanted. The

fall of the house of Usher… my house hinges on this decision… If I don't do this, I'll be dead anyway," Jon answered. Ryan gasped as if pain overcame him.

"I never thought it would come to this. I don't think I'll ever forgive you for this," Ryan pushed passed him.

"Ryan," Jon tried.

"Don't bother," he said slamming the door as he left.

Jon looked over at Steven as soon as Ryan left. "I'm right, aren't I?" Jon asked. "To choose Beth, I mean. He really wants her. Courtney is just collateral. He would kill her after Beth just to prove a point. We might have time. Beth is his true target. Tell me I made the right choice."

"I'm not here to say you did right or wrong, I'm simply here to help you figure out the best approach to your decision," Steven explained. "But I'll tell you this, I know where the riddle came from," he held up the book. "It's a poem Poe wrote called *The Sleeper*. It's an ode to his beloved in her tomb."

"Forest, vault," Jon put it together. "Oh jaysus, I know where she is."

CHAPTER FORTY-THREE

Paul hung up the phone and grinned down at Courtney.

"Liar," Courtney ground out around the gag.

"Dear me," he mocked. "Because we criminals are always so truthful. So, who do you think he'll choose?" he asked.

Paul indicated to Quinn standing beside her, to remove the gag. Quinn pulled on the knot. Courtney winced when he yanked some hair out.

"Gently," Paul scolded. "You wouldn't want to end up like our poor unfortunate Mr. Dupin or Mr. King who she was so eager to shoot a couple weeks ago."

Quinn let an obscene word slip through his lips while looking down at Courtney.

"Now, now, no name calling," Paul said. "Why don't you go and check the perimeter? Ms. Shields and I are going to have a chat."

Quinn sneered and left the room. Paul turned to Courtney. He pulled a chair out from a table nearby and sat in it backwards.

"Don't mind him," Rob said. "He's just a little upset because his brother has yet to be found."

"His brother? You mean Bradley Henderson?" She

questioned.

"Not only beautiful but smart too," Paul grinned. "And don't even try to tell me the police have him like Jon did. It doesn't work with me. I know full well that you don't know where he is either."

"What makes you so sure?" she asked.

"Because I have an eye in the police and I know he's not been picked up yet. Besides that wasn't his job."

"What was?" she asked.

"Are you interrogating me, Detective?" he asked. "You forget what I do for a living? It's not going to work."

"All right, fine," she went on. "How did Quinn Henderson get out of protective custody?"

"He had one of the best lawyers and he escaped again during the prison transport. Those cops never get out much, they're done in by a pretty face," he winked.

"I knew it was you," she replied.

"Did you?" he asked.

"The only *possible* person it could be," Courtney said. "Someone close enough to us and yet far enough away that we would never suspect. Someone in our confidence. How does it feel to play Scott?"

"My, my," he mocked. "Have I been that transparent? My daughter didn't think so," Paul went on. "I sat opposite her at all those meetings. She used to come in and sit in my office and talk to me about her day like any daughter would but she never once figured out who I was."

"You reinvented yourself and now you're striking at the very heart of Jon's family," she summarized. "Why?"

"Because revenge is sweet," he said. "I can't tell you how excited it made me every time Kim would talk to me. She told me once I was like the father she never had. She was just as dumb as my wife. We were a wonderful little family, until Jon and Carol messed everything up making Beth get that restraining order on me. I know she never wanted to. She loved it. She loved me."

"You are sick, you know that?" Courtney replied. "What about your family? Your current wife and kids, hell I went to your anniversary party!"

"Yes, you did," he grinned. "I do care about Lisa and the boys, but there are so many times she backtalk's me and I want to discipline her like I did Beth... Beth never did it again after that. Lisa nags and nags and nags, sometimes I want to shut her up..." he looked away. Finally, his empty eyes turned back to Courtney. "We're not unalike you know."

"Oh? And how is that?"

"We both love from a far."

"Meaning Jon?"

"For you," he answered. "For me... I've always loved Beth."

"You had a piss poor way of showing it," she said.

"I just could never control myself around her," he stood and walked away. "She wanted it, don't think she didn't. She loved it."

"She hates you," Courtney said.

"I'm always with her," he replied turning back. "She has never gotten rid of me. Even when Jon took the family, the life and the respect I should have had. So in recompense I took *his* life. Carol was such a sweet woman, I was very sad not to have spent more time with her before she died. Like I'm doing with you," he smiled softly and sat back in his chair.

"So, once wasn't enough?" She asked. "What do you hope to achieve? His death?"

"He'd welcome that."

"His downfall, then," She said. "No matter what lies you spread, no one will believe you. He's too well known."

"Is he? Or is that just the face, one of many, he puts on for those who don't know him?" Rob asked. "Some could even say I am well known in my circles. Would anyone believe I am the one behind this? Me? I'm a church going, tax paying, family man. But Jon? He's a loose cannon. It's amazing what the right kind of stimulus can do."

"No matter what you do to me," Courtney said. "He will not blame himself."

"Are you sure about that?" Rob asked. "Because what if he doesn't try to save you?"

"I'm a cop, *she's* a civilian. I want him to save her."

"Do you think Ryan will see it that way?" Rob asked. "Because I sure don't."

"This wasn't about using me to tear Jon down. You were going to use me as a catalyst for Ryan to tear him down."

"Like you said, the house of Usher, cannot be defeated from without, only from within. Enter an angry Italian Irishman with a grudge against the patriarch."

"Ryan will understand," Courtney stated.

"And once I inform the police of what I *saw him doing* the other night," he made air quotes around the phrase. "I will be hailed as a hero while Jon's precious legacy will crumble around him."

"What are you talking about?" She demanded. "What lies are you gonna spread now?"

"Well, think about it, were you ever with him when a murder was committed? Was anyone? I don't think so. Jon had motive and opportunity. Motive? He's lashing out. It's coming up on the anniversary of his wife's death, he feels like he's cheating on her by screwing my wife, so he takes out his anger on helpless victims," Paul explained. "Wasn't he alone when John Doe was killed? And didn't that guy bare a remarkable resemblance to one of the men who killed his wife? And when precious Anna was kidnapped, wasn't he alone? What about the amontillado in your apartment? Didn't you give him a key a year ago just in case? And… well… do I even need to spell out the motive for Pastor Hollywell?"

"Just because you spin these crimes to suit your deranged

agenda, doesn't mean anyone will believe you," she spat.

"No?" Paul asked. "Perhaps not. But after your body is found, do you honestly think Jon will refute any evidence against him? He'll curl up like the coward he is and take it all. My job will be complete," he sneered. "And don't worry he'll have one of the best lawyers…" he gestured to himself. "Scott will come groveling to me begging me to help him. But unfortunately, this case will be a little out of my league and I'll lose it just by that much," Putting up his forefinger and thumb to show the amount, Paul grinned.

"It won't work, I will stop you," she said.

"Oh? And just how do you propose to do that?" He asked. Before she could answer Rob's phone chimed a text.

"Well, well, looks like the plan is already working faster than I thought," turning his phone toward her, he revealed the photo he had just received. Ryan punching Jon in front of her apartment.

"Ryan! No!" She screamed.

———◦•◦———

Jon and Steven drove in silence. They both knew where they were going and they both knew why.

"If he kills her," Jon gripped the steering wheel tighter.

"I know," Steven said. "But the little I know of Courtney, she can take care of herself."

"Can she?" Jon asked. "Maybe Ryan's right. I'm abandoning her again."

"No, Jon, you're leaving her to her own devices to catch the criminal behind this. If you knew how many times I had to do that, I'm sure your opinion of me would be lowered," Steven said.

"I doubt that," Jon replied. "You do what you need to do to keep us all safe."

"And what exactly are you doing?" Steven asked rhetorically.

"But I'm not keeping *everyone* safe," Jon said. Steven did

not answer. "We're here," Jon pulled into the cemetery where Carol was buried.

"Do you have a family vault?" Steven asked.

"No," he answered. "Just a couple plots. Carol always hated the idea of being filed away or being above ground. She had a thing about being returned to the earth."

"Anything near there? A mausoleum or something?" Steven asked.

"Maybe," Jon replied. "I'll drive toward her grave, you keep an eye out. Between the two of us, you're more the Poe scholar."

"Wait, there!" Steven exclaimed. Jon slowed. "Roget; a Poe work."

"I remember that one well," Jon replied. "One of the ones with C. Auguste Dupin. And it's by trees, could be considered a forest."

"And it's a vault," Steven added remembering the riddle Paul gave them over the phone. "That's gotta be it. Go ahead and park," Steven said.

Jon complied but before they got out of the car, Jon turned to him.

"Are you sure you want to do this?" Jon asked. "It's dangerous and you have a chance to have a family. Maybe you should wait here."

"No," Steven answered. "He has my mother. I'm coming with you."

"I love her, Steven," Jon said.

"I know," Steven answered. "We'll find her." For the first time, Jon saw vulnerability in his eyes. Having always seemed aloof and obviously able to take care of himself, Steven never showed his softer side. But with the possibility his mother was dead or dying, Jon saw just how scared he really was.

CHAPTER FORTY-FOUR

"Do you expect me to be afraid of you? You and *The Masque of the Red Death*?" She taunted.

"Shh, shh," Paul soothed her hair. Standing over her, dressed in a red suit with a red skull mask, he looked intimidating. "I thought you'd enjoy it. It is, after all, one of your favorites."

"What are you going to do?" Courtney asked as they tied her wrists down to a table.

"Oh, don't worry," Paul went on. "I'll make sure it's a lovely funeral. Many a tear will be shed."

Courtney swallowed and gritted her teeth as Quinn tied the ropes tightly around her ankles.

"I'll make sure I comfort Ryan, too. I have someone waiting in the wings for him. She is very anxious to see him again," Rob said.

Courtney looked up at him, anger and suspicion clouding her eyes. "Who?" She demanded.

"Oh," he sighed and smiled stroking her hair. "Don't you worry your pretty little head about it, although you have already met her." Courtney remembered the statuesque blonde who brought her something to eat earlier. "He'll be well taken care of in her arms and that will make Scott hate him, which in turn will make Jon more alone."

"Never," she said. "Absolutely never. They would never turn on each other."

"We'll see," he smirked. "You weren't there about ten years ago when they would have sliced each other's throats given half the chance; at least Scott would've. He always was the jealous sort. As I've said many times before, it's amazing what the right kind of stimulus can do."

"That should be your epitaph," she replied. He chuckled. "You know, tell me, all those times you were right by us, all those times you could've killed us or him in a freak accident, why now? Why did you wait?" Courtney asked.

"I had to stay in character," Paul chuckled. "And you know all about that, don't you? I remember seeing you in Jane Eyre."

"So, tell me, this, what are your plans for Scott?" she asked.

"Oh, those have already begun. In fact, you'll see just how — well... I guess *you* won't see at all," he chuckled.

Quinn nodded at Paul and left the room. Paul sighed.

"It's time. Oh, my dear, I hope you know just how jealous I am of you right now. All these years studying Poe's work," Paul went on. "It must be quite thrilling for you to be smack dab in the middle of one. This one was specifically designed for you. I heard somewhere it was your favorite," Paul smiled slightly and stroked her hair again. "Now, you will remember to scream loudly for the camera, won't you?" He said indicating the video camera mounted on the wall. "I'll be sending a copy to your fiancé."

He kissed her cheek and headed for the door.

"Wait," Courtney called him back. He turned. "Tell me this, is Beth safe?"

"'Ahh, my dear Fortunato, you are luckily met,'" he quoted.

"No! Oh, god, no!" Courtney cried when she figured out where Beth was.

"Oh yes," he sighed dreamily. "It's been fun Courtney, do give my best to Carol when you see her. But I have a queasy stomach when it comes to blood, so if you'll forgive me. Goodbye, Courtney."

———————

After several failed attempts to open Roget's crypt, Jon and Steven agreed they had to rule it out. Steven's hand shook slightly as he walked back to Jon's car.

"We'll try the next one," Jon said seeing the slight tremor.

"We only have an hour and a half left," Steven replied. "We don't have time to search each and every vault, there must be hundreds."

"We're too far from Carol's grave for this to make any sense," Jon said.

"We're running out of time," Steven shouted.

"Listen to me, Steve, it's not too late and that white car has been following us since we left Courtney's apartment. Don't look now," Jon stopped him. "Pretend to cry and hug me." Steven did as Jon said but Jon strategically moved him so the white car was over Jon's shoulder when he held him.

"Paul's surveillance team?" Steven whispered not breaking Jon's hold.

"More than likely," Jon replied. "Can you see if there's anyone inside?"

"Two men," Steven answered. "Can't make out anything else but they're watching us."

"Then we need to see what happens when we get closer to Carol's grave," Jon said. "You have your gun?"

"In the back of my pants," Steven said.

"Good," Jon replied pulling away and touching Steven's face. Steven pretended to wipe his tears away and nodded.

"They're taking pictures of us," Steven revealed.

"Makes sense, he wants to know where we are at all times,"

Jon said. "Oh god, Courtney," once again, Jon's decision weighed heavily on his heart and mind. "Get out of there."

"Get out of there," Courtney heard Jon's voice and froze.

"Jon?" she breathed. Just as she heard his voice, her heart slowed, and she controlled her breathing. With one final deep breath, she assessed her situation.

Her wrists and ankles were tightly tied to old sailor rings drilled into an old, but still solid, table. She looked around the room. It was dark, but she could still see a little of the room. There was a workman's table near to her, impossible to reach bound and there was a second-floor above her. She was in a warehouse, that much she could tell by the style of the structure around her. But, everything to her right was pitch black.

Then she heard it.

A great grinding sound like something heard at a construction site, followed by a great swooshing sound. She felt the wind of the object before she saw what it was. Her heart lodged in her throat. Her vision blurred around the edges and sweat broke out along her back.

A gigantic pendulum was swinging six feet above her.

Courtney needed no more motivation than her memory of the story gave her. Knowing the pendulum was sharpened at the bottom and was designed to lower slowly, cutting the person on the table in two, Courtney went to work. Twisting her wrists to get out of the bonds that held her, they burned and she could feel her flesh ripping off. She did not cry out. She did not want to give Paul the satisfaction of breaking her.

The pendulum swiped back and even though she felt the air slice around her, she kept working the ropes. Her heart nearly gave out when she heard the *chink* of metal indicating the pendulum being lowered one gage closer to her.

It may be getting closer, but the ropes were getting looser

— or was that just her imagination? Still, she kept trying. Accustomed to the burn now, her wrists were numb. The only thought that entered her mind was to get out of there alive.

"Fight," she heard a woman say. "He can't lose you too." Not knowing who it was that spoke to her; it wasn't Beth's voice, nor was it the woman she had met earlier that day, she silently asked for help.

"Jon," she breathed.

"Courtney," she heard Jon's voice again. "Think."

"They're still following us," Steven replied looking at the reflection in the visor mirror.

"How about now?" Jon asked, turning down another road.

"They're backing off," Steven said. "Whatever you're doing, it's working."

"It's Carol's grave," Jon replied, pulling to a stop. "See anything that might work with Poe?"

Steven's eyes left the visor mirror and scanned the vaults. "There —" Steven pointed. "Montresor; I forget which story, but I know it's a Poe."

Jon parked the car and as they got out, Steven's eyes watched. They had pulled off and were waiting, watching them.

"Eyes out," Jon said.

"Agreed," Steven replied.

Jon passed a flashlight to Steven as they reached the Montresor vault.

"Jon," Steven indicated the top of the mausoleum.

Jon looked up to see a large stone raven at the peak. "Looks like we're in the right place," Jon said. Steven nodded as Jon reached out and tried the door, it pushed open with a squeak.

CHAPTER FORTY-FIVE

That is getting way too close, Courtney thought as the whoosh of air from the pendulum swaying back and forth moved her hair. The swaying was getting faster the closer it got to her.

Her wrists hurt, her bonds felt slippery, but she didn't want to know why. One final tug.

Ah! Her left hand was free. She fell back for a second in relief. The pendulum swayed back. When it was safe, she worked on the bondage that held her right hand. Blood dripped down her fingers and onto the rope. Luckily it didn't take much to get that hand free and as she heard the next *chink* of the pendulum lowering yet again, she laid flat against the plank table. When it swayed away, she shot back up working the ropes holding her feet.

She could barely work. The blood from her rope-blistered wrists had trickled down her fingers. Laying back when she heard it coming again, god, she didn't want to die, she nearly shouted. *So close. Too close,* she thought.

As soon as it was safe, she went back to working the ropes that bound her ankles to the table. They wouldn't budge. Her fingers were going numb and her heart pounded with fear, adrenaline and pain. The next chink of metal resounded in the silence. She screamed.

This is it. She thought.

She knew how low the pendulum was. *This is it,* she thought again, trying to resign herself to the fact she was going to die. Closing her eyes for a moment, she took a deep breath waiting for it.

"No!" the same female voice she had heard earlier cried out.

The swoosh of air just above Courtney made her gasp. Opening her eyes, she saw the pendulum wasn't nearly as close as she thought.

"Get out of there! You're almost free!" she heard.

"Who are you?" Courtney asked as she looked around her.

"Just do it, Courtney! My husband can't lose you too," then the voice was gone.

Carol? Courtney wondered. She had no time to think about it, she had to keep working.

Frantically looking around her, she saw a broken piece of glass right below the table, if she could just... reach.

"There's nothing here," Steven said as he swept the beam of his flashlight across the room.

"There's gotta be," Jon replied. "You said yourself, we're in the right place. Keep looking."

"I'm telling you there's nothing here."

"That's not possible."

"We're running out of time."

"Beth has to be here."

"You know who would know?" Steven said ominously, pulling out his gun from the back of his pants. "The people who followed us."

"Wait," Jon grabbed his arm before he could leave.

"No, Jon," Steven yanked his arm out of Jon's grasp. "We don't have time to think about this we have less than an hour."

"Shh, listen," Jon ordered. Steven went silent. "Do you hear it?" Jon asked.

Steven nodded. It was faint, but it was a scratching sound. Steven inhaled sharply.

"Oh god, Montresor. I remember. Jon, it's *The Cask of Amontillado*. She's in the walls!" Steven cried. "Mom!" he yelled.

Both Steven and Jon rushed to opposite sides and listened. Putting an ear to the wall, Jon closed his eyes listening intently.

"Steven, over here!" Jon called. Steven rushed over. The wall was complete stone. Without thinking, they started to push. It wouldn't budge.

"Wait," Steven stopped and looked down. "Jon, look," he pointed to an engraving on the wall. "A raven."

Jon breathed in and slowly, touched the eye of the raven. It sunk in and the wall opened revealing wooden slats. Immediately, Jon and Steven tried to pry them off with their bare hands.

"In my car there's a crow bar. Go!" Jon ordered. Steven ran. Jon pulled out his Swiss army knife and went to work. "Beth? Can you hear me, baby?" He kept calling to her. Finally, he was able to pry one slab far enough away to be able to use his hands. Once the wood splintered and gave way, he shown his flashlight into the opening. "Beth?"

"Jon?" he heard.

"Oh, thank God," he cried. "I'm here, baby." He worked on the next slab.

"No, what are you doing here?" She demanded.

"It's all right, I've got you," Jon replied.

"Oh no, no, you shouldn't be here! You should've gone after Courtney! She's the one they're going to kill! They knew you were going to save me! I prayed they were wrong!" Beth cried.

"What are you talking about?" Jon asked stopping for a moment to look at her.

"This whole thing was centered on breaking you. They

were going to kill Courtney and then frame the murders on you. Jon, you should've gone after Courtney! Go! It's almost too late!" Beth cried.

"I won't leave you," Jon said.

"You have to!" Beth replied. "I'm fine. They left me oxygen. Go!"

"I don't even know where she is," he answered.

"Yes, you do," she replied holding his gaze intently. His breath left him just as Steven ran in with the crow bar.

"Steven, I need you to go," Jon finally ordered. "Go save Courtney, there's still time."

Steven looked at him then toward the opening in the wall.

"She's fine. I got this. I can't be in two places. I need you!" Jon said.

Steven tossed him the crowbar. "Where?" he barked as he headed back toward the car.

"The warehouse where Carol died," Jon called after him.

CHAPTER FORTY-SIX

Steven drove with the police lights and siren blaring. He hated leaving his mother but if there was a way to save Courtney, he was going to do it. Dialing a number as he drove, he waited for Ryan to answer.

"What?" Ryan finally picked up the phone.

"Where are you?" Steven asked.

"Where do you think?" Ryan demanded. "I'm trying to find my fiancée."

"Just listen," Steven ordered. When Ryan didn't answer, he continued. "I know where Courtney is. I'm going there now."

"Where?" Ryan pressed.

"She's at the same warehouse Carol died in," Steven replied. "Can you meet me?"

"We'll be too late," Ryan moaned.

"We have twenty minutes. I'm fifteen minutes away. It'll be close, but we just might make it."

"I'm leaving now," Ryan said. "We'll probably be there the same time. Pray to God we're not too late."

Come on, Courtney urged as she sawed at the ropes still holding her ankles. It was hard to do much when every five seconds she had to lay back in order to not to get hit. One of the ropes finally broke and the bond gave a little.

Again, the pendulum swung. She worked on the next strand of rope. Another chink in the lowering mechanism and the ropes finally gave way.

She rolled to the floor just as the pendulum reached the point where it would have started to cut into her. Wiping her hands on her jeans, she almost screamed. Looking down, her hands shook and she saw nasty cuts on her palms from the glass. She ripped her already torn t-shirt and wrapped her hands in the cloth. Taking a moment to catch her breath, she finally got up and raced to the other side of the room.

Steven and Ryan pulled up to the warehouse with exactly two minutes left on the three-hour deadline.

Tossing Ryan Jon's spare piece from the glove compartment, Steven lead them in through the side entrance. It was dark inside as the only light came from the poorly blacked out windows. Ryan saw the thin beam of light peeking out from under a door to their right. Tapping Steven's arm, he pointed. Steven nodded, and they headed in the direction.

Courtney's wrists and hands were screaming with pain, but she continued down the long passageway. She didn't know where she was going but she had found another shard of glass one with a better point on it and took it, wrapping it in part of the blood soaked, torn cloth of her t-shirt. There was only one goal, not to let them find her and take her back to that contraption.

Survive, Courtney thought and oddly it was Dave's voice ringing in her ears. *Come on, Courtney, if you could get out of that situation, this one shouldn't be that hard. What will they do next?*

———⧓———

The hallway came to a dead end with two doors. Ryan and Steven looked at each other.

"Split up," Ryan offered.

"No," Steven shook his head. "Not with everything that's been going on."

"We don't have time to argue," Ryan said.

"Then listen to me and we won't. Now, let's try the door on the right first," Steven answered.

Ryan huffed and followed as Steven opened the door. It was pitch black, but Ryan started forward anyway.

"Wait," Steven said, his arm shooting out, stopping him. "Do you feel that?"

"What?" Ryan looked at him.

"The heat," Steven answered.

"So? It's a little warmer, so what? Let's go," Ryan said pushing past him.

"Wait, no," he held Ryan's arm. "I remember this one, it doesn't go well."

Ryan looked down and pulled out his cell phone. Shining the light down to his feet, he saw a few more inches in front of him was the end of the floor and it opened to a giant pit.

"*The Pit and the Pendulum*," Steven said. "Let's try and stay out of the pit."

Ryan swallowed and nodded. Looking down, he couldn't see the bottom. He backed up and went with Steven to the door on the left which opened to another long hallway. Steven went first, finger on the trigger of his gun.

"How do you know where you're going?" Ryan whispered.

"I don't," Steven replied. "But I figure, if that's the pit..."

"Then where's the pendulum?"

"It would have to be further down and out of the way."

"Oh god," Ryan swallowed the bile rising in his throat and strained his ears to listen for any screams. "How did you know that was the pit?"

"You felt the heat?" Steven asked. "It was considerably warmer in that room." Ryan nodded. "In the story, the man is tied to a table as the pendulum swings. He is able to escape, but he can't go anywhere because the walls start to close in on him and glow red hot."

"Do you think Courtney is at the pendulum?" Ryan asked. Steven didn't answer. Ryan's breath was slow and stuttered. "Then we're too late."

Steven heard something ahead of them and gripped his gun tighter, not wanting to think of what Ryan was going through. He knew the pain, but he could not relive it. Courtney needed him at his best.

The hallway turned left at the end and slowly they walked. And onward, he led.

CHAPTER
FORTY-SEVEN

Courtney's vision was slowly fading, her breathing was ragged, her ears were ringing, her legs were wobbly. She was weakening but she had to press on. Rounding a corner, she came face to face with one of Paul's men she had seen earlier. She shrieked when he grabbed her. She fought, slicing at him with the piece of glass and catching his throat. She cut through his jugular and felt the spray of his blood on her face. He grasped his throat and fell to his knees. It was war and she was numb. Grabbing the knife she saw in his belt, she took off running.

She ran and ran, not heeding where she was or where she had been. Every time she tried to remember or think, her brain would cloud, and she couldn't remember what it was she wanted to remember.

She heard shouting from behind her. They had found the man she had killed. Running. Running. Running. Jumping at shadows, she continued on. Following the hallway, dodging left at an entrance and right after that, she tried to elude them.

Finally, she turned to what was left. She slowed as her body begged for her to rest. She knew she couldn't stop. Looking over her shoulder, to make sure no one followed her, she turned back as

Quinn walked around the corner. He was just as surprised to see her as she was to see him. But soon the same obscene name he had said earlier, escaped his lips again as he charged her.

"This is for August," he said.

"Then join him in hell," she replied as she dodged him and smashed the palm of her hand against his face. He doubled over, his hands clutching his broken nose. "This is for Jon," She used her elbow at the base of his neck and slammed his head against her knee. He crumpled to the floor, unconscious.

The hallway up ahead bent to the right. Clutching the knife, she kept going. When she turned the corner, she came face to face with two other men. Instinctively, she raised the knife. One of the men grabbed her wrist to stop her. She cried out in pain and backed off.

───────

"Easy!" Steven shouted.

"Courtney!" Ryan cried. "Oh my god, thank God!" He rushed to her. Finally, her senses came back and she realized her fiancée was holding her.

"Ryan?" she asked.

"I'm here. Are you okay?" he asked, pulling away to look at her.

She nodded dumbly.

"Is Paul dead?" Steven demanded.

"I haven't seen him since he…" she trailed off as she realized the true horror of her situation.

"We know about the pit and the pendulum," Steven replied.

Her brows furrowed.

"We found the pit," Ryan explained. "We figured the pendulum wouldn't be too far away."

"It's not," she answered. "At least I don't think so. I don't know how long I've been running."

"You haven't seen him since when?" Steven urged.

"Since he tied me to the table and tried to use the pendulum," she replied. "Where's Jon? Is he okay? And Beth?"

"Jon's with mom," Steven explained. "They're both fine. We have to go. Follow me."

Steven led the group back up the way they came and once they reached the main level, Courtney clutched Ryan's arm.

"Be careful," she said. "I was up here for a little while. The men walked around cautiously. I think it's rigged to blow." Steven gave a hand gesture acknowledging her. "Where are we?" She whispered.

"We'll tell you later," Ryan answered. "Right now—"

"Well, well, well," a voice in the darkness sighed. "Isn't this nice?"

Steven ducked into a darkened alcove behind them and Courtney and Ryan peered into the darkness.

"Courtney, my dear," Paul's voice continued from the darkness. "I watched your escape with great enthusiasm! You even had me rooting for you."

"We're leaving," Ryan said.

"Oh, Ryan," Paul chuckled. "I guess I'm not surprised."

Ryan took a step forward, but Courtney held him back.

"Please," she whispered in his ear. "Be careful."

He nodded and didn't move again. "You've lost," Ryan went on. "Let us go."

"Lost?" Paul replied. "I don't think so. I may not have succeeded in killing Courtney, but there is little you can do to prevent the rest of the plan and I still have a black queen in play. Oh, and let's not forget the little thing I've done to Scott and the business."

"Who are you? Why do you think that?" Ryan demanded.

"Think?" Paul questioned. "I don't think, Ryan, I know. Because I did it," Paul stepped into the light and Ryan stared. "I know," Paul went on sarcastically. "It's hard to imagine, isn't it. But a little plastic surgery goes a long way. What do you think?" he turned, around showing off. "This is the new me!"

"Tom Roberts?" Ryan questioned in disbelief.

"In the flesh," Paul answered. "Isn't it great? You really didn't know, did you?"

"What have you done?" Ryan demanded. "Scott trusted you! He treated you like a second father! You helped him build his law firm! You are his partner, for god's sake!"

"I know, and it was like a dream come true," he grinned. "Imagine my good fortune!"

"What have you done?" Ryan demanded again.

"A lot," Paul shrugged. "But mainly, Jon won't be able to look in the mirror without knowing he couldn't protect his family. He lost Carol. Scott is ruined. Mat is gone. His own friends won't know him. And that woman he's been enjoying? She can't get rid of me. I'll always be there."

"Really?" Steven's voice came from the shadows right behind him. "I don't think so." Paul gasped as Steven rammed a long knife into his back and pulled upward. "Run!" Steven commanded. Ryan grabbed Courtney's arm and took off toward the door.

Paul slowly turned to look at Steven. Pulling the knife out, twisting as he went, Steven stabbed him again when he faced him and this time, twisted enough to nearly cut his heart out. Paul grabbed his shoulder as Steven pulled him in close, ramming the knife to the hilt.

"Say hello to the devil for me... daddy," Steven whispered in his ear.

Paul stumbled backwards, and Steven watched as the life drained from his eyes. He fell to the floor. But just as Steven took a breath to let it all sink in, he heard the click underneath the floorboard. Paul's dead weight had triggered a trip pad.

Steven took off running.

Ryan and Courtney raced out of the warehouse and around behind Jon's car. Once they were safe, Ryan's eyes and hands flew over her, checking to make sure she was all right. Courtney pushed him away.

"I saw what you did, Ryan," she said. "I know you fought with Jon."

"What?" Ryan was confused.

"Don't deny it," Courtney replied. "What did you do?"

"He wasn't going to save you!" Ryan confessed.

"I saved myself," Courtney answered. "But you need to know, you can never come between my partner and me. He knows what's best for me as I do for him. I've never come between you and the doctors you work with. I ask the same courtesy. Jon is my partner."

"I'm your future husband," Ryan said defiantly. "And I need you to listen to me!"

"With that attitude you just might not be," she replied. "You can't control me, Ryan."

"I don't want to control you! I want to love you!" he cried.

"Then love me for who I am!" she exclaimed. "Love me for me and take all my faults! This is who I am, Ryan. You've always known this. I love you but dear god, don't smother me!"

The building burst into flames throwing Courtney into his car. Racing to her, Ryan grabbed her in his arms and held her to him. When she didn't open her eyes immediately, he shook her.

"Courtney!" He screamed.

"I'm fine," she winced. "Oh, my head."

"Don't get up," Ryan said. She looked up at him. "Please, baby."

"Better," she replied throwing her arms around his neck. "I love you. I'm sorry. I just... I'm very..."

"Hey, hey, it's me," he said. "I may not be as good as Uncle Jon in solving this sort of stuff, but I will love you until my last breath. Nothing will ever stop that."

"I don't deserve you," she sobbed.

"Let's not go there," he replied. "I'm trying to let you win this argument, but if you start talking badly about my fiancée then we're gonna have a problem."

"I love you so much!" she pulled him down and kissed him. "I thought I would never be able to do that again."

"Me neither," he answered, kissing her again.

"Oh my god," she pushed away from him. "Steven!" Courtney yelled.

"Steven!" Ryan called too. Helping her up, Ryan called for him again.

"Steven!" They finally shouted together when they saw the rubble of the warehouse still on fire. "Steven!"

"What? What?" Came an annoyed answer. Steven finally rounded the corner of the last standing piece of the structure.

"Oh," Courtney breathed. "Thank god!"

"We thought you didn't make it out," Ryan replied.

"Sorry to disappoint," Steven groaned.

"I think we should get Courtney to the hospital," Ryan said looking at her wrists.

"Good idea," Steven answered. "Think I could join?"

He stumbled as he walked, and only then did they see the shrapnel sticking in his side. Courtney's eyes grew wide.

"I think that would be a good idea," Ryan replied calmly. Courtney couldn't move. He had saved her, and he was injured.

"Just one thing," Steven said.

"What is it?" Ryan asked.

"I think I'm gonna pass out," Steven fell forward unconscious. Ryan caught him as Courtney raced toward him.

CHAPTER FORTY-EIGHT

Slowly Steven woke. Blinding light glared down at him, he blinked his eyes tightly and tried to open them again.

"Steven," he heard his mother's voice. Smiling slightly, he looked over. Beth, Jon, Mark, Kim, and Scott stood around his bed.

"Hey," he said softly. "Who's dead?"

They all chuckled and he heard the sob from his mother and sister.

"Not you, luckily," Mark said, even his voice was tight. "Though you've had plenty of tries."

Knowing Mark had seen him at his lowest, Steven said nothing about the slight reproach and instead, tried to sit up.

"Easy, easy," Mark replied as he and Jon helped him. Steven looked down at the bandages wrapped around his abdomen and side. As if reading his mind, Mark continued. "They were tired of having to cut open the hospital gown whenever you sprung a leak, so they omitted it altogether. And to be honest, I think most of the female nurses wanted some eye candy as they walked by."

"Heh," Steven chuckled. "I must've blacked out, what happened?"

"You sustained shrapnel to the side and abdomen from the

blast. You've been out since they brought you here. That was yesterday morning," Mark explained. "No serious damage but you did lose a lot of blood."

"Yesterday?" Steven asked. "Then that makes this…"

"Sunday," Jon confirmed.

"No," he breathed rolling his head back against the pillow. "I… Ryan and Courtney, are they all right?" Steven asked.

"They're fine," Jon answered. "Courtney had some abrasions to her wrists, ankles and hands but it could have been much worse. Her parents are with her."

"We're just so glad you're okay, sweetie," his mother hugged him gently.

"Likewise," he replied, taking a deep inhale of her lavender shampoo. "You all right?" Pulling back, she nodded. "Good," he tried to smile. "Could I have a few minutes with Jon?"

They nodded and left the room. Once they were alone, Jon pulled up a chair and sat beside the bed.

"Everything okay?" Jon asked.

"Paul's dead," Steven replied.

"I figured," Jon answered. "You're sure?"

"I watched the life leave his eyes," Steven explained. "His body triggered the explosion. I made it to the stairs. Protected me from most of the blast."

"It's hard to believe he's finally gone," Jon replied.

"I know," Steven answered. "And remember," he moved and groaned slightly. "My way is quicker and less painful."

"Say that again when your morphine wears off," Jon teased.

"Not funny, Jon," Steven replied, laying his head back on the pillow. "How's Mom?"

"She's shaken, and she won't like small spaces anytime soon, but it wasn't Paul who took her so, fortunately we don't have to worry about regression. I've called a friend of mine who is a phycologist. Beth's agreed it is time to get Paul out of her head.

They have an appointment set for Wednesday."

"Good," Steven replied. "I hate to see her in pain."

"We both do," Jon answered.

"Do you know where my phone is?" Steven asked. "I want to call Amber and Josh. Apologize for missing the game."

"It was destroyed in the blast. It was in your pocket on the side where the shrapnel hit. Mark has it, he says he's going to take it in and get a replacement for you."

"Shit," he muttered. "I need to call her."

There was a slight knock at the door. Jon called for them to enter. His brother Patrick walked in.

"Good to see ya finally awake, Steven," he said, his thick Irish accent shining through.

"It's good to finally be awake, Patrick," he replied.

"Grand, well, there's a couple o' people outside, eager to see you," Patrick locked eyes with Jon, knowingly. Jon grinned.

"I can't see anyone right now. I'm really very tired," Steven answered, his eyes halfway closed already.

"I think you'll want to see them," Jon replied. Patrick opened the door at his brother's nod. Josh ran in carrying a trophy as Amber walked behind him.

"Hey, Buddy," Steven lit up when he saw him. Josh climbed on the chair Jon had conveniently left for him and hugged Steven. Jon walked over to stand with his brother.

Amber's relieved smile rested on Steven, then she turned to Jon and Patrick.

"Thank you," she said.

"No worries," Jon answered. "He needs his rest though, fifteen minutes?"

"Understood, and thank *you*," she said softly to Patrick.

"You're very welcome," Patrick replied. "He's a good kid," he winked at her. "Yours is too." She snickered through a smile, thanked them one more time before walking over to Steven. Patrick turned and held the door open, but Jon paused a moment. He watched Josh talking to Steven about his game as Amber walked over to the bed. The look in Steven's eyes when he saw her was one Jon and Patrick knew well. It was the look of a well-loved man and one who loved well in return. Amber leaned down and kissed him just as Jon and Patrick left the room.

"I'm not happy with you, Jonny boy," Patrick said as soon as the door closed.

"Oh? And what did I do now?" Jon asked.

"What did you do?" Patrick replied shocked. "You nearly got yourself killed and didn't tell me."

"I'm a cop, Rick. If I called you every time I nearly get myself killed, your phone would be ringing off the hook."

"I still don't like that you didn't clue me in on this whole thing."

"It was an open investigation."

"That's shite and you know it," Patrick replied. "This is a continuation of last month when Riley was chasing after ya, wantin' to be steward. I was there then and I'm here now, it's in between I don't care for. Being kept in the dark is not my idea of communication."

"I'm sorry I didn't call," Jon apologized. "But Rick, seriously, I can't be expected to call every day."

"Not every day but at least give me a warning when you go off on your own," Rick asked. "I'm your brother. I love you. I want to be there for you, unlike I was all those years ago. Let me."

"Love you too, brother," Jon replied. Rick pulled him into a hug and held tightly for a fraction of a moment.

"May I interrupt?" Courtney's voice drew their attention and they pulled back. Jon locked eyes with her.

"Of course, love," Rick smiled. "We'll talk later, Jon." Jon nodded once, his eyes never leaving Courtney's. Rick walked away and for the first time in what felt like years, Jon and Courtney were alone.

"Courtney, I," he started.

"Shh," she replied. "Please let me." He nodded. "I'm sorry Jon. I pushed too hard. I didn't know Steven apart from what you and Ryan had told me. He seemed larger than life to me. I got a little jealous and I shouldn't have. I'm sorry for what I did, but I'm not sorry for what I said." Jon knew immediately what she meant. "But perhaps you need a break from me. We see each other every day. Maybe we should try and just be future uncle-in-law and future niece-in-law. Maybe if we don't see each other all the time, this awkwardness between us will go away." Jon grabbed her and held her tightly against him

"No," he breathed. "I don't think I could do that."

"But maybe it's the only way," she said. "I will not take back what I said."

"And I don't want you to," Jon replied.

"You don't?" she asked.

"No, but now you had your chance to talk. Now it's my turn. Courtney, I was sick the whole time I couldn't protect you. I left you alone, you were hurt and nearly killed because I didn't listen to you. I have asked you to blindly follow me so many times and when you asked me to follow you, I refused. That will *never* happen again. I swear to you, if you ask me to trust you, I will until my dying breath. I am so very sorry. I pushed you away when I should have kept you close and listened," he took her wrists in his hands and raised them to his lips. Kissing the bandages that wrapped her cuts, his eyes were fixed on the wounds. "It will always be a black mark for me. I will never forgive myself."

"I forgive you, that should be enough," she countered.

"It's more than I deserve," he replied.

"Hey, partner," she looked up at him, ducking down to make him look at her. "It's over now. We're both here and thankfully… in one piece."

"Too soon," he shook his head.

"Yeah, that was kinda bad, wasn't it?" she asked laughing. "But I have to make light of it. If I don't, I'll wallow, and I can't do that."

"No, you can't," Jon confirmed. "You're not a wallower. But I should have listened to you, not rebuked you and I should have figured a way to save you both."

"You did," Courtney said. "And there is no reason you should have chosen me over Beth. You care for me, love me even, but she... I knew you could never go through losing the woman you love again. I wanted you to choose her."

Jon looked down. "Courtney, I cannot tell you how much it means to me to know you care for me that way, but I've never been one of those men who pine for their glory days and try to relive them at 50 and 60. I am very content in my life right now. But the choice I had to make was a choice I never want to make again. It brought out some very difficult emotions for me and I hated every second I couldn't be there for you. But I think the main question is, can we both live with where we are now?"

She looked up into his green eyes and smiled slightly. "You know how I feel, Jon," she started. "But I absolutely love Ryan. When I was tied to that table and I thought my life was going to end, I thought about a lot of things. I heard your voice urging me to get up and get out of there, but it was Ryan's face I saw when I closed my eyes. I longed to see him smile, to hear his voice, feel his kiss. I'm not ashamed of what I said to you. I do love you. You've always known that. But Ryan is the man I *want* to marry, the man I want my kids to call dad, and the man I want to grow old with. You and I were never meant to be together, and I know that now."

"This hurts more than I thought it would," Jon breathed.

"Probably because you feel you're losing Carol again. I promise, that is not happening."

"You're right, but it'll always feel as if I betrayed your trust.

If you hadn't been able to get out of there. If you hadn't been able to…" Jon's voice trailed off as he looked away.

"Let's not worry about what would have or could have been. I'm all right now. Beth is all right. Paul or Tom or Rob or whatever, is dead. Let's enjoy this time," she said. "How's Scott doing?" Courtney asked, looking over at him talking with Kim. "I mean, a man he's looked up to for most of his professional career turns out to be the man who killed his mother, attempted to kill you, and has done something to ruin his firm."

"I'm not sure," Jon answered. "He puts on a good face, but I really don't know."

"Well, one step at a time, right? Now, I just want to go home to my parents' house and crash," she said.

"Good, I don't want you alone," Jon replied.

"I don't think Ryan will let me out of his sight," she said.

"How about dinner when Steven gets out of the hospital?" He offered. "Maybe next Saturday?"

"Sounds like a great plan," she said smiling and wrapping her arms around him. When she finally let go and slowly walked away, she stopped and looked back at him. "Oh, and by the way," she started. "I told you so. I told you it was Poe."

"This is for you, Rob," Meredith said as she shot back an ounce of tequila. "I will finish what you started. Don't worry. Jonathan Greene will pay for what he did to you."

"Hey there, beautiful," she heard a man walk up to her. "I've never seen you in my city before."

"Your city?" She asked looking at the man who walked up to the empty seat by the bar.

"Sure is," he answered ordering a beer from the bartender. "What brings you to Minneapolis?"

"A bit of business, a bit of pleasure," she replied.

"I think I can help with the pleasure bit," he said.

"I think you can help with it all, Mr. Pellegrino," she said.
His eyes shot up.

"You know me?" he asked.

"Eammon O'Malley and Viktor Redorvsky say hello."

CHAPTER FORTY-NINE

Jon walked through the main door of Meridian Street Lutheran Church. It wasn't a long walk to the sanctuary, but to Jon it seemed to get longer with every step. Reaching the doors, he heard a voice and debated going in.

"You got this far go," Jon whispered, his hand stretched out for the doorknob, but he pulled back after a moment. "What's wrong with you?" Jon berated himself. *Go on, Jonny,* he heard Carol said. Breathing deeply, he opened the door.

Father Isaac stood at the pulpit addressing an empty church. He stopped speaking Jon walked in.

"Is the sanctuary open, Father?" Jon asked, his voice tight. "I'd like to talk."

"The sanctuary is always open, son," the old man said stepping down from the pulpit. "I was rehearsing Pastor Hollywell's memorial service sermon."

Jon sat as Father Isaac motioned to the pew. "When is that?"

"Wednesday evening," Isaac replied.

"I'd like to come, if that's all right," Jon said.

"All are welcome," Isaac offered. "But I'm sure you didn't

come here to talk about the Order of Service."

Jon shook his head and the old man waited. "Last time I was here, I said things to you you didn't deserve," Jon began. "Things I'm ashamed of. I came here today to ask your forgiveness and to tell you I was wrong to treat you the way I did after all you did for us, for me and for Carol. I am sorry."

Isaac covered Jon's hand with his. "Jon, you had just lost your wife. Half of you was gone. You had every reason to be angry and you took it out on the person you trusted could handle it. I was just worried about you afterwards and I prayed you would speak to me, but I knew you couldn't. That's why I asked Pastor Hollywell to go visit you. I knew you wouldn't open the door for me but for someone to help your son? *That* you would never forbid." Jon looked over at him surprised.

"You lost your helpmate, the woman you loved, the mother of your son, the woman you thought you would grow old with," Father Isaac continued. "You held it all inside and I was worried it would kill you. In a way it has. I remember a man so full of life and love and now the one I see before me is empty. Your life and love was ripped from you and you had every right to question and be angry. I only wish I could have helped you more." Jon took a shaky breath. "God called an angel home," Isaac went on. "It's not fair, it's not even logical, but it happened." Closing his eyes, Jon felt a single tear roll down his cheek. Isaac was quiet for a moment as a second tear followed the first. "Tell me something, have you ever cried to Scott?" Jon shook his head. "Why not?"

"Because, I'm his father," Jon cleared his throat and wiped his eyes. "I need to be strong for him."

"Forgive me but he's hurting just as much as you are. Especially now you're with someone else, he needs to know you're still in pain," Isaac said. Jon looked up at him surprised. Isaac smiled. "I wasn't always a priest, son. My wife and I have been in love for many years," he answered. "I thought, at first, it was your young partner. She's a lot like Carol. In fact, that's what startled me when you both walked in. It was like seeing you two together again. But then I realized she was with Ryan… Is it Beth?" Jon nodded slowly. "Good," Isaac replied patting his hand. "And does she make you happy?" Jon nodded again. "Is Scott all right with this?"

"He seems to be," Jon answered.

"If I may make a suggestion," Isaac said gently. "He needs to know how you feel. He knows you're strong, now he needs to know you're hurting."

"I've held it in so long," Jon breathed. "I don't know how to let it out, especially to him."

"All you can do is try," Isaac said.

"Thank you, Father. It's nice to be able to talk to you again."

"I've missed our conversations, Jon."

"As have I," Jon answered. Isaac patted his hand again but changed the subject. "I guess I should go," Jon said standing. Isaac stopped him with a gentle hand on his arm.

"How long has it been since you prayed?" he asked.

"Too long," Jon breathed.

"May I?"

CHAPTER FIFTY

Jon and Scott stood at Carol's grave, both placing a bouquet of roses on the ground. When Scott straightened, he looked over at his father and noticed a single tear slide down his cheek. Mesmerized, as he had never seen his father cry over his mother's death, it tugged at his heart and he placed a hand on his father's shoulder, squeezing gently. Looking over at his son, Jon let the second tear fall.

"I love your mother, Scottie," Jon said. "I always have, and I always will."

"That was never a question, Dad. And you know Mom would want you to move on, be happy," Scott replied. Jon looked down at his wife's grave finally letting the tears fall. He lowered to his knees, Scott following, and they held each other tightly as they both cried.

Finally, pulling away, Jon framed his son's face, stared deeply into his watery brown depths and smiled. "I am so lucky to have you, son."

"I'm the lucky one, dad," Scott replied. "Not many fathers would welcome their son's back with open arms after everything I put you through."

"You are my son, of course I always welcome you back. I love you, Scottie."

"I love you too, dad."

Kissing his son's forehead, Jon pulled him into a tight hug not letting go until they heard thunder in the distance.

When they pulled back, Scott asked the one question that burned in his mind. "Does Beth make you happy?"

"Very much so," Jon stated.

"And Courtney?" Scott asked gently. "I know it's not my place to ask but if you're happy with Beth, why? Why did you let her do that?"

"Honestly? She looks so much like your mother and for a time I... pretended Carol was back. I'm not proud of it, but that's why. We've discussed it and, what you saw, will not happen again." Looking back up at his son, Jon saw Carol reflected in his face. "She is not your mother, I know it. I want to be with Beth, for the rest of my days, I want her by my side."

"Good," Scott grinned. "For a second I thought you were going to turn into Uncle Mat."

Jon laughed. "I'm not that bad."

"Have you heard from him?" Scott asked.

"Just when he landed. It's too dangerous for anything else right now."

Scott nodded and looked away. "I was hoping he would be at my wedding."

"Maybe he will be," Jon replied. "But he did ask me to get something for you. He had it in a secret place in his house. I am to give it to you on your wedding day."

"Can I ask what it is?" Scott asked.

"Nope," Jon shook his head. "Not until your wedding day. But I don't think you'll be disappointed."

"Don't you have to be somewhere in a little bit?" Scott asked after a brief pause and thunder again rumbled in the distance.

"We have some time, in fact, I have something I want to show you and something to ask of you."

"Okay, shoot," Scott said.

"I… need to show my best man something."

Scott stared at him, then realization dawned. Scott let a silly grin spread across his face and he grabbed his father to him hugging tightly, thumping him on the back.

"She hasn't said yes, yet," Jon laughed.

"Oh, come on," Scott teased. "She will."

"Wanna see the ring?"

"Absolutely!"

CHAPTER FIFTY-ONE

Viktor Redorvsky saw the lightening streak across the night sky. Hunching into his coat, he turned to his friend.

"I think it's gonna rain," Viktor said.

"Yeah?" Sergei looked up. "What are ya gonna melt or somethin'? We're almost to my place."

Viktor was going to miss him. As hard as it was to lie to him, Viktor knew Jon had a plan.

"Any more on the college front?" Sergei asked.

"No," Viktor spat.

"Why not?"

"Because dad didn't seem to like the idea."

"You know he didn't only because he wants you where he can manipulate you," Sergei said. "If you have a chance to get away, do it. I'll help, you know I will."

Viktor sometimes wondered why Sergei was his friend. As his father's second-in-command, Sergei, was set to inherit the *business* as soon as Viktor was out of the scene.

"I know. But dad's made his displeasure perfectly clear," Viktor said rubbing his still sore ribs.

"Hey," Sergei grabbed his arm gently and cupped his face

forcing him to look at him. "Listen, I know what you're going through. I wouldn't want my kid to be raised in this life but it's the only life we know. Give your dad time to adjust to your new ideology. I'm not saying he'll come round but he might just need more time. Then get away. Get far away."

Viktor nodded but the hairline fracture on his cheekbone, from father's displeasure, throbbed.

"You're probably right," Viktor answered walking away. "But I still don't understand his discipline style. I got it after the *first* broken rib."

"How do you think it made me feel? Watching. It made me want to tear their damn heads off."

"It doesn't matter," Viktor shrugged off.

"Doesn't... doesn't matter?" Sergei breathed in shock. "You know how I feel about you, why would you say that?"

"I'm sorry. I'm hurting, and I wanted to hurt someone. I didn't mean. I'm just scared, Serge. I don't know what to do."

"I know," he walked over to him and framed his face for a moment then pulled him into a hug. "Does this have anything to do with what you told me last night? I wondered why you wouldn't tell me what's going on."

"Partly, but I can't, I'm sorry."

"Hey, I love you, you can tell me anything."

Viktor looked up at him and tried to smile. Sergei had only ever said that once. It felt good to hear it but also made him question his plan. Pulling away from him, he walked on.

"I'm here. Talk to me," he pressed.

"I know but I can't."

"Why not?"

"You're married, and you're damn near old enough to be my father."

As terrible as it was to throw that in his face when Viktor knew Sergei only married to unite the families and it had nothing to do with love.

"I'm not that old and it never stopped you before. Besides, we're divorcing," Sergei stated without emotion.

"What? Why?" Viktor asked.

"I think you know why. She figured out I wasn't interested."

"But you didn't... tell her?"

"She doesn't need to know everything. She had her own problems she never talked about," Sergei walked away for a moment and gazed up at dark storm clouds. "I guess that's my problem, huh? Nobody talks to me."

"It's not that I don't want to—"

"Then what's stopping you?" Sergei turned his cognac colored eyes to Viktor and waited. Viktor took that moment to memorize him. His dark brown hair closely trimmed around his ears and sides of his face. The small peak it made on top without any product. The tight beard that colored his sun-kissed skin. The way his light blue collared shirt opened at his neck with three buttons undone. The thick woven belt he wore holding his dark blue slacks and the dark blue blazer, straining over his muscled chest and arms, with his usual handkerchief stuffed inside the outer pocket on his chest. Sergei was the only person who took an interest in him. Ever since he was young, Sergei was there. Never as more than a friend until Viktor realized his own feelings.

Tears filled Viktor's dark blue eyes and he pressed his full lips together stopping the show. Sergei watched him, a myriad of expressions crossing his face. Rushing to him, Sergei pulled him into his chest and held on. The second his familiar cologne teased his senses Viktor let the tears fall.

"I'm sorry," Sergei soothed, stroking the back of his head. "I know something is up, but I trust you, Viktor. Whatever it is, I back you. If you have a chance to get out of this life, take it. Don't think of anyone but yourself."

Viktor shook his head. "*If* that's a possibility, I'd want you to come with me."

"You know I can't do that. But I would gladly face prison time if it meant you were safe."

"I'd be there when you got out," Viktor promised, wiping his eyes.

"Not if it hurts you. Live and don't look back. Love who you want, be what you want, go and do what you want and don't think about me. Promise me, Viktor."

"All of those things are standing right in front of me," Viktor revealed.

"No, they're not. I want you to meet someone your own age. Girl, boy I don't care but get out of this life and live."

"You know how confused and messed up I am. How do I explain it to others? I don't know what I want, I only know I want you to be there," Viktor said.

"I'm not one you can be with. I love you but that's as far as it goes. There's no happily ever after for me," Sergei said.

"That's not fair," Viktor whined.

"No," Sergei shook his head. "It's not, but as your dad would say, it's just business."

Suddenly, IMPD officers swarmed them. Lights flashed, people ran, a woman sitting outside in the patio of a restaurant screamed. Viktor wiped his face and looked up at Sergei. He sighed and raised his hands over his head.

"What did you do?" he breathed.

"I'm sorry, it's the only way," Viktor said. "I need to get out and he's going to help me."

"Go far away," Sergei breathed.

"Down on the ground now!" He heard from every cop around them, but one voice stood out.

"On your knees!" it shouted. Viktor locked eyes with Jon standing a little way away. "I said on your knees!" Jon shouted walking closer aiming his gun at Viktor.

"Vitya," Sergei urged as he knelt with his hands behind his head. "Get down."

He shook his head, looking back at him. "My father wanted me to prove to him I'm tough, I'm ready to take over? Well, here's my chance, Sergei," he said not taking his eyes off him. Nodding as he understood, Sergei waited until Viktor broke eye contact. Viktor ran toward the cop Sergei had seen briefly the day he dropped Viktor off at a house, after he was beaten up. Sergei closed his eyes, flinching when he heard two pops of gunfire, but the sound was different. He was shooting blanks. Then all was quiet. Opening his eyes, he was not prepared for the sight before him. Viktor lay on his back, theatrical blood seeped out of his shirt, but even as tears assaulted his eyes at the gruesome performance, Sergei saw Viktor's chest rising and falling just slightly and looked up at the cop.

Jon looked over at Sergei and nodded. Right then, Sergei realized his part to play. Screaming at Jon, he surged forward and cradled Viktor's body to him. After shouting at him to come back and that he would be all right, Sergei pulled Viktor up into his chest and rocked him back and forth.

"Be careful," he whispered and felt the slightest touch of Viktor's lips against his jaw.

One week later...

Jon found his party seated at a table at Fogo de Chão after he hung up with Viktor and Keelan in Ireland. The fake shooting incident the other day had hit national news but fortunately, he was out of the country before that happened. Beth looked up at him when he approached.

"Everything all right?" She asked as he sat down beside her.

"Perfectly," he smiled.

"This is a wonderful treat. Thank you, Jon," Courtney's

mother said.

"It's my pleasure," Jon replied, glancing at Courtney. She smiled softly at him as the waiter came around to fill their wine glasses. After everyone was served, Jon stood and raised his glass to propose a toast.

"I would first like to say thank you to my family. It means a lot to me to have this many people sitting at the table with me. Please drink to the health of my son, Scott and his current and future happiness with a woman I consider a surrogate daughter." Kim smiled at him and took Scott's hand one of the few times he had it out of the sling. "And I ask you drink to my nephew Ryan, who has always been there for us in every way imaginable. *Ti amo, nipote*," Ryan looked up at his uncle.

"Love you too, *zio*," he said. Mending the fence between them had taken a lot of wine, whiskey and shouting but it happened.

"His health and happiness with the woman who means a great deal to me. My partner has always been there for me, she has always trusted me, sometimes in situations where we have nothing to go on but my gut instinct. Courtney, you know what this means," he raised his glass to her and drank. She smiled at him and nodded. "Rick, I want to thank you for wanting to be there for me, even if I don't always remember it," Jon said. His brother chuckled.

"Aye, ya lazy dope," Rick called. "And don't you be forgettin' it neither!"

"*But*," Jon stressed nearly rolling his eyes. "I truly want to thank someone who kept me level headed throughout these most difficult times. My son, Steven," Steven looked up at him and smiled. "Without his help, I don't know what would have happened. So please join me in drinking to his health, quick recovery, and happiness. *Sláinte*." Everyone sounded *cheers* and *clinked* their glasses together.

Before Jon sat back down, he held up his hand indicating

he had one more thing to say. "I'm sorry to monopolize the time, and I know we're all anxious to get to that filet mignon, but I have one last thing to do. Something I've waited far too long to say," he looked over at Scott who grinned and nodded. Then his gaze landed back on Steven who nodded once. Jon reached in his pocket and produced a powder blue box. Kneeling in front of Beth, the entire section of the restaurant went quiet and turned to watch. Beth's hands flew to her mouth in shock and tears rolled down her cheeks.

"Beth, love, you have been my rock for so many years. You have kept me sane. You have always been there for a late-night chat or a swift kick up the arse. You know what it is I lost thirteen years ago, and you have never tried to compete with her. You have only ever tried to soothe the pain of losing her. I know Carol is looking down at us and smiling right now. I feel it in my heart. I don't want to go through life alone anymore. Not when I have such a helpmate by my side. I want to make something that is far too long overdue, permanent," he opened the box and the gasp echoed around the room, but Beth's reaction was all he cared about. The five-carat, round cut, diamond ring called to him the one day he went browsing in Tiffany's while waiting for Scott to meet him at the mall food court for lunch and he knew it was the one for her. Beth froze staring at the ring then her eyes went up to Jon's.

"Elizabeth Nixon... will you marry me?"

To Be Continued...

Be sure to check out the conclusion of The Greene and Shields Files: *Old Sins Cast Long Shadows*. Available now!

ACKNOWLEDGEMENTS

I hope you enjoyed this continuation of Jon's and Courtney's story. I certainly enjoyed writing it. Edgar Allan Poe has always been one of my favorite authors and it was a pleasure to research his works and write them into this story. Poe's genius inspired my first publication in the form of the poem, *Onward, Onward, Onward He Led* featured at the beginning of this novel.

As I was sitting to write the sequel to *Blood is Thicker Than Water*, many attempts were made but none really clicked. Pulling out the book containing my poem, I reread it and all of the sudden I had an amazing idea (at least, I thought it was an amazing idea). Use Poe as the theme. Chess was used in Blood, as Jon mentions, as clues for him, I wanted to showcase Courtney's strength in this one by using something she saw and understood.

I hope you will keep an eye out for the third and final novel in the trilogy available now. Until then, thank you all for taking Jon and Courtney into your hearts!

A big thank you to my editor, Ashton Clark for his keen eye and quick wit. And a big thank you to my family who have always supported me in my writing and understood when I was not sociable because "I have a deadline!" Love you all!

Read on for a sneak peek at The Greene and Shields Files: Old Sins Cast Long Shadows!

The Greene and Shields Files
Book Three

Old Sins Cast Long Shadows

M. KATHERINE CLARK

Prologue

Zoe stumbled to her car, the blinding pain blurring her already clouded vision. Her hands shook as she tried three times to get the damn keys in the ignition. Finally, the old ford started up.

The moon's rays were obscured by the snow clouds and the white flakes shown in her headlights. Her car swerved when the worn tires hit a patch of black ice.

The pain in her side grew more intense. She had to get help. Pulling out her cell phone, she dialed a number only to hear nothing as the call couldn't connect to a tower. Looking at the screen, she cursed the No Service icon at the top.

Cursing in frustration, she leaned over, crying out when her side collided with the gear shift. The satellite phone was in the glove compartment. It rang. Rang. And rang.

"Dammit, answer!" she shouted.

"Zoe?" his voice came over the receiver.

"Finally! Listen, Skylark is blown. He knows, Steven. He – shit!" she screamed when she saw the oncoming headlights of an eighteen-wheeler.

"Zoe? Zoe!" Steven shouted.

VIKTOR REDORVSKY SHOT DEAD BY POLICE

IND – Viktor Redorvsky, son of Russian businessman Viktor Demetrovich Redorvsky, was shot dead by police yesterday while walking home with a friend. According to eye witnesses, Redorvsky, 18, was walking along the alleyway between Chatham Tap and his friend's apartment complex. Redorvsky and his unnamed friend were then swarmed by IMPD officers and a firefight ensued. Redorvsky was shot dead and his friend was wounded. Redorvsky's father was subsequently arrested by the Organized Crime division of the IMPD. His hearing is set for later this month. Police are asking anyone with any information to please step forward and inform the IMPD.

Chapter One

Viktor rubbed his eyes as the words of the article on his laptop blurred. He looked at the clock in the bottom corner and yawned. Before he could shut the laptop down, there was a knock at his bedroom door.

"Who is it?" He called.

"Keelan," a voice said.

"Come in," Viktor replied.

The door opened and Keelan O'Grady leaned against the doorframe.

"Still worried your father will find you?" He asked.

Viktor shrugged. "Force of habit."

"Are you all right?"

"Couldn't sleep," Viktor admitted closing the lid of his laptop.

"Jet lag after a month?" Keelan asked.

"No," he answered. "Something else."

"What's wrong, Greg?" Keelan asked.

"Couldn't you call me Vitya?" Viktor asked. "I mean, I appreciate my new life, but I miss being called by my real name."

Keelan shook his head. "Probably wouldn't be best," he stated. "Viktor Viktorovich Redorvsky is dead, remember?"

"Yeah. It's strange seeing my obituary," Viktor sighed.

"What's wrong?" Keelan asked. "Are you homesick?"

"It's hard to be homesick when you've never had a home," he answered.

"I can tell something's on your mind, lad," Keelan said. "You know you can tell me anything."

Viktor sighed and opened his laptop. Keelan pushed off the doorway and sat on the side of the bed.

"This," Viktor said as he played a news video.

An older man was speaking outside a courthouse in front of several reporters.

"These police have made mistake. I am an honest businessman," Viktor heard his father's Russian accented voice and suppressed a shudder. "They arrested me on word of two men who have, for some reason, disappeared and cannot be found. The judge had no choice but to let me go. And these police will see just how powerful I truly am."

"Mr. Redorvsky, is it true one of your arresting officers killed your son Viktor last month?" One of the reporters asked.

Redorvsky stopped and looked at the reporter.

"My son was innocent and not given fair trial. The cop who shot him will pay. They will all pay…" he looked directly into the camera. "I know who you are. I will find you. You cannot escape me. I will return favor."

———————————

Detective Courtney Shields woke in a panic, her heart racing, sweat making her hair stick to her neck. Looking around the darkened room, she tried to calm her ragged heartbeat. Her recurrent dream since her time beneath the sharpened pendulum was still vivid in her mind. Swallowing, she took another deep breath.

"Courtney?" Ryan's voice came from beside her. Looking over, she took his hand as he reached toward her. "Are you okay, baby?"

She shook her head. Predawn light broke through her bedroom window outlining Ryan's silhouette as he lay on his stomach. Moving slightly, he leaned up on his elbow and stroked her face.

"What's wrong?" he asked.

"I keep having a dream," she replied.

He sat up fully and her eyes went down to his bare chest. Taking her in his arms, he slowly stroked her back.

"What sort of dream?" he asked.

"I'm back at the warehouse, under the pendulum," she answered. "And I can't get out."

"But you did," he said. "You did get out."

"I know," she replied. "But it doesn't help."

"What can I do?" he asked.

"You've already done it," she said. "Just by being here."

Slowly, he leaned them both back on the bed and held her tightly.

"Do you want to talk to someone?" Ryan asked. "Uncle Jon swears by his shrink. Maybe you could talk to him?"

"That might not be a bad idea," she replied.

"Did you talk to the Police Psychiatrist?" he asked.

"Yeah, but it didn't seem to help," she said.

"It's not been long enough," he replied. "You need more time."

Nodding, she stroked the fine hairs on his chest.

"I'm glad you're here," she said. "I'm glad we're together."

His arms tightened around her and he kissed her hair.

"Me too," he answered. "You aren't worried we didn't wait?"

"We waited long enough," she replied. "I needed you that night and you were there. I don't think I could face this without you."

"Me too, baby. Are you sure you want to go back? Maybe you could call Dave and tell him you're not ready."

"You can't take another sick day to be with me," she snuggled deeper into him. "And I need to get back out there. I've had nearly a month off. I need to get back to it."

"I'm here if you want or need me," he replied.

"I always want you," she teased looking up at him. Shimming her way up to be eye level with him, she kissed his lips and distracted them both until the alarm on his phone went off. Groaning, he tapped it quiet. "Do you really have to go in?" she pouted as he rolled out of bed and grabbed his clothes.

"You just told me not an hour ago that I couldn't take any more time off," he laughed.

"I know, but that was before you distracted me," she replied.

"And I would distract you again," he knelt on the bed and leaned forward. "If I didn't have an ER filled with patients."

"And they are all in need of your special attention," she said. "As I am."

"That is completely different special attention and I plan on lavishing you with it as soon as you get home," he said.

"Home? I don't recall inviting you over tonight," she answered.

"You didn't," he teased. "I just thought I would help you out and invite myself."

"And what if I wanted to invite another hot doctor home for the evening?" she asked.

"You'd have a hard time finding a hotter one," he kissed her.

"That's true," Courtney laughed, then, smacking his

shoulder, she continued. "Go, take a shower, before I tie you to my bed."

"Don't tempt me," he winked.

"Go, I'll get coffee going."

"I love you," he said softly. "And I want you to call me if you can't do today, okay?"

"I will but I'll be fine, baby," she replied. "Jon will be there and Dave, so I'll have all the protection you could hope for me. I need to get back. I need to do something."

"I know you do," he said. "Just be careful."

"I'll call you when I have a break, okay?" she offered.

"Perfect," he replied. "And I'm making dinner tonight."

"I love your short shifts," she teased.

"Me too," he answered.

"Any word on the promotion you interviewed for two months ago?" She asked.

"Nothing yet," he replied. "Fred said it could take a couple months. They have to make a show of interviewing other candidates," grinning, he raised his hands in innocence. "His words not mine."

"Assistant Head of Surgery," Courtney whistled low. "Sexy."

"Yeah, it is," he teased. "I'd be working with Fred most of the time so it's not like I don't know how to handle him."

"He's a good guy," she said.

"He is," Ryan agreed. "I gotta jump in the shower. I love you." Kissing her once more before heading to the bathroom, he flicked on the overhead vent and light.

Courtney listened to the sound of the water gushing and then the shower start. For a moment, she reveled in Ryan's love. After their first time together, they agreed not to tell anyone. She wasn't ashamed but she wanted to keep the newness and forbidden desires to herself.

But when the memory of her would-be-shower-garrotter from last month came back to her, Courtney allowed herself five seconds to get through the fear as the police shrink told her. Taking a deep breath, she stood, grabbed one of Ryan's oversized sweatshirts he had given her and headed to the kitchen. Brewing a pot of coffee, she was nearly done with his omelet when Ryan walked out dressed in his usual suit.

"Damn, I love you," he teased kissing the back of her neck, exposed by the sloppy bun she had pulled her hair into.

"You are lucky," she replied.

"I know I am," he poured two cups of coffee and grabbed the hazelnut creamer from the refrigerator. Making a latté for them both, he watched her move about in bare feet and nothing but his old Notre Dame sweatshirt. "You are making it very difficult to want to go to work today."

"That's my job," she swayed to the music playing in the background on her vinyl record player. "Besides I have to keep you away from all those pretty little nurses."

"Which do you mean? Maybe Mrs. Reed? Oh, I know! Mrs. Phillips, the lady who is old enough to be my great grandmother."

"Mmhmm," Courtney teased. "I've had my eye on her for a long time. It's always the quiet ones."

"I'm gonna have to tell her you said that," he said. "She'll get a kick out of it."

"Tell her I know exactly what her plan is, playing the sweet little old lady act," she bit her lip. Ryan saddled up behind her, pulled her tightly against him and kissed her neck.

"I like this little jealous streak of yours," he whispered in her ear making her shudder. "But you don't have to worry about Mrs. Reed or old Mrs. Phillips, why would I want them, when I have you to come home to? You are my life, Courtney Shields, and soon you will be my wife." Turning in his arms, she wrapped hers around his neck.

"And you are mine, Ryan Marcellino," she answered. "You have seen me at my best and my worst and you are still here. I love you."

"And I," he kissed the tip of her nose. "Love you."

"You better, now, would you eat this delicious omelet before it gets cold?"

"Wouldn't want that," grinning, he broke away from her and straddled a kitchen barstool, watching as she cut the omelet in half placing one half on her plate and the other on his.

Chapter
Two

Sitting in her car, looking at the elevators leading to her precinct, Courtney took a deep breath. It had been nearly a month since she had stepped into that elevator and even now the nerves built inside her. She was a good cop, but after something so devastating, so traumatizing, she wasn't sure she was ready to return. One more deep breath, she breathed in the eucalyptus scented car freshener Ryan bought her. It calmed her and gave her courage.

Grabbing her handbag, keys, the two coffees and the two dozen donuts she had stopped to get, she locked her car and walked briskly to the doors.

"Hold the elevator!" she called as it started to close. A hand shot out and stopped the door from closing. "Thanks." She breathed then looked at her elevator mate. "Scott? Oh my god, what are you doing here? Are you in court?" Giving him a quick awkward hug with her hands full, she made sure not to spill the coffees on his Armani suit.

"Hey, Courtney," her partner's son replied, offering to take the donuts for her. "Dad said it was going to be your first day back.

How are you doing?"

"Great," she answered. "Feeling better at least."

"Good," he grinned. "I get it, you know? If you ever need someone to talk to, let me know. I'm here for you."

"Thank you," she answered. "I will probably take you up on that."

"That cousin of mine taking care of you?" he asked.

"Completely," she answered. "But, how are you? What are you doing here?"

"I'm feeling great. The doc says I'm back to ninety percent rotary function."

"That's fantastic!" she cried.

"And the wedding is nearly planned," he replied. "Kim is a saint putting up with my work schedule. There's been a shit load to do; I'm lucky if I make it home by midnight."

"That's tough, but she loves you so it's easy," she stated. "Are you in court today?"

"You could say that," he answered. "Dad wants to sit in on the Redorvsky hearing so I volunteered to join him."

"That's nice of you," she replied.

"Hey, it's a free lunch," he teased. The elevator dinged as she laughed and they both stepped out. Applause greeted her as they rounded the corner into the bullpen. Shock changed to a soft smile as Courtney thanked them for their welcome back. Jon and Dave stepped out of their offices joining in the applause. Finally, after everyone quieted down and she showed Scott where to put the donuts, she reached her partner and boss.

"Hey, kid, you look great," Dave started. "How do you feel?"

"Nearly one hundred percent," she replied. Once the door to their office was closed, she handed them both a coffee and hugged them.

"It's been quiet and peaceful without you here," Dave

teased. "There's no one to raise hell."

"Gotta keep you on your toes," she retorted. "And here I thought about calling in sick."

"You could have, there's nothing pressing to do," Jon replied. "Scott and I are heading over to sit in on Redorvsky's hearing. You're welcome to join us."

"Oh, no thanks," she answered. "I think I'll get a start on stuff here."

"If you're sure," Jon replied.

"Bad luck it falls on the same day you return," Dave tsked.

"Oh, come on guys," Courtney started. "It's not like I'm going to run off."

"Right, well," Jon began. "Thank you for the coffee. I'll be back up as soon as it's over."

"You guys go, go to lunch," Courtney said. "You've earned it." An uncomfortable pause built around them until Scott spoke.

"Hey Dave, you had that thing you wanted to show me in your office, didn't you?"

"I did?" Dave asked. Then after a beat, he nodded. "Oh, right that thing. Yeah, come on. I'll be happy to show it to you."

Jon looked down as the men left the room and chuckled silently.

"Wow, not very subtle, were they?" Courtney asked.

"My son, the man who thinks he knows what's best for everyone but himself," Jon replied. Turning to her, he held her gaze for a long moment.

"You cut your hair," she said.

"Yeah," he admitted. "I was ready for a new look. They cut a little too much on the sides, but I like it, so does Beth."

"That's good. I like it too."

"Thanks," Jon replied. "Really, how are you?"

"It's been a month, Jon," she shrugged. "When I said we needed a break, I didn't expect you to take it so literally."

"I wanted to give you and Ryan time. I remember what it was like to be newly together," he replied.

"You know?" she asked.

"It's kinda hard not to," he answered. "I am pleased for you both."

"But I don't understand why you kept your distance from me. Ryan has told me you had him over several times and met him for lunch. You never once reached out to me," she said.

"Because I didn't want to influence you," he answered. "We said some pretty damning things, Courtney. I needed to make sure our feelings were merely because we are in the line of fire together and we depend on each other."

"And were they?" she asked.

"My phone wasn't ringing off the hook either. You have to understand, as much as things will be the same between us, things are different now and we have to work through them. I think it's a good thing you and Ryan are together, it shows he is where your heart truly lies."

She looked up at him and finally whispered. "But I missed you."

Jon sighed and pulled her into him tightly. "God, I missed you too. But I couldn't do that to you or Ryan. We needed space."

"And now we've had it, and now I am fully with Ryan," she said into his chest. "I know my… infatuation caused a lot of chaos. I'm sorry. I do love you, Jon but not like that. We're partners. I think a partnership is a lot like and can be confused for a relationship but that's not what I want with you."

"I don't either, to be honest," Jon replied. "I'll admit there was a time when we first met I thought what if, but it was brief. Courtney, I have, at times, projected my late wife onto you and it's not fair to either of us. I think that's why your confession was so difficult for me. It was like I was losing Carol all over again. But you are not Carol and I am so very happy with Beth as you are with

Ryan. Can we leave it and see where we go from here?

"Yes," Courtney nodded. "I realized after I said it, it was childish and I have strived for so long to make everyone see me as an adult but I realized I couldn't be who I wanted to be living in a fantasy world. I thought I knew what love was but now I do and I realized what I felt for you was infatuation, admiration and companionship."

"That is partly my fault. I pretended for a while Carol was back. I know now that was a wish and desire I had no business putting on you. Can we go on from here?"

"Gladly, partner," Courtney beamed and squeezed his hands in hers.

"Now, I do have to go. I'm going to be late. How about tonight, when we're off duty, we go to Chatham Tap for a Guinness?" Jon asked.

"Oh, I would, but Ryan is making dinner tonight," she answered. "Raincheck?"

"Knocked out for my younger, cuter nephew, eh?" he shook his head dramatically.

Courtney threw her head back and laughed. "If you think of it that way then we've not made any progress."

"True," he winked. "But truthfully, how are you?"

"That conversation will take more time than the five seconds we have until Scott comes back through that door and tells us you're going to be late," she said and sure enough Scott popped his head in from Dave's office.

"If you two are finished, we're going to be late, Dad," he announced.

"You really are pushy when there's a free lunch in it for you," Jon said.

"Of course," his son teased. "I'm a growing boy."

"Growing boy, my arse," Jon answered.

Made in the USA
Middletown, DE
14 September 2021